# GOBLIN FRUIT

MYSTERIOUS CHARM: BOOK 2

CELIA LAKE

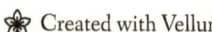

# ALSO BY CELIA LAKE

**The Mysterious Charm Series**
Outcrossing
Goblin Fruit
Magician's Hoard
Wards of the Roses
In The Cards
On The Bias
Seven Sisters

Find a complete list of all my books at celialake.com/books.

Sign up for my newsletter to be the first to hear about future books and learn about fascinating bits of research. Happy reading!

## ABOUT GOBLIN FRUIT

**Addictive potions challenge even the greatest minds.**

Lord Geoffrey Carillon is known to be a pleasant and harmless man. Apparently fully recovered from the Great War, he sees to his responsibilities as Lord of Ytene when he's not at house parties, balls, and other social events. When an inquiry agency needs his particular talents to investigate a mysterious and highly addictive magical drink, he's happy to lend a hand.

Lizzie Penhallow wants the simple things: her sister's health and safety, food on the table, and enough money to pay the bills and keep their home in Cornwall. After her father and uncle were lost on an disastrous expedition (along with a lot of other people's money), she's had a difficult time getting anyone to hire her. Lizzie knows she needs to meet the high standards of her employer to keep her job and she has no time for distractions. Even charming aristocratic ones.

There's just one problem. Lord Carillon has the access

she needs to keep an eye on her sister and help her new employer solve a deadly and complicated problem. She can work with that. There's no choice. Even if it involves house parties, gossip, and some quite suggestive dancing.

**Join Carillon and Lizzie in 1924 as they explore the mysterious goldwasser drink in *Goblin Fruit*.**

# ONE

## MARCH 1924, AN ESTATE NEAR GRIMSBY

"Magical items go on the third to tenth tables, Mr Carter. And Mr Iyer, look at your hands. Mirrors, non-magical, silver. Over there." She pointed with the end of her pencil before sticking it back in the bun at the nape of her neck.

"Yes, Miss Penhallow." It came out in stereo. One lanky blond man went left, one, shorter and dark, went right.

Iyer was Indian, she knew, but she regretted she'd not had the chance to find out more about his background. She knew the name was Brahmin, but not how his family had emigrated, or when.

He was one of half a dozen helpers, sent from the auction house. Well-bred, earnest, too young to have fought in the Great War, but old enough to be apprenticing.

They were in the husk of what had been a large estate at Grimsby, looking out to the east and the ocean. Its exceedingly elderly owner had died last month, and the building itself was too far gone to save. It might stand for five years, or ten, but sooner or later the foundation would shatter and the whole thing would slide into the sea.

So here were the young bright men from the auctioneer to fetch and carry, putting a polish on their knowledge of obscure magical and luxury items. And here was Lizzie in charge of the lists and inventory and filling out a great many cards for the auctioneer's reference.

Some were in lots, the household goods, the wood-work stacked in piles in the stable yard under tents. Others were to be sold individually. There were debts to pay off, and cousins who hoped to get a little money out of the death. Which meant, of course, identifying the things that might attract high bids. Or at least moderate ones.

As for her, Madam Porter had made it clear to her that this would be a trial run. She had one chance to prove her skills were as good as the scant two references she'd been able to provide claimed. If she did well, there might be steady work in it. If not, it would be back to trying to piece together jobs from people who clearly distrusted her because of her family.

She needed the steady work. She and Laura both did. There weren't many other options going at this point, not if they wanted food. It'd be months yet before the garden picked up.

"Miss Penhallow? Can you check this book? I don't remember it being on the list."

It pulled her out of the contemplation she had no time for. "Of course, Mr Cohen. Let me look." He handed her the book with a little half-bow. She peered over the top of her glasses at the gilded title on the spine, then thumbed through the list on the table. "Alternate title inside. Fourth shelf, third row down, fifth book in. Alphabetical by title there."

That got a prompt "Yes'm," as he went off. The young

men were very deferential to her, she'd noticed, and she wasn't quite sure why.

The Great War, though, was between them. They had not even been at Schola when it began, most of them. She had been out and finding her own ways to serve. With paperwork, not fighting, but still. Perhaps that was what made the difference.

It was an unfamiliar set of shoes on the worn floors that alerted her to an intrusion, and she stopped wool-gathering and looked up sharply. They were not supposed to have visitors.

"Good afternoon!" The voice was bright, cheerful, undeniably English and aristocratic, that slight clipped drawl like nothing else in the world.

She took a breath, first, deliberately bringing to mind the training she'd had for the event. Take a breath. You're in charge. Don't rush on someone's account if you're supposed to be there and they aren't. Another breath, then she said, clearly, "The auction is not open to visitors yet." A half-beat, a glance at the clothing, and then a "Sir."

He was well dressed, she'd give him that. A deep blue walking suit of finely woven wool with the long cloak favoured by those who didn't have to pass in non-magical circles. Blond hair, blue-grey eyes. The cane he showed no sign of needing and glasses, however, were a bit much and gave him the air of a slightly foolish man.

She almost labelled him absent-minded, but no, it wasn't that. He seemed without a care in the world, as if the War had utterly passed him by. Clearly wealthy, clearly a man of leisure, to be here in the middle of the day and no appointment.

"I've permission." The response was bright. He didn't flatter or dissemble, and that was novel. "Here, my card, and a note from the solicitors. I'm leaving for business abroad tomorrow and need to instruct my man."

She reached out to take the cards, turning them so she could read them, and then raised an eyebrow. "Lord Carillon." She would be polite, of course. She read the note he presented, then murmured a charm and pressed her thumb to the corner. The deep blue flush confirmed that the signer was the person whose name was on the card. "Your request is in order, but I am afraid we are not yet fully arrayed."

It was, after all, Wednesday, and the auction was Friday. She was superb at organising, but the process took time and they'd only started Monday. Even if he was a man of some influence, to arrange that permission, he could not present a pretty note to bargain with the hours.

The man waved a hand. "I'm interested in a specific set of things. Not a long list. If I could look - not touching, of course, bar books if I may, I collect old ones. Among other things. I do admit an interest in the wine cellar. Perhaps one of these young men could keep an eye on me?"

Lizzie glanced along the line. The young men had all paused, quite attentive, and not at all doing their work. Except for Mr Allery, who was coming up from the wine cellar, carefully levitating a case of port. There was something here she was missing, but it was not as if she could ask.

"I am Miss Penhallow." She glanced among the young men, almost missing the slightly raised eyebrow she expected when people heard her name. She ignored it as she always did and said "You may have your pick of an escort, except for Allery. We need his particular skills. We have a list of the wines you may consult." Her voice was precise. "Mr Michaels, the list?" It was placed promptly in her hand. She looked it over and then handed it to the earl.

He made a slight bow to her, and considered his

prospects. "You'd be one of the Minister of Materia's sons, yes?" he said, addressing Mr Iyer, who made a slight bow and murmured, "Yes, sir. The youngest, sir."

This got a beaming smile, and the easy confident comment, "I remember meeting you, a party, some years ago. Come along, then, and tell me about things." Lizzie raised an eyebrow, watching the very deliberate bonhomie. The two went off to toward the bookshelves along the back wall, and Carter came up to her.

"Miss Penhallow, did you ever see Lord Carillon play bohort?" It burst out of him like he couldn't restrain his interest.

Allery snorted, from where he was setting the port down. "Pavo, you. There's rather a difference." Lizzie waved a hand at them, but Carter went on.

"Father saw him play the Apprentice League match in 1903. And the one in 1911. That one that went on for eight hours."

Lizzie rubbed her nose for a moment. "Good then, was he?"

"Is, ma'am." The response came from all directions, including Cohen behind her. Carter continued, with a gesture to the others to shut up. "He still plays. There was a break, during and after the War. But he did a charity match for wounded soldiers last October. Started a new stud farm. Gossip is he wants to restock the pavo horses properly." He considered. "I guess he does other things too." Those were clearly less interesting. Pelson added, almost awed, "He inherited Ytene."

Lizzie glanced over at the man. There was a certain limberness there, perhaps. Not that that was a thing that particularly recommended a man. Ytene was one of the great estates, she knew, but not what else made it interesting. Besides, that was not her work today. Or this week. She brushed her hands off, with a brisk, "Back to work, all of you. We are on a deadline."

She bent to her own tasks, taking notes, and when Lord Carillon left an hour later, she nodded and wished him safe travel, out of habit.

The young men, of course, immediately flocked around Iyer, asking this question, and that, and which books did he look at, and did he say anything about the pavo season.

Iyer said nothing at all useful about the man. She gathered at least some of the titles he'd been interested in had to do with bohort and pavo, but Iyer didn't mention specifics and they weren't books she knew well. She gave them precisely two-and-a-half minutes by her watch before clearing her throat.

They all jumped, and she said, once again in a rather clipped tone that she hoped did not sound peevish, "That is for the pub after work, gentlemen. Or wherever it is you go. We've a long list to get through yet. Mr Carter, that box. Mr Iyer, the other hand objects like that mirror." The others wheeled and turned back to their tasks.

# TWO

## TRELLECH

"Miss Penhallow?"

It was the end of the following week. The auction had gone well enough, she'd thought. There were two days of writing out complete forms and overseeing the packing for items being sent to their new owners.

Then she had heard nothing, until a note asking her to present herself Friday morning at half nine, at Madam Porter's offices in Trellech.

Lizzie was wearing one of her better suits. It had been her mother's, once, and Lizzie loved the rich sapphire blue. More to the point, it was the classic style that did for a formal meeting with a woman of terrifying reputation. A suitable felt hat, with a cream ribbon band.

She rose, as smoothly as she could, picking up the leather portfolio from the table beside her. She nodded at the assistant who gestured her inside a small door to one side.

It was not the formal office setting she'd expected, the one she'd seen on her first interview here. Instead, two chairs were pulled up, looking out a large bay window across the fields and down to the river.

"Have a seat, Miss Penhallow. I understand you like a jasmine green tea. We've quite a nice one if you'd like a cup? We'll likely be talking for a bit."

Lizzie blinked, then gathered herself. "Of course, Madam Porter, how kind." They were automatic phrases, but she tried to put warmth behind them, despite her nerves.

"Jasmine tea for both of us, Eleanor." Madam Porter said, moving to settle into one chair. Lizzie looked at her closely; the woman seemed ageless, but was always impeccably dressed, and more than that looked utterly at ease in the tailored robes.

There followed a brief discussion about the auction, how it had gone, the details of Lizzie's report. Madam Porter made it quite clear she'd not only read it in detail but asked about a few specifics.

"And what did you think of the young men? Speak honestly, please."

Lizzie paused, gathering her thoughts. "Ma'am, my review of their work was in my report. I presume you would like me to provide a more - subjective evaluation?"

Madam Porter smiled. "Exactly."

Lizzie took a breath and then said, "They're still very young, in the ways that matter, ma'am. Used to doing as they were told, but also to freedom. It took me a little to figure that out. I've not done much with people young enough not to have served in the War."

That got her a nod. "Quite." Very precise and clipped.

"Cohen, I think, has the most potential. He noticed - as I reported - several discrepancies and minor but important details as we were processing items. He certainly asked the best questions. Thoughtful. Incisive."

"No difficulty working with someone of his background?"

"No, ma'am, of course not. And it was easy to arrange things so he could leave enough before sunset on Friday."

She gathered her thoughts about the others, trying to decide who to mention next. "Iyer is charming, but easily distracted. If he learns to focus better, he'll do quite well. He has a good eye for quality, especially the more indefinable aspects that come from materia choice and artistic preference."

That earned her a laugh she couldn't figure out how to interpret, but Lizzie pressed on. "Allery has a delicate hand. Agreeable, cordial, but not chatty. I think he'd prefer more solitary work, long-term, and flourish with it. Restoration work, perhaps. Carter gets carried away, and I'm not sure how that'll work out for him, but he's good-hearted and that's something you can't teach. Pleasant to work with. Michaels has a knack for reawakening materia. If I had any say in it, I'd be guiding him in that direction, there are few enough people who can do it well. But he could be prickly when redirected."

"Pelson?"

Pelson had dropped three different things and broken one. Fortunately, as it turned out, a vase of utterly no value. "One is inclined to suggest a speciality in large marble sculpture, firmly bolted to the floor. But I think there's something else going on there. A block, in his magic, some Silence oath that's hampering him, something..." She tapped her fingers on the arm of her chair for a moment. "Something out of tune."

This earned an arched eyebrow, followed by, "Oh, that's

quite interesting, Miss Penhallow. Thank you." It was not clear if she intended to say more, because at that point there was a soft knock, and her assistant coming in at Madam Porter's clear "Enter."

Even with green tea, there was a certain amount of fussing. Less about sugar and cream or lemon, but more about letting the tea breathe and inhaling the delicate fragrance. There was silence for a few moments after pouring, and then Madam Porter settled back, with a "Do you have questions for me?"

This was the delicate point. Lizzie had, in the grand scheme of things, a long list of questions she'd like answers to. Whether she'd done well enough. What they were looking for. Where Madam Porter got her information. What this office was. Why Madam Porter had handled the job instead of someone from the auction house. Where the tea was from.

She asked none of them. She took a sip of her tea, and then swallowed, and asked, "Do you have questions about my decisions or skills as applied to the work, ma'am?"

This earned her a laugh, and a "Oh, do relax. This is an interview, but I should reassure you. I am quite willing to offer you further work. The discussion will determine what kind of work. You're a clever woman, I'm not telling you anything you don't expect."

This was not at all what Lizzie expected, actually, not that bluntness, and she paused, before venturing, "Ma'am, I know my skills are good. But I have not found a - suitable place to use them."

That got a nod. "No false modesty with me. I need my staff, every single one, to be clear on what they are capable of, and what they should not attempt. Do you know much about the agency?"

"The public information, ma'am, of course." She had done her research. "You have a select staff, hired out to offices who need temporary staff for particular projects, or to fill in while a trusted staff member is on leave. Sensitive matters, normally, not that people discuss what, just that you fill positions beyond what a secretarial pool could manage."

"And why did you apply with us? The truth, please."

"I'll not deny I need a position, and something steady." She considered explaining why and didn't. For one thing, Madam Porter likely knew. "I enjoyed the specialist work I did during the War, but my family situation - I'm quite sure you know - has meant few people would give me an opportunity."

That got her a nod. "And what do you make of that?"

Lizzie shrugged. "A certain amount of frustration, at people judging without asking me directly. But that is something I expected, it being a thing people will persist in doing. I thought, given your reputation, you might at least give me a chance to prove myself."

That gets her an honest laugh, with warmth in it. "They do, don't they? Your analysis is correct. I would say what we actually do as an agency is use people's assumptions against them, for the good of our clients. I am selective what cases we take. It is not, you understand, a simplistic choice of good or evil, as some would judge it. More like, oh, the Prometheans versus those who are lawful but static."

Lizzie contemplated. "Prometheus did not end well."

Another laugh, and a, "No. But we do not play for quite such stakes as fire, or with such beings as the gods. As a rule." She tapped her fingers on the arm of the chair. "I do intend to take you on, but there are two different assignments I am considering. Do you know anything about those under the mountain, the Belin?"

Lizzie blinked. "I'm afraid not in much detail, ma'am. I have a little more experience with their cousins in Germany, I accompanied my father there on a trip about a decade ago. I wasn't part of the actual negotiations, of course."

That gets a nod. "I think it can benefit more from your skills than the other. You'll be working in the Ministry, here in Trellech, if that's not a problem."

"Not if they are fine with me, ma'am. I'm living in Cornwall, but we have a portal in the village."

That got a snort. "They're quite aware of your skills and think you'll do well. And I understand your younger sister has a secretarial post in town? You'll likely be able to meet for lunch from time to time."

That brought Lizzie up short for a moment, but of course Madam Porter would do her research. "She is, ma'am. Simple office work, but a good way to begin. She's excited to be working." Her poor health had meant Laura hadn't worked yet, for all she was approaching thirty.

That brought them around to the practical arrange-ments of salary and hours, and what Lizzie should prepare for Monday. They made plans to meet so she could be intro-duced to the office and staff. Lizzie was sent home to read up on the Belin, several borrowed books under her arm.

# THREE

## TRELLECH

"I presume you intended for me to get a look at Miss Penhallow on her way out, Vivian?"

Carillon watched Vivian Porter's expression change from her usual measured and enigmatic smile to a broader amusement. "I have her report about you. I'm curious about what you might have to say about her."

"And what did she say about me?"

"Tsk. That'd be telling."

Carillon laughed and settled down. "I saw the books, so I assume you're keeping her on."

Vivian shrugged her shoulders and then smiled. "I won't hide that from you." They both knew she was hiding other things. "She did very well with the auction."

"There are mutterings about her family."

"Geoffrey Carillon, you know perfectly well there are mutterings about any family anyone's ever heard of, and then some." A gesture.

Carillon spread his hands. "Point. She is Hendrek's daughter, though?"

"She is. No one's heard from Hendrek or Kenver or

anyone else on that ship for years. The young women are on their own, and no one to speak for them. Lorelei - that's the younger - has been in poor health since she was a child, and Elspeth feels responsible for doing well for them. Family home in Cornwall, with a portal in the village, thankfully, though I gather Lorelai has a room in town here."

He nodded, and then said, "I assume she's not why you invited me into your den?"

"Afraid the fox will develop a taste for owl, then? Honestly, Geoffrey. We've known each other long enough for that not to be the thing. Also, your talons are quite sharp when you loose them."

He made a sound, in his throat, and then was glad to be interrupted by the tea service. There was a little fussing over the details, Eleanor left, and then Vivian smiled, over her cup. "Your impressions of her, then?"

Carillon considered. "Competent, from everything I saw. Clear about the scope of her authority, and not afraid to walk up to the edge. She kept the bright young men in line very nicely. I lingered in the hallway, listening, after she thought I'd left. She let them talk about me for two or three minutes before reminding them to get back to work. It was measured, a deliberate choice, and a sensible one."

"And which you did they see?"

"Oh, the easy-going harmless man about town." Carillon waved a hand. "You know the thing. A bit foolish. Asking about the pavo manuscripts. Actually, there was a rather nice one, my man of business got it for me."

"And they didn't see the other side of you?"

"No. Iyer didn't notice me paying particular attention, either. Three manuscripts that should not see the open market and didn't. Private sale before the auction opened, government prerogative." His voice had turned flat. "At least some of us will have no more of the poison air and bogs of death."

Vivian went quiet. People always did when he let that show, the places the world had been torn apart that they tried desperately to ignore. He kept it hidden, under the smiling lord who favoured pavo and a fine port and a good book, not too complex. Because even Vivian went still and awkward, and she was the one who most understood.

He paused, deliberately took another sip of his tea, keeping his voice pleasant. "Miss Penhallow was entirely on top of matters, as much as anyone who was not a specialist in the particular academic fields might be, and then some. She'd correctly identified the books as needing expert review."

"Just not that you were the person reviewing them."

"Exactly." He settled back in his chair. "This is not why you invited me over, Vivian, we know that."

"Related, actually." Vivian leaned forward, then reached for the portfolio on the table beside her. "Have you heard any gossip about a new alcoholic drink, by chance?" Vivian waved her fingers, the little delicate trail he had to admire. She knew how to use her gestures well.

Carillon tilted his head, considering. "Drinks. Drinks. Not wine. Not..." He taps his finger. "Tibbie Morland mentioned something in passing. He's got a new office on Trivium Way, the north end." He grimaced. "I'm not fond of Tibbie."

"More money than sense, then."

That got a laugh from Carillon before he relaxed slightly. "Rather, yes. He's a few years younger. His brother was tutored with me." He tapped a finger on the arm of the chair. "He didn't fight in the War. Did something here, I forget what. Has wheezy lungs, always has. And rather a lot of business, since he wasn't fighting."

"Is it the not fighting you disapprove of, or something else?"

Vivian was always too sharp. Carillon paused, so she wouldn't see quite how sharply that hit. "It's one thing not to have fought. Plenty of good men didn't fight, or not at any of the front lines. But Tibbie made rather a point of profiting, and rumours are it was at the cost of other men's lives. Other people's lives."

"And that you don't abide." Vivian's voice had gone quiet. "I could have a profile on him done, if you want to know."

Carillon shook his head. "Save your staff. For the moment. He asked if I'd stop in, and I'll toddle along there after we're done here and see about that. But that doesn't answer your question."

"I've been asked to assist with investigations into something new that's turned up. No one's quite sure what the issue is, it's - diffuse. We think there's a drink involved."

"Vivian, darling, it's 1924, and we're in Albion, not the United States. People come up with a dozen new drinks every time there's a house party."

She laughed at his tone. Carillon prided himself on being note-perfect with that drawl and the sharp brightness of his voice. One couldn't play among the glittering Bright Young Things without it. Or the older circles who wished they were bright and young and deathless and knew they weren't.

"You have a point. But do have a rummage round, would you? Anything interesting in the drinkables line. I have a young woman or two on the task as well, but you hear different things, you always do."

"Your Miss Penhallow?"

"That," she said "Would be telling. You know I don't." She was amused enough he suspected he was right.

"What's this drink supposed to do?" He drew out a small pocket notebook, working on making a quick note in the personal shorthand he preferred. It wasn't so simple as a code, those were too easily broken, rather a series of personal references and associations, combined with a mix of symbols.

Vivian peered at it as she always did before she shook her head. "Nothing about it is simple. The observed evidence suggests that there's something addictive in the drink. A single drink relaxes, more than the alcohol content suggests. More on a par with opium. Dreams and fancies. But one drink won't do much more than that."

"And what happens if you have more than one drink?"

"That's the part we're not clear on. But we've had more than one person turned up with a deficit in their magic. When questioned, the drink is one of the only shared possibilities. So say the healers, and they're baffled. Not an easy thing to resolve. Even extended rest in a suitable healing environment is very slow."

"How long has this been around? And what kinds of people are the patients?"

Vivian shook her head. "We've been seeing cases for the past six months. One or two at first, but we're up to two dozen now. Different backgrounds, nowhere they've all been. They all talk about drinking something that tasted fabulous, being given a bottle of it for some reason, taking it home. Finishing the bottle over a week or two."

"Tracing magic revealed nothing?"

"Whoever made it took steps. New cauldron. New tools. New bottles. Nothing of them touching it. We suspect the bottles we know about were made in the same batch."

"And we don't have the bottles?"

"No. A few of the patients thought they'd kept them, but we couldn't find them at the homes. Only two, and they didn't have enough drops left for testing."

Carillon made a sour face. "That by itself is suspicious."

"Which is why I'm setting you on the problem. If you can fit it in between your clothing fittings and your pavo practice and - whatever you're doing with yourself this week."

"Breeding and training at the barn. Fortunately, my stable manager's very sound. But I do need to be there for a few days this week and next."

Vivian shrugged. "It's a pressing problem but not currently urgent. And besides, we're scarcely able to twist your arm, given this is all entirely unofficial. But if you'd apply your skills, we'd be the usual kinds of grateful."

Carillon inclined his head, considering what that might mean this time. Books. Materia. Artefacts. Quiet backing for projects he particularly wanted completed. He'd have to consider what to put on the list.

# FOUR

## TRELLECH

"Good afternoon!" Carillon had taken just enough time to go by the family townhome in Trellech and change into something suitable for a lunch out.

The young woman at the front desk was vaguely familiar. Blonde hair, almost sunny, draping over her shoulder in loose waves with the kind of artless natural curl many women of his acquaintance would spend an hour and a dozen charms to achieve. Her pale green dress was more suited to later spring, but the colour flattered her, bringing roses to her cheeks. She'd matched the dress with a cream shawl, the embroidery shifting from bare green curling vines to blooming flowers and back to vines.

She looked up, and smiled at him, and something in the smile seemed familiar. The angle it gave to her cheekbones caught his memory. Ah, that was it. This must be Lorelai Penhallow. It was the eyes that did it, the particular shade of blue like a late summer sky.

Mind, her sister looked quite different. The glimpse he'd had of her, at the auction and today, Elspeth had been quite severely dressed, in deeper jewel tones. Oh, he'd noticed her fondness for the deeper colours, a green tailored dress at Grimsby and a rich blue suit today. But she'd had her hair pinned back in a tight coil at the nape of her neck, and glasses as a wall between her and the world. Without the glasses, he could see the blue eyes quite clearly.

She repeated the "Good afternoon!" brightly. "Welcome to Morland Limited. How may I help you today, sir?"

Carillon considered for a moment and then withdrew a small visiting card case from his front coat pocket. "Oh, pardon, I was woolgathering. I'm an old friend of Tibbie's," he said, amiably. "He wondered if I was free for lunch, sometime, and I was free today, so I thought I'd pop round."

This got the young woman blinking down at the card, and then a charming "Oh, Lord Carillon, of course, he mentioned you." It had Carillon wondering if Tibbie had, or if Lorelai was more skilled at dissembling than she appeared. "Please have a seat. I'll inquire about his availability. It might be a few minutes, he's engaged in business."

"Of course. It's no bother to wait." The woman went off to knock on the door to the back office, then slipped inside.

Carillon settled into an armchair that seemed likely comfortable, but discovered after a moment that he had been mistaken. Something about the length of the seat or the angle of the cushions didn't quite work. He picked up a magazine - some frippery about the current fashionable magical luxuries - while he tried to decide if this might be intention or accident.

They left him alone for ten or fifteen minutes, before the woman returned to her desk with a little delicate cough, and a "Your Lordship? Mr Morland would be delighted to lunch with you, but he'll be about twenty minutes more. Would you prefer to wait, or come back?"

"Oh, I'm glad to wait." Carillon did his best to be charming about it. "I didn't have an appointment, after all."

"May I offer you a cup of tea or an apéritif?"

This got a wave of his hand. "Oh, tea, if it's not a bother. Still, a tad brisk out there, isn't it, even if spring's on the way?"

Lorelai smiled, and said, "Oh, a bit, yes, sir, and I do feel the cold."

"May I ask your name, perhaps? You're new in the office, aren't you? Well, I mean, I gather the whole office is new, isn't it?" Best charming voice, utterly harmless. Nothing to see here.

That got a pretty blush as intended. "Lorelai Penhallow, sir, but most people call me Laura."

"That's a Cornish name, isn't it? The Penhallow, I mean. Lorelai would make you a siren."

That got a bit of a flutter from her. Not at all his taste, but he could see how it would suit some people. It was certainly as much 'summer of English loveliness' as one might wish to order from a catalogue, though perhaps a little out of season, it still being April.

He got lost in his train of thought for a moment until he caught the tail end of her explanation. There was something about a place name, why she was named after her mother's side of the family, that her mother didn't care for the Cornish forenames.

"My sister, she's Elspeth, properly." A little smile "More distinguished than Elizabeth, don't you think?"

Carillon made a non-committal noise, and they went on like that for another few minutes, about nicknames and odd names he had come across in his travels. It was one of many topics he stored up for times such as these.

Eventually, there was a noise from the inner offices, and

the door opening, and a "There you are, glad to see you, old man. Now, Laura, darling, we'll be out at lunch, likely a long one. Will you be all right here by yourself, dear?" Tibbie had filled out, turned florid in the past couple of years, and with a clear fondness for fanciful clothing, draping sleeves and impractical fabrics. The deep red with gold threads did him no favours.

Carillon stood, with a "Tibbie, glad it worked out," and waited while they sorted out the utterly tedious minutiae of an office pretending to be more prosperous than it was.

He was quite sure the callers named would not be showing up in such numbers as Tibbie implied. Not when the office had been utterly quiet the entire time he was there. There had been no messages on the pneumatic tube, no messengers, no morning mail, no callers besides himself. But the dance for his benefit was educational, so he waited until Tibbie had given all the instructions he seemed inclined to give, and then tipped his hat. "Miss Penhallow, a pleasure."

They went down the street, and Tibbie murmured, "Do you mind my club, old man?"

Carillon did, rather, as he'd never cared for Tibbie's club. Too much boasting and noise. But he wanted the man at ease, so the Boar's Head it was. They were seated at a table in the dining room, the privacy curtains lowered, and then Tibbie took his time with the menu.

Carillon was patient. Once they'd finally placed their orders, he said, "So, you said you have a grand new project. I did want to see you today, I'll be back in the New Forest most of the next two weeks. Stable matters, you know."

He knew Tibbie didn't, which was convenient. And, of course, 'stable matters' could and did cover many things, even with people who knew more.

"Plenty of things need rebuilding after the War, yes. Stables too, I suppose."

"And business interests - it's been good to see some of the shop fronts reopening, now there's a need for more than War goods."

Which was where Tibbie had made a lot of money, not that Carillon was commenting on that. It was, however, why he'd not rushed to renew the acquaintanceship.

"Ah, well, yes. And that's where we come in. There's a man - quite a clever conk of one, one of you Owls, I believe, a good bit older than we are. Must be in his sixties, now. Well, he came up with this simply fantasmagorical drink. A new kind of distillation, it's all about bringing one's fantasies of travel and luxury to the surface."

Once he was off on the topic, Tibbie was rather effusive. Carillon kept things rolling along with the occasional "Oh, really?" and "Do tell me more," until the larger picture began to emerge.

Tibbie, of course, was not going to tell all about the actual process. Frankly, Carillon didn't think he knew it or could explain it. That was someone else's job. Tibbie's was to look right, and bring in investors, and be jovial and agreeable, and he was hoping Carillon might be interested or know someone who was.

Carillon made the proper non-committal noises. Money tied up at the moment, but he'd see what he could get free. Depended how the repairs at Ytene were going, of course, a lot to see to there.

Having an ancient property was a tremendous help when people asked you for money. You could invent any number of problems with the drains or the walls or the wood rot. Ninety-nine out of a hundred people wouldn't know how much it might cost, or how urgent it might be.

The ones who did know weren't the ones asking for money as a rule.

It was a bit more promising to ask about what kind of investors they were looking for. Tibbie was quite effusive on that point. "Lots of us chaps have made names for ourselves, separate from what our families might have done. And really, there are many people, perfectly charming, interesting, throw the most interesting parties. People who don't come from the First Families, even the Second or Third, but who want to make their way in the world a bit more brightly. That's the sort we want, Gee. Not that we won't take the old families like yours, of course. Good solid foundation, the people who've been around for yonks."

Which gave him a picture of what Tibbie was after, even as he was making a face at the childhood nickname. Bright Young People with more money than sense, and their parents, eager to make a name and have their Bright Young Children marry well.

He'd heard enough, by the end of the lunch, to have the definite sensation there was more going on. Nothing he'd heard was suspicious by itself, but he could feel the shadows, something underneath what Tibbie had said, that didn't quite add up. Especially with Vivian's comments about the loss of magic, though that would of course not be the sort of thing one might mention to an investor. The trick would be getting access to a better source of information than Tibbie.

# FIVE

## TRELLECH

Lizzie hummed under her breath Thursday at lunchtime as she walked down the street to meet Laura for lunch.

She'd not seen her sister since Sunday afternoon. Laura had taken a room in a boarding house, in a reasonable neighbourhood, claiming the portal journey exhausted her. The coin for it was scarce, but with both of them working, they could manage. More or less.

Lizzie was still at their home in Cornwall with all the complexities of getting to Trellech each day. Waiting for the portal was tedious, and of course, she waited for the cheaper times to save money. Then there was the walk home, which was getting more pleasant, but still had patches of mud and ruts in the road to avoid.

Once she got home, there were chickens to tend, eggs to find, and the garden to prepare around her actual work hours. And the household spirits to feed. The cream didn't put itself out, someone had to do it. It was queer to have the house empty even though she and Laura had not lived together for most of their adult lives.

She tried not to think about that, the unrelenting chilly dankness of a stone house on a sea cliff, and instead went back to thinking about work.

The new job was, in a word, fascinating. Overwhelming, of course, but that was only to be expected when dropped into an entirely new field with only two-and-a-half days to prepare.

The location was rather poor. Their offices were in a dull corner of one of the less decorative Ministry buildings. The building itself was tucked behind a faded door in a crooked alley on the southwest end of the Ministry district. Nothing notable, nothing historically interesting. Just dull eighteenth-century stonework.

The people in the office were quite another story.

They definitely had quirks. The head of the office vastly preferred the Welsh habit of using a patronym rather than a surname.

She hard startled the first few times she heard "Verch Hendrek, take a note, will you?" But something about the format was almost comforting. Others who knew her wanted to write her father and uncle out of her history, and here it was, right up front. Hendrek's daughter. She still wasn't sure how she felt about being called that, but she would not argue with Iolo ap Rhys. Not about that, anyway.

Lizzie was there as a replacement for Audrey, who'd left to have her first baby. No one expected her to come back to work, and Lizzie was there to keep things running until they made a long-term hire. Which might be Lizzie, or might not.

She was not yet at all sure which she'd rather.

Iolo ap Rhys, the head of the office, was a large burly man with wiry dark hair and a rather chaotic beard. He was, however, one of the most sharp-witted men she'd met, including her father and uncle. He had been very direct with her in their first conversation that Monday morning, explaining.

The office dealt with negotiations relating to various materia sources, especially the Belin, what less well-educated folk might refer to as Welsh dwarves. There were a dozen or so other non-human races who provided materia in the British Isles. And of course negotiations with others from many further places, but since Trellech and Schola were both in the Belin's territory, they had a great deal of priority.

At least for this office. Their role was to manage the various details of the treaties and formalities. After all, someone had to be in charge of any problems that fell into the areas covered by the treaties. Quietly, without fuss or bother. It wouldn't do for people to be reminded that their materia depended on negotiations with legendarily difficult fairies. They might fuss and make trouble, or, worse, try to deal with them themselves.

That's why there were half a dozen staff with a range of skills and the office manager. Two who had the languages needed to manage detailed treaties across several countries. Two with materia expertise, who could do analysis on raw materials. Two generalist researchers. They all chipped in with reports and tasks though. That was something Lizzie hadn't expected. Some of them had been pleasant, others purely business-like, but no one had been too much of a problem, which was a surprise. She had been prepared to have to deal with rather more difficulty.

Everyone outside the office thought they did something very tedious with minor accounting details. Lizzie had been thoroughly instructed to avoid telling anyone what she did. She had even been coached, the first day, in the best ways to avoid saying anything of interest. They'd rehearsed the sentences that would make anyone except an actual accountant yawn and turn away.

Which made what she would talk about at lunch tricky. She hoped she could lure Laura into talking about her work instead.

Lizzie walked past the law courts on the right, the statue of Iustitia holding her scales high. She turned along the back side of the clubs on the left. She felt more than saw the ground change from the older cobblestone near the Ministry onto the flatter pavement designed for carts and deliveries, the proper high street. She walked down the broad avenue for a good quarter mile, taking in the bright paint on the shops, a rainbow of jewel tones and carved signs. She made her way past everything from apothecaries to drapers to toys to stationary, each one finding some way to advertise their wares.

At the market, she veered right, taking the fork that led to the posher shops, the ones focusing on clothing and jewellery and furniture. She paused for a moment in front of one dressmaker, looking at a beautiful deep ruby dress and velvet cloak, with a little sigh. Not for her, that kind of impractical clothing. Where would she ever wear it?

Three doors down, four, then up the staircase. When she knocked on the door and got a bright "Do come in!" she found Laura putting on her coat, with a bright "Lizzie! Mr Morland's already gone, or I'd introduce you. He was looking forward to meeting you, but something came up - an urgent appointment." She sounded very impressed.

There was something a little queer about Laura, Lizzie thought for a moment. It was a hint of something faded, but then she blinked and shook her head, and it wasn't there. She covered by saying, cheerfully, "Oh, I'd not want to keep him from that! Do you know a good place for lunch, or should we guess and try something new?"

"There's a nice little cafe, down at the end of the corner. Not too dear? Though, um. I'm short until tomorrow?"

Lizzie sighed and nodded. "More expensive in town, I know. I'll pay." That or her sister had overspent her budget again.

They walked out, and down the street, not arm in arm like some sisters might, but companionable. Lizzie watched as Laura nodded and waved and said things to half the people on the street, then murmured, "You seem to have met a lot of people already?"

"Oh, Mr Morland likes me to get to know people. And we're wanting recommendations for all sorts of things. Carters, warehouses, suppliers. He has me asking after glass bottles, now. Lots of visits to apothecaries." Laura wrinkled her nose. "I still don't care for the smell."

"Of course not." Lizzie was never quite sure what Laura felt about her time in various sanitariums. It was not a thing they'd talked about, that Lizzie knew how to ask about. They turned into a small cafe, little round tables designed for two. "This is charming." Any excuse for a new topic.

Laura waved at one woman behind the counter, and they took a seat. The usual fussing with the menu and ordering took up a few minutes, and then Lizzie said, "So, the work seems to agree with you?"

Laura lit up, and Lizzie got to hear another good ten minutes of explanation of what the work was like, and her employer, and he was very interesting, Laura insisted. Her role, clearly, was to sit at the desk and be pleasant to visitors.

"Do you get many visitors?"

"Well, no. Not yet. But when things take off properly, we will. There was someone last week, he was very pleasant. Meeting Mr Morland for lunch. They went to his club. You know how men are about clubs."

Lizzie snorted. "Rather ridiculous, really." The Schola house clubs all welcomed women, of course, but it was mostly men who spent a lot of time in them.

"I'm glad it's not too busy. Gives you a chance to get used to it. It must be odd for you, yet, keeping set hours?"

Laura said, "Nice to be out of the house and talking to different people. That's the thing I rather missed about the sanitaria. Always people to talk to, different people." There was another hint there, something that rang a little false, a sour note in Laura's innate cheerfulness.

Lizzie nodded slightly, and let Laura go off into a story about one nurse, at the place in Switzerland.

"And the work's not too many new things?" Lizzie had worried about that. That the days would be too long, or that Laura would be asked to do too much.

"No, Lizzie, silly. Besides, I like having the chance to do things on my own. Mr Morland was quite clear, I can set things up as I like, so long as I can find the files when I need them."

Lizzie was even more dubious about this, there were so many ways coming up with a system on the fly could go badly. She didn't know where to begin with something Laura might hear. She was stuck thinking about it when she caught half a sentence and realized she was woolgathering.

"Pardon, I didn't quite catch that. You said a party, this weekend?"

Laura laughed, and it was good to see her so cheerful, only Lizzie wasn't quite sure about her going out like this.

"Oh, yes. A grand party, a masked ball. Mr Morland said I'd be quite welcome. People have to come in pairs.

There's a nephew of his, or a cousin, or a son of someone he knows, anyway, a bit younger, but he's glad to escort me."

"In pairs?"

"One of the conceits of the party. You show up in a paired costume, but nothing - matchy, you know? Just things that actually do fit. Cleverest costume wins a prize at the end of the night."

"And you - it's not too much for you? Going out, something like that? When you've only just started working." Lizzie regretted it as soon as it was out of her mouth, the look Laura gave her.

"I'm quite fine, thank you. The healers said so." Laura was very prim about it, her mouth tight now. It was clear to Lizzie that she'd mis-stepped. Again.

"I - " Lizzie put her hand up, and said, "So." There was an awkward pause, as she tried to figure out what to ask. Eventually, she had to fall back on "What are you thinking about for a costume?"

That at least kept the conversation going through the meal, between Laura's thoughts and the discussion of other paired costumes, and how obvious they might or might not be.

# SIX

## A COUNTRY HOUSE, EAST COAST OF ENGLAND

Saturday evening, it was clear out, and mild for mid-April, especially for the east coast. That was about all the evening had going for it so far.

Carillon was decidedly uncomfortable. He couldn't lean forward. The holly bush he was behind might tear the costume he'd gone to some lengths to procure. It was a proper Arlecchino, late Italian form with moons, stars, circles, and triangles sewn on a proper mediaeval jacket and trousers. Soft cap to cover his hair, and a leather mask that covered the top half of his face.

Only he had no partner. Which was the rub. He'd made a try at the gate, and they'd turned him away. Pairs only.

He kept going through the list of people he could talk into attending on incredibly short notice. Someone who he could trust to help with what he needed and not get in the way or throw a fit. Someone who had a journal for communication, a workable costume, and sufficient access to a portal to get here, to boot.

In the middle of the third pass through his mental black

book, he heard a sound three or four bushes to his right. It wasn't the right rustling to be an animal or bird.

Carillon froze for a moment, then there was the sound again, soft, not enough to make anyone on the path into the Hall notice. His joints complained when he straightened but he stood, long enough to peer in the direction of the sound. A woman's figure, by the shadow. There must be some reason she was there, and he moved as quietly as he could to join her.

She was hiding by a softer bush. He discovered this by tripping over the blanket the woman was sitting on and toppling face-first into the branches. Yew, maybe. Springy, nice resinous smell.

He clung to his dignity with the thought that at least he'd not cried out when he toppled, so they didn't attract more notice. She hadn't either, just stared at him, her eyes gleaming in the reflected light from the hall's windows.

Carillon took a breath, then another, then said "Pardon, madam. Were you wanting to go to the party?"

He caught her sharp inhale, then a "Yes. But they're only interested in duets tonight."

That made him chuckle, low under his breath. "I had the same problem. Have you a costume?"

She eyed him. "A mask. Nothing to match you." She was wearing the mask, a simple white satin eye mask. A dress, rather ordinary, thirty years old, pulled out a trunk by the smell of camphor.

"That won't match me. But. Mmm. May I apply some charms, m'lady?"

That sharp inhale again as if he'd crossed some imaginary line of expectation, but then she nodded. "Should I stand?"

He considered. "Let us retreat, m'lady, back past the stone wall, there, down the road past the turn. There's a lamp there, and we can arrange ourselves properly. Do bring the blanket, it will make a grand petticoat if I can coax it along."

She blinked at him, but with the mask on, it was hard to read the rest of her expression. She stood, gathering the blanket and keeping an eye on the table and staff handling people coming in. Once she had everything in hand, she backed off behind a tree, then another, down the road.

He gave her a decent head start, then followed her lead. Once he got around the corner, he spotted her waiting in a curve of a stone wall, under the lamppost. He made a bow with the cap in hand, and murmured, "M'lady. Would you be my Columbine?"

She frowned. "Not my style." Her tone was sharp.

"That is what makes it a costume." He gestures with the cap at her dress. "You'd make a fair enough Victorian governess or some such, but that's not a match for me."

"And I've no low-cut bodice to fall out of and frills lying around either." Her tone was dry and sharp.

"Goodness, do you think Columbine's all chest and laughter? Oh, she's a soubrette, but it's the women who have the wits in commedia, m'lady." He paused, rummaging in his memory. "Duchatre said something, that by her keen and active wit, she was able to hold her own in every situation, and..." He paused, thinking of it. "Emerge with ease and dignity from the most involved intrigues."

It was a decidedly dubious look she gave him, even through the mask's interference. And in that moment, he laughed and said "They've fripperies on the entrance table. You need a fan. To tap on your wrist and snap. Do you have hairpins? I'm not the world's worst lady's maid. And I can do for your dress, with a few charms."

"Nothing - I don't want people - assuming." Her voice broke off.

"If you'd rather not. Chemise, we'll be using that, turning your dress into a bodice, but nothing exposed. Lifted, that's a bodice for you, well, an Italian one, but we're not emulating Gloriana, are we?" He grinned. "Difficult to move in, besides, Gloriana's idea of fancy dress."

She blinked at him. "You know a fair bit about historical dress, sir."

"I go to rather a lot of costume parties. Best to know what's not tiresome to wear."

The woman considered that for a moment, then gave him a sharp nod. "Do your charms. I can do the hair after."

He nodded and then took a step back to consider her. She decidedly had a more Renaissance figure than the current flapper styles and angles. He considered, then extracted two silk handkerchiefs from his pockets, then more cautiously the wand he carried with him, tucked into a sheath on his leg. He tapped each piece, murmuring over them, watching them bloom into long lengths of filmy fabric. Once he was satisfied with the feel, another charm gathered them along one edge.

He considered, then said "Will you accept a petticoat, m'lady? Something to puff out your skirts. I'll do that next. Do you need this dress to come back like it was afterwards?"

She frowned, then said, "No. It's a dress I don't much like out of the costume box from when we were children. But it fit."

What that implied about her wardrobe at home was an intriguing question. He nodded and set to work with a dozen layered charms, pressing fingers into the fabric to hold it and thicken it, then to shape it.

She flinched each time he came close to touching her directly, and after the second time, he murmured a quiet comment about the specific thing he was doing. He waited for her to exhale and then continued.

It took about twenty minutes, but the end result was rather striking, if not at all historically accurate in some details. Oh, the outline was there, well enough, a well-shaped bodice that lifted her breasts without being indelicate. Much of her skin was hidden by a cream muslin chemise, sleeves attached by ribbons charm-woven from threads.

He had lightened the colour of her dress to a pale but piercing blue that echoed the colour of the eyes behind the mask. It gave her a virginal and pristine shimmer.

"If you'd do the hair, m'lady?" She frowned but reached to undo the tight bun, tucking the pins into her hand, and then pinching strands and pulling them gently out, to leave ringlets. They had a odd curl to them, he couldn't place why, but when she'd gathered and pinned them, it largely disappeared.

He considered, then said "One last charm, m'lady, and one for me." And then he blew on his hands, murmured a charm he'd learned from a carnival showman, and blew shimmering powder that landed on her. He brushed his fingers along patches to make them shine the same way, the glitter spreading slowly on the cloth to fill each shape. "There we are."

The lady looked back at him, steady now that the fussing with clothing was done. "Not quite. Can you make the base of yours shift to a blue, and darker? Twilight sky, perhaps?"

He blinked.

"Can you?"

"M'Lady?"

"It will look more like we're paired. Not matching, but - a set. As it is, we look like we bumped into each other and made a go of it. They'll ask fewer questions. And they saw us both before, and you still look much the same."

He saw the logic of it at once now she'd spelt it out, and nodded. Two more charms, then. One to deepen the colour of his costume, and then one last touch of the shimmering glitter, to make his mask turn from dull brown leather into silver.

Carillon was rewarded with a firm nod and a slight smile. "I would be most glad of your escort, sir." And then a softer, more hesitant, "What should I call you?"

He considered for a moment "Let us keep the facade. I am Arlecchino. You are Columbine or Columbina."

She nodded. "Columbina."

Carillon bowed low to her. "Columbina, may I escort you, then?"

It was a short parade back up the road, and to the table at the entrance to the grounds. This time, they were welcomed, given a brief explanation of the grounds, the available facilities, where events were taking place.

His Columbina claimed a fan without either asking or prompting. She took in the gathering in the lantern lights, before turning to him with a "Gentle Arlecchino, I find myself curious about the grounds, before we turn to the dancing."

Carillon nodded and offered her his arm again. As they walked across the grass, he was glad he had not altered her sensible ankle boots. She murmured, "I would like to see what the gossip in the lady's withdrawing room is like, once we have established ourselves."

It reminded him that she had some purpose for being here she had not even hinted at, but he merely nodded once more. Perhaps she might share a tidbit, from that mysterious and highly informative space he could not enter.

## SEVEN

### A COUNTRY HOUSE, EAST COAST OF ENGLAND

Lizzie was not quite sure how she'd got here. Wanting to know what Laura was up to was nosy, but within the usual standards for a worried older sister.

Hiding in the bushes was not like her at all. Neither was agreeing to be escorted by a strange man who'd nearly fallen over her. On the other hand, here they were, inside the gates.

Arlecchino was an acceptable escort. He'd been careful to ask for permission. More than that, he'd listened to her suggestions and instructions, and not argued when she was right.

It had felt odd to do the charm curls on her own hair rather than Laura's. But she supposed the entire effect was working, the way other couples were looking at them, the little smiles and bows and nods that showed they were included.

Her escort was leading her on a short promenade. From the forecourt, they'd come down a path, around the side of the house, toward a lake and summer house. Chilly for that, normally, but there was a great bonfire burning on a curve of land by the lake.

Down to the left, the path led into the garden, with what looked like statuary. Some people were standing and talking and drinking, others were dancing. Some others swayed to some beat only they heard, and a few were draped over benches and passed out, even as early as it was.

Lizzie was doing her best to look out for Laura, who had not decided on her final costume. One could rule out those with darker hair or skin, and there were plenty of both in attendance. Not that some people weren't using the more thorough kinds of cosmetic magic, but she rather thought they weren't something Laura had access to. Still, blonde and pale skinned left maybe a fifth of the party, and it was full of people.

They wandered past a few rather ordinary pairs. Several pairs of twins, either Castor and Pollux or Romulus and Remus, it could be a little hard to tell. Three suns with three moons, which made her lean over to her escort and murmur "I wonder what would happen if people came as the moons of Mars."

That got a prompt "Phobos and Deimos? We'd be running in terror if it were done right. Not at all the done thing for a party." It came with a laugh, though, and a "Well spotted. I'm wondering about that vulture and snake over there."

Lizzie followed his chin, the line of his gaze, down to a clearing by the lakefront, well-lit, to where two women were dancing. One was plump, done up layers of black and white feathers that shifted and shook. Her partner was the sleekest femme fatale of a flapper she'd seen in months in a body-hugging scale-covered dress that shimmered turquoise, coral, and gold in the torchlight. "Oh, my, that's a thing."

They were gorgeous, not just the costumes, but how they were with each other. There was a certainty and flirtation that came through even from a distance. Her escort smiled "Ah, I suspect they'd be a pleasure to talk to. Let's see if we can work around to it, shall we?"

Lizzie nodded, she couldn't resist the chance, and as they wandered that way, she murmured, "I'm wondering if it's something Egyptian, perhaps? They went in for animals rather more than some."

There was a little scuffle, off to their left, two men with swords - unedged, she hoped - and mediaeval women. Gwenevere, Iseult, ladies in towers. Nothing she had any desire to watch or be near.

Steady progress brought them down to the dance floor, where the two women were still dancing, the scales and feathers shimmering and catching the light. "Do you dance, Columbina?" came the murmur at her ear as the previous song ended and the next began. It was music she'd not heard before, with something of jazz improvisation in it, but more structure, better to dance to, brass and a fiddle and insistent drum beats.

"Well enough, with the right partner."

That got a laugh, and she felt the slight pressure of a skilled dancer in the hand on her back. She thought she'd forgotten what this was like, from before the War, and before everything else changed. Back in the days when she went to glorious parties, danced with charming young men, and had a delightful time.

He spun her out expertly, catching her hand, and pulling her back. He had the good sense not to try anything fancy, she liked that about him. Flashy, oh, yes, spins always were, but it was a fluid thing, not tight and precise.

They came back together, palm to raised palm, and she

used it to press and spin, blessing the boots that gave her a stability that shoes wouldn't. That let her pivot, step, twist, and twirl under his arm.

The music was faster than she'd been used to before the War, and it took them a turn around the dance floor to get a proper sense of how it went. Then they settled into the dips and flourishes, and then they set into the dancing with a proper will, figuring out each other's little preferences. He liked a tap of the toe on the floor behind him, she liked rising to the balls of her feet, the little minute jumps and kicks that ruffled her petticoat.

No one who knew her now would recognise her, dancing. Her feet belonged to a time before the War and everything changing.

In time, the spins and turns and movements of the dance lead into a pause, and the band was taking a break, apparently. Her Arlecchino had steered them near the vulture and snake, and gestured for a waiter with a tray of drinks, handing one to her, and then cheerfully, "Your tastes, ladies?"

The other two eyed them, and Lizzie offered a, "We couldn't help admiring your costumes. So well designed. Egyptian, yes? I'm afraid I don't know the symbology properly?"

The two exchanged a glance, and it was the one in feathers who languidly stretched out a plump arm and extracted a glass from the table. She replied slowly, her voice a rolling alto, some accent Lizzie couldn't quite place, "The joined kingdoms."

They passed a little time in conversation, and they warmed, Lizzie thought, as she asked a few questions about the costume design, details. Her escort was well-mannered, not staring at exposed skin, but not ignoring it either.

Appreciating it, that was what he was doing. It was meant to be appreciated.

The vulture-lady stood after a few more minutes and murmured, "I should see to that feather, darling," to her partner, and Lizzie stood. "I have a hem I need to mend - and I've got skill with a needle. May I give you a hand?"

That got a laugh. "Oh, if it's offering to help, we can use that." Something in that made Arlecchino's shoulders twitch, but he nodded. "I will look for you anon, Columbine," he murmured, with a bow, and they broke off in three different directions.

Lizzie and the woman in the feathers turned to the house, her escort along toward the garden. The snake woman was drawn into a question by someone else she clearly knew and sparred with regularly.

The withdrawing room was actually several rooms. They settled on a silk covered bench once they were inside, and the other woman pointed out where feathers were coming out. Moulting.

Lizzie rummaged in the pockets of her chemise for a moment, drawing out the small sewing kit she'd brought. Five minutes later, she had a line of others who needed a hand, and all the gossip she might want.

There was no sign of Laura and people weren't using names, but she kept hearing threads of similar things. A new drink, goldwasser, something that made one dream and fancy and yearn to wander. Hard to come by, though people at the party mentioned getting tastes.

Lizzie had plenty of desire to wander already, that was no temptation. She'd had it in her blood since she was born. Lizzie let the murmurs about visions wash over her, before jerking her attention back to what was going on, when someone murmured something about "Morland's new business." She couldn't quite hear everything, but the fragments she caught suggested there was something going on there, perhaps associated with the drink. Perhaps not.

Then she lost the thread, as a bunch of giggling flappers, a decade her junior, came staggering in, all shrill laughter and brittle sharpness. Not long after that, she slipped back outside and went looking to see what her escort had got up to.

She came back across the terrace, looking down into a sunken garden, with what initially looked like statues. She realised only part way across that many of them were couples, intertwined and clearly amorous. More than amorous. She passed too close to a trio on a bench by the stairs down, one of whom reached out to her with a "Want a tumble, pretty lady?"

She whirled away. She did want. But not like that. Not at all like that, thank you, with a stranger at a baffling party.

Lizzie made it out to the lawn again, looking for that flash of silver among all the other flashes of colour and light. She was still looking when there was a smooth voice, at her elbow. "A drink, Columbina?" She startled and then found it was Arlecchino. "Nothing odd in it, I promise. Sparkling water and syrup."

She eyed it warily, then passed her hand over it, murmuring one of the charms her uncle had taught her, and nodding at the slight golden glow. Her escort cocked his head, without quite asking a question.

"My uncle was a rogue of several stripes. Taught me all the things someone could do with a drink when you weren't looking."

"A useful education, Columbina. Here, I was hoping to overhear some of that group over here, if you'd indulge me?

It's a paired dance, and I find I quite prefer you as a partner."

"I've not stepped on your feet?"

"Nor thrown yourself at them, or into my lap wanting rather more than a dance."

Lizzie had to laugh at this, and he led her off into a swirl of comments, only about a fifth of which she understood. A few, though, made her worry more about Laura and what Laura's employer might be up to. Lizzie could only tuck them away and hope they would be a help at some point.

Two hours later, her quite mysterious Arlecchino escorted her to the portal, with a murmured "Columbina, a most pleasant evening to you." Without, she noted, trying to hear the destination she murmured to the portal keeper.

Courteous, but distant. She had had far worse evenings. Not that it mattered, she'd be unlikely to see him again.

# EIGHT

## YTENE, IN THE NEW FOREST

"Rufus, what on earth is keeping you?"

"Sir, getting the mare, sir."

"Do not give me that mild subversiveness, Rufus. If I'm being an idiot, tell me."

"Sir." And then Rufus grinned and replied, "Only got two hands, sir."

"And you can't hold a horse and do other things at the same time. I'll get the bucket."

Rufus snorted, the sound matched by the black mare he was leading. "Let me get her settled, sir."

Carillon laughed and went to go fill the bucket, coming back to catch Rufus checking the mare. The right amount of give on both ties, enough she could move her head but not so much she could catch a leg, or that their new stallion could.

"There's a good girl, Nox. There, now. You've done this before. Know just what to do. Your last little filly's all grown, and right gorgeous she is, and it's time for another one. There, good girl, just like that, settle on down."

Carillon came up, with the bucket, levitating it to hang

on a hook set in the wall, with a, "There we go. Ah, yes, she's lovely. Settling down nicely? Should I go get our boy?"

Rufus nodded. "If you'd not mind, sir."

Smithy was a stunning copper chestnut who thought extremely well of himself, but who was not as difficult to handle as he might be. Formally known as Hephaestus of Bells, he was not the brightest of their herd, but their mares more than made up for it. It was a work of a minute or two to get him led over to the breeding barn. Carillon grinned to watch his ears pricking as he realised what his next task would be.

He was doing his best not to be distracted. Distraction was a dangerous thing when you had worked up horses at hand. And yet, his thoughts kept drifting to the party, to what his mysterious Columbina had shared of the gossip. To what on earth he would tell Vivian next they met.

They got through the breeding smoothly enough. It took them a bit to settle Smithy and the mare back in their stalls, and talk through which of the other mares might come into heat next, leaning over the fence and watching them, chatting about the foals, and their prospects.

"You said you wanted to train up for pavo, sir? What does that involve, precisely?" They'd talked about it, but not recently, and Rufus had more context now for the horses.

"Have you ever seen a pavo match, Rufus?"

Rufus shook his head. "Not a thing played in the village, and I didn't on leave, either. Bohort, plenty of times, but not pavo."

Carillon nods. "It's like bohort, and not like. Older, probably. Pavo's how they used to train for war, the knights on horseback. Agility, obedience, specific skills. And then of course, people wanted to play who didn't have highly trained livestock, and that is how bohort came to be."

Rufus snorted. "And then they complicated that all up. Setting puzzles that most folks can't solve with magic. Well, some of them."

"I like a good bohort match, honestly. The ones that rely on wits. Though I don't dare play where most people can see me. Gives too much away, watching a bohort match where people are relying on wits and knowledge rather than showy skills. So, I prefer the Schola rules or Westbury, but I'll only play Richmond in public, and that rarely."

Rufus laughed at that, and Carillon was grateful again for the steady practicality of his barn manager.

He considered, watching one foal frolic for a moment, kicking up her heels, then said "Anyway. Pavo, teams of five, all mounted, though it's permitted for one person to be unmounted at a time. The same sorts of challenges as bohort, collecting flags or moving items to specific locations, or solving puzzles with magic. There's a larger element of speed and accuracy because of the horses. Less emphasis on challenging objects, again, because of the horses, things that might cause damage."

"What sort of skills, then?"

"Agility - wheeling around quickly. Steadiness. Obedience. A good mount for pavo can gallop, come to a halt, hold while you do something with one of the fixtures, and then take off again and weave through poles or obstacles or jump a fair height. Sometimes you have to ride a pattern to trigger the next piece, or do something at speed."

"Is there a preferred size, or breed?"

"Smaller's better. Some people vault on and off. I can't manage that anymore, my shoulder won't take it. But even if you don't, there are sometimes things where leaning over is easier if you're lower to the ground. Sturdy legs are good.

That's why I was thinking the New Forest ponies would make good stock."

"With a little judicious outcrossing." Rufus nodded at their shiny copper stud, a sturdy Welsh Cob who'd bring height and strength to their mares.

"Exactly." Carillon beamed. "I can lend you a few books if you like."

Rufus grimaced and considered. "I've not got over much time for reading, sir. Still working on what we'd agreed, the other lessons."

"Oh, I'd not get in the way of you learning to herd your magic sensibly. Only as you've got time. And no neglecting Ferry. A young wife is a lovely thing, I gather."

They watched the horses for a few minutes before Rufus ventured, "Do you see anyone, sir?" and Carillon looked at him sharply.

"My, you'd not have said that two years ago."

This got Rufus tapping the brim of his cap. "Lot can happen in a year, sir."

Carillon considered, then said "It can, yes. Do you have a reason you're asking in particular?"

Rufus looked out at the mares for a few breaths, and then he said. "Heard people wondering, sir, if you were. In the pub, at the market. Some of it was just idle gossip, you know how people do. But some of it was, well. Wondering about the future."

"Which would be more reliable for people here if I settled down and had a family and a promise of the next generation." Carillon winced. "That didn't work out so well for mine."

"So we do better," Rufus said. "Be bloody hard to do worse, wouldn't it?"

Carillon made a sudden gesture, flicking his fingers, the

one he'd picked up in his travels, averting bad luck, then shook his hand out. "Don't say that. It tempts fate."

Rufus retreated into himself, and Carillon had to pause and take a breath. "Sorry," he said.

"Sir." Very distant, now.

"Shouldn't take my temper out on you. Not your fault."

"Sir." It was a little warmer, perhaps.

Carillon paused, watching the horses again for a minute. Carefully, not looking at Rufus, he said, "Does the village gossip have any ideas about who I should be seeing?"

That got a small chuckle and Carillon let out a breath. "Plenty. Many of them not that practical. You'd be wanting someone who likes rural living if you're going to make a go of the stables. We've the portal, but still."

Carillon nodded. "Plenty of people would rather live in Trellech or even London. Not here. And I admit, the old place still needs care."

"Several people thought a wife might oversee a bit more of that. Hire more crafters in. Good for the village, that kind of thing."

Carillon made a little gesture with his hand. "True enough. Though Benton's managing the house well."

Rufus snorted more loudly, enough to startle one of the foals. "Benton's keeping the place running, but that's different than shaping it, making it a proper home, and you know it, sir. You say as much every time you come to the cottage."

This got Carillon looking at Rufus again, more intently. "You have got outspoken." It was curious.

"You've given me reason to be, sir. Encouraged me in having opinions. And Ferry has too."

"Well. No time for courting at the moment. I'm working on a project. Consulting."

"That's the thing that's got you in Trellech?"

"It is. Possibly some other places, too. There's a party coming up - well, I suppose I should bring someone to that, but it's tricky to figure out who to bring to something you're investigating."

"Not something I'd know about, sir." Rufus was definitely more amused.

"If I need an expert in escaping from a tithe barn, I will definitely be consulting you and your lovely wife."

"Sir." Rufus was back to decidedly contented now. Which was good. Carillon hadn't meant to upset him.

"Not all of us are so lucky as to meet someone who suits us that well by accident."

That got a quieter murmured "Sir." and a long pause. Finally Rufus started talking, quietly and amiably, about one of the younger mares, about whether it was worth switching her from breeding to training.

# NINE

## TRELLECH

Tuesday after work, Lizzie turned the opposite direction out of the Ministry buildings, off toward the river valley and Madam Porter's building. She wound past the older Ministry buildings, past the warehouses, to where the house sat overlooking the borderland area, down to the Wye River.

It took her a good twenty minutes at a fast walk, which gave her time to think about her workday, and a meeting they had pulled her into. The Belin were upset, but no one, even ap Rhys, could figure out why.

It was some obscure phrasing, something that hadn't come up since before the Great Vowel Shift. There were notes, in three different and obscure dialects of Middle English. All complex enough that they'd spent the afternoon poring over lexicons and annotations, and her neck and eyes now ached. And they not only hadn't figured it out, but they might well not. Not everything was in books.

It was a relief to be out in the April air, even if it was a bit damp, and to get a good walk before another meeting.

She wasn't sure why Madam Porter wanted to see her.

She'd made her weekly report on Friday, but it hadn't had much. Nothing about the party but that was on her own time.

Once she arrived at the trim house with the blue-green trim, she knocked as she'd been instructed, and the assistant let her in. "This way, please. Green tea again?"

Lizzie nodded, and drew off her hat and light cloak, handing them over to be hung up, before Eleanor showed her into the sitting room. There was the usual fussing of bringing the tea out with a few scones, and Lizzie sat forward on her chair, unable to relax.

"Nothing you've done wrong, but I wanted to give you some additional information."

"Ma'am?"

"I gather from ap Rhys that the Belin are quite unhappy. He inquired whether I had any additional sources of information. What can you tell me?"

Lizzie took a breath, to settle her mind and organise her thoughts. Not that she hadn't expected something of the kind.

"We haven't quite sorted the problem, ma'am." She laid out what they did know. That the Belin were restless, that it was not a problem that had come up recently. She drew out her notebook and mentioned the texts they'd consulted, the ones they were working on translation and annotation for.

Madam Porter listened, leaning forward intently. Here and there she'd ask a question, sharp and clarifying, but she followed the decidedly obscure theory readily.

"What do you think would solve it?"

Lizzie inhaled, then said, "Figuring out what it is they're on about, obviously. But barring that - ma'am, I couldn't help thinking, this afternoon, that if someone's doing something, maybe there's a sign of it somewhere else." She hesitated, then said, "I heard something this weekend, and it doesn't seem to fit, and yet..."

"Go on." It was more an order than an invitation.

"I was at a party, this weekend, ma'am. Um." She flushed. "Wondering what my sister was up to. I didn't see her, at least not to be sure of. But I heard some things."

This got a little gesture. "That pairs party? How did you get in?"

"Um. That's a different story." Lizzie suddenly felt clumsy. "In the withdrawing room, I was helping with some mending. It's a good way to hear things."

"It is. Clever of you."

The praise made Lizzie look up, and smile, and then continue. "Someone said something about a - run on certain metals. Whoever she was with elbowed her, shut her up, right after, and then other people came in and I couldn't hear anymore. Gold varieties, mostly. Coinage, specifically, but not just any coin?"

Madam Porter made a small noise, considering. "Tell me what else you heard, if you would. Even if it seems to have no connection."

Lizzie glanced up, and the other woman was leaning forward, now. "Ma'am," she said, and then half closed her eyes to recall the sequence, and told what she remembered. Who she'd helped, the costumes, what she'd said.

She found that the costumes created a memory palace effect for her. It was easier to remember what was said because she associated with a striking design or the feel of fabric between her fingers. The mention of the goldwasser. The gossip about some odd thing with jewellery. Something from someone in one of the banking families, she thought one of the Scali. She said what she remembered as clearly as she could, with comments about how clear it was or wasn't.

Madam Porter paid close attention, then asked, "Is that your usual level of recall?"

"Ma'am, I think the costumes made it easier. To keep things in sequence because I was helping people who were memorable." She would be honest.

That got a snort, and a "That would do it. Still, well done. People who've had memory potions have done worse. Do you feel that's complete?'

Lizzie nodded. "Ma'am."

"Tell me how you got into the party, do." Madam Porter leaned back, more visibly relaxed. "While I'm thinking about the next step."

Lizzie swallowed, paused for a sip of tea, and then explained how she'd rummaged an old dress out of their dress-up box at home. She'd tried and failed to get in, and then a man in a commedia costume had fallen over her, and they'd joined forces.

"Did you exchange names? Does he know who you are?"

"No names, ma'am. I called him Arlecchino, at his suggestion, and he called me Columbina, at mine. He sounded much like any other well-educated man from the magical community would, the accent wasn't distinguishing. Three or four inches taller than I am in boots with a heel, not heavily built." She considered. "I might recognise him by his dancing, but not by his face or voice."

That got an outright laugh. And then, "Tell me about his dancing, then."

Lizzie blinked but agreeably said, "Lightfooted. A good sense of rhythm. The most identifying thing was a little tap on the ground behind him, with the toe of his boot, in the decorative beats. He favoured turns and twists, and..." She considered. "I wonder if there's an old injury, to his left shoulder, he did the more complex moves with his right, but that might just be chance."

That got a nod. "I believe I know who it was. I'll make inquiries, but you may hear a little more about it." Madam Porter looked somehow very satisfied. "What did you think of him?"

That was a good question. "A good dance partner, ma'am, and a good partner in other ways. I liked how he - didn't press me for my reasons for being there. We talked a little, between the dancing. He didn't tell me why he was there, either. I shared some of the gossip from the with-drawing room with him, and he told me a few things he'd heard in the smoking room."

Lizzie paused for a moment, considering how to frame the next part, then said "I didn't tell him all of it. He asked if I'd heard anything about a new drink, and I didn't see the harm in telling him that. But of course, I didn't hear more than the name and a few sentences. I didn't tell him about the metal, or that comment from the woman I thought was from the Scali."

That got Madam Porter tapping her fingers on the arm of her chair - a rare overt sign of thought, Lizzie realised.

"Your escort. If he's the person I think, would you be willing to work with him again? Something similar, an entry into spaces you would find difficult to get to yourself, in exchange for your ears in places he cannot go?"

Lizzie blinked, then said, carefully, "I would need to know more details before I could agree or disagree, ma'am. I don't even know enough, right now, to know what reservations it would be sensible for me to have."

That earned her an open laugh. "Oh, well said. Let me see if I can get hold of him, then, and discuss some further steps. What's your diary like for next week, another teatime meeting?"

Lizzie considered, then said, "Monday or Wednesday would be easiest, ma'am, or I could do a modest length lunch on Tuesday."

They left it at that, with Lizzie making the walk back to the portals near the centre of town not quite sure what she'd just agreed to.

# TEN

## TRELLECH

Carillon tapped the invitation on his leg, waiting for Vivian to join him. She'd suggested he come to her offices for lunch, without explaining why. She never explained herself.

And then he'd been seated in here, with a cup of perfectly made tea to start, and a "Madam Porter will be a few minutes, Lord Carillon. There's one other party who will join you for lunch."

He was thinking about who it might be, and how to frame his response when he heard a noise from the other room. It came from the more formal office, a startled sound, loud enough to carry through the adjoining door.

It quickly stopped, or rather went back to a faint sound he presumed was a more ordinary conversation. Several minutes passed, and then the door opened, and he immediately and reflexively stood.

"Lord Carillon, this is Elspeth Penhallow. You've met at least twice."

He bowed, equally reflexively, at the hand she

presented. "Miss Penhallow." And then his brain caught up with the sentence. "Twice?"

Vivian settled in a rustle of folds, and said, amused, "She described that habit you have of tapping your toe behind you when dancing quite precisely. Also, her suspicion you'd had some injury to the left shoulder in the past."

Carillon blinked at her, then at the younger woman, before letting her hand go. "Miss Penhallow?"

She looked back at him, quite steadily. "I prefer Lizzie to Columbina if you please."

That at least gave him something to work with. "Lizzie. I'm Carillon to most people. Unless formal titles are called for."

Lizzie gave him a precise nod and settled in the third chair. Vivian's assistant brought in the lunch cart, all tidy sandwiches and tea and a plate of small cakes.

"Nothing too exotic, Geoffrey, but the ones there are that curry and chicken you like. Miss Penhallow - or may I call you Lizzie, in this case, if you prefer it? - the others are cress and cream cheese, and salmon paste." Vivian was prompt in getting things moving.

They sorted out their meal with a minimum of fuss. Carillon was glad to see that Lizzie was neither a fussy eater nor birdlike about her food. She made her selections, one half of each type of sandwich. "I hope you don't mind my being a bit speedy with my meal, I need to be back in the office inside the hour."

Carillon raised an eyebrow inquisitively at Vivian, and she waved her hand. "She's working for ap Rhys. On a matter that appears to be more related than I'd thought originally. Hence this meeting."

Suddenly things made rather more sense. "If that's so,

why not tell me we'd both be at that pairs party? It would have saved us some fuss dressing."

Vivian laughed, and Carillon was surprised at the openness. "Oh, Geoffrey, I had no idea she'd be there."

Lizzie swallowed the bite of sandwich and said, "I wasn't there for that particular question but on a personal matter. Madam Porter tells me that the information about the goldwasser was, however, quite helpful."

Carillon nodded. "Oh, quite, yes."

She paused, considering, and he leaned forward slightly, wanting her next question. "May I ask, then, what use you think I might be in the investigation?"

That brought him up short, and Vivian gestured at him. "Explain what brought you."

He nodded and set the invitation on a side table. "I was invited to a rather grand sort of party, and it would be preferable if I were escorting someone. It's that sort of thing, where people will be paired up." He considered, then said, "And you would be quite helpful, gathering the sort of information you did at the last one. Your mending skills got rather a lot of detail I have no access to."

Lizzie tilted her head, visibly considering. "What precisely is involved? I'm afraid my wardrobe doesn't stretch to the sort of clothes that would be at a party like this. All my good things are from before the War."

It was how she said it that caught his attention. Some women, especially those who liked pretty things, would be bitter about that, or accusatory. She was wistful. This was a thing she'd known well enough to know she liked it.

He waved a hand. "If that's the concern, I'd be glad to arrange credit at whatever dressmaker you prefer. Or to advise on the sort of thing that will likely be there. It's a crowd I don't run with much, I'm a bit old for them, but I know what they favour."

He earned that little tilt of her head again, and he watched her glance at Vivian. She replied, "Our client would be glad to cover the clothing as part of the expense of the investigation, but I believe Carillon would best be able to offer advice on what would be suitable. They understand that being able to move in the relevant circles is a necessary expense."

Carillon nods. "I can provide suitable jewellery from the family pieces. There's quite a few that aren't notable or memorable, but quite the thing."

He watched Lizzie consider this, and then nod. "For the right image." She paused, then asked, "Would you tell me more about this party, and what you want me to help with? Before I agree for certain?"

That got a chuckle from Carillon and the murmured "Of course." Vivian waved a hand for him to explain, with a murmured, "I trust your judgement, Geoffrey."

He settled in his chair, considering how to begin. "Vivian approached me about a problem that her client had noticed, several people who had accepted a bottle of a new drink, and found their magic drained over time."

"The goldwasser?"

"So it seems. We've not been able to get a sample of it yet. Bottles disappeared from the houses of people who went in for treatment, or they had already gone out in the trash."

That made Lizzie furrow her forehead. "Go missing?"

"Most of the people who were most affected, their memories are a bit fuzzy."

She considered. "Does... does the magic come back?"

Vivian answered this. "We think so, but we're not sure

yet. Slowly, though, if it does. What's drained in a matter of a couple of months may take years to return."

This got a face from Lizzie, something entirely overt about her emotions, which was quite in contrast to the professional prim air she'd had so far.

"May I ask what you were investigating, Lizzie?"

She looked up sharply, and Carillon could see her figuring out what to tell him. "I was looking for my sister. She's got in with a fast crowd, and I was worried."

"Not the matter you're working with ap Rhys about?"

She shook her head. Vivian considered, then said, "The Belin are restless, Geoffrey. No one's quite sure why, though it appears to be a matter that's not come up for some time."

"Commentary in Latin?"

"Dialects of Middle English." That was Lizzie again, promptly. "We think it's something to do with what might be phrased as the proper life, the word that keeps coming up is cwick, which is living or alive. It's where we get quick-silver from, for mercury, but it's not quite like that?"

He considered, then nodded. "It sounds like this might be connected. Not for certain, but definitely worth investi-gating. And coming to a party with me won't take you from your regular work, at least."

Lizzie shook her head. "When's the party?"

"Saturday week. Time for you to find a dress and such. May I meet you after work to make the arrangements?"

"Tell me what sort of thing would do, and I'll sort it out myself. I can write if I need more details."

Clearly, she did not want him too near her selection, but he nodded. He spent a few minutes outlining, quite precisely, what kinds of dresses would position her correctly. Nothing too much of the flapper, it would neither suit her figure nor the kind of woman who'd be his escort. Modern, shorter, but not quite so faddish.

At a quarter past one, Lizzie looked up and said "I need to go back to work. I'm sure you've more to discuss, Madam Porter, do let me know if I should come back and see you?"

Vivian waved her hand. "After the party, unless something new turns up. Do take care, Lizzie."

Carillon had hoped he'd have a chance to speak to Vivian further, but as soon as Lizzie was gone, Vivian was standing. "I have a client coming at half one, and a few things I need to have ready before then. Thank you, Geoffrey, I'm sure the information will be most useful."

# ELEVEN

## A COUNTRY HOUSE, WILTSHIRE

Carillon had arranged via a series of brief notes to meet Lizzie at the portals in Trellech. She had been entirely unspecific about precisely where she lived. He only knew it was somewhere in Cornwall because of a brief mention of her living in the family home.

He waited, a bit nervously, wishing he'd kept the taste for a cigarette after the War, but the smell brought back unwelcome memories more times than not. He'd withdrawn to one of the waiting nooks, hoping she would not be terribly late, when someone came up to him, hooded. The figure was wearing a black cloak, undistinguished, and something rich and red underneath. He blinked several times and then watched her pull the hood back.

Oh, there were cosmetics there, and the sort of fussy things women did with their hair these days, but that was Lizzie. He immediately stood extending his hand. "Miss Penhallow. Lizzie. Or would you prefer to be Elspeth for the party?"

She considered, extending the hand in delicate silk

gloves for him to murmur over. "Elspeth, I think. The name suits the dress better, don't you think?"

"I look forward to seeing it in its full glory. Shall we?"

She nodded, and when he turned, she tucked her hand into his elbow quite precisely. He walked with her in silence halfway to the portal they needed, then murmured. "Your note said you were familiar with formal party etiquette."

"Before the War, but yes. Not high court, but the proper forms."

He nodded. "It's not a sit-down meal, so we won't be separated. I would like you to excuse yourself at some point to hear the gossip among the women, and I will do the same among the men. Games of chance, smoking room, and all." He considered her, and realised suddenly he found her harder to read than Vivian, which was quite an accomplishment. He had no idea if she was nervous, excited, focused, or what.

She snorted. "And you want what from me? Am I to be utterly enchanted with you? Hanging on your every word?"

"Oh, by all the Green Men, no," he said, amused at how she put it. "They're rather used to seeing me with decorative women, some quite opinionated. But consistency through the evening would be a help. I'll play along with whatever you do, but it's easier if it's the same thing or an arc."

That got her quiet, she was considering the implications. Just before they got to the portal, she murmured, "A little overwhelmed at being at such a large gathering, we've newly met, but found each other intriguing enough to attend this party together. Say we met when we did the first time, at the auction, if anyone wants an explanation. I liked your attention to detail and manners, even if you were rather out of season."

Carillon laughed. "Oh, that will do quite well, yes. Do you expect any difficulties? Old beaux I should be aware of? It's likely there'll be several women I've been associated with there, but I don't expect any of the likely ones to be difficult."

That got her looking up sharply, and a, "You'll find some way to identify them to me, then. As relevant. I don't like being made a fool of."

"One of your lines?"

"A quite reasonable one, don't you think?"

And then they were at the head of the line, and she was all amiable pleasantries with the keeper, as Carillon passed the invitation with the settings over.

The portal was the usual rush of rapid change, the surge of pure magic around them. Not everyone could tolerate it or would choose it, but she followed promptly behind him and didn't need a moment to steady herself.

The portal had brought them out in the courtyard of the house. "Not unlike Ytene." he murmured. "The layout." The lights of the great house burned brightly, illuminating the stone of the courtyard, he could hear music from this side, and whiffs of food. "Though this is - mmm. Georgian, I believe."

That earned him an amused snort. "So, much younger than your house."

He replied with a cheerful, "Oh, yes, and I am quite a snob about that."

It was all to the good, to have them both laughing and amused as they walked up to the front door, and he passed the invitation to the footman. He read it, checked with a little press of the thumb and a flicker of magic. "Please do go through, Lord Carillon. The lady's name?"

He replied for her, as expected, "Elspeth Penhallow, thank you."

"You may leave your cloaks just inside, the buffet is to the right, dancing to the left. The gaming and withdrawing rooms are back past the stairs to left and right."

Carillon nodded, and led his partner inside, murmuring, "Let us circulate through the food first, and then the dancing for a little, and then split up?"

She nodded, and he helped her off with her cloak, handing both his and hers over to the housemaid tending to them. He turned, startled by Lizzie's dress, which was a deep red verging on orange. He suspected she'd not favoured that colour before, but it suited her. There was a translucent veil of a shawl over her shoulders, pinned in place. He'd wondered if she'd known the customs, that revealing skin was a sign of trust in a world where a poison or enchantment could be brushed along one's arm or shoulder very easily without one noticing. The hands, though, were bare, as gloves at such a party would be considered an insult to the hostess.

He bowed slightly to her as he reached to take her hand. "My pleasure to escort you." She ducked her head and let him lead her to the right.

Carillon paused at the entrance. There were long buffet tables set up along the wall. Smaller tables and chairs were clustered along the side of the room by the windows, charmed lights hanging down to illuminate and flatter. He took in the room immediately and murmured, "One of my former partners there, now Mrs Amelia Forsythe. Married, mmm. Middle of the War, I forget when. Another there, Mrs Beata Knully."

Lizzie tilted her head. "Your former partners, all likely to be married?"

He nodded. "It's been a while since I've been out with anyone for more than an evening. Years." He could feel her relax slightly.

"And on decent terms, you said?" A pause, as she considered something. "You used their given names."

"Yes. I don't believe in women giving up their identity in marriage. Untraditional of me, but one must have one or two foibles. Mrs Andronicus Forsythe is also rather horrible as a name, don't you agree? Or Mrs Cadwallader Knully."

That made her laugh, and he had to grin back at her. "See? They'll both be quite pleasant, I'm sure."

Lizzie nodded, and then said, "Well, we shouldn't linger in the door. Do introduce me around as seems best?"

He made another half bow to her, and they began a circuit of the room. He was delighted to see she understood the art of picking food for conversation. Bite-size nibbles, nothing that might drip on that lovely dress, or the veiled skin above it, nothing that would be indelicate to eat. Across the room, someone, rather younger, had got that wrong, to the visible amusement of those she was with.

They made their way down the table, until he drew up close to Amelia, in order to say, "Amelia, it's been an age."

"Carillon, goodness, I had no idea you were coming!" Her voice was as florid as ever. "And who's this, then?"

"Elspeth Penhallow." Amelia was good-hearted, but she was also a terrific gossip. If they got things going the right direction here, she would spread it through the party inside half an hour.

"Penhallow. The explorers?" That was an arched eyebrow.

Lizzie shifted slightly. "My father and uncle, yes. I'm

afraid I've not been much out in society since..." She let her voice trail off. "Well."

It was quite the right tone to take with Amelia, who clucked sympathetically, and said, "Oh, goodness, dear, how brave of you. Though Lord Carillon is a most gallant protector if you need that sort of thing. How on earth did you meet?"

Again, Lizzie found the right sort of words with no need for prompting. "Oh, I was organising the auction out at the Foxon estate at Grimsby, a month ago. Carillon turned up wanting to look at some books before everything was properly sorted."

"Pavo, of course." Carillon chimed in easily.

"We've only seen each other twice since, but I just couldn't resist his invitation here." Which had Carillon wondering if she'd enjoyed seeing him, or not. Her tone was bright and cheerful, but he noticed how precise her words were.

Amelia swept the conversation off into an amiable comparison of who Lizzie knew, and who she might be interested in meeting. It left Carillon free to murmur at intervals, add a comment or two, and then bring her around to meet others.

About half exclaimed rather profusely at his escorting someone, and someone not at all known in this part of society. The other half, apparently, were more than a little puzzled that she'd dared to come out or had chosen to, it wasn't quite clear. It wasn't clear to him, either. The more he watched her reactions, the more distracted he was trying to figure out how she'd learned her very competent social skills.

One man drew him aside, as she was being introduced to a brightly dressed clump of women. "Never thought she'd be at a party like this, old man," he said. "Leander put rather the kibosh on that."

The name was enough to trigger a faint memory. One of the sons of a minor aristocratic family, the Sibleys. Their eldest son had died early in the War, and he half remembered hearing some gossip about the next son marrying, but he couldn't recall what happened after that. Not that it mattered. It is not as if he'd let a Sibley dictate his choice in partner.

# TWELVE

## A COUNTRY HOUSE, WILTSHIRE

The next hour was a flurry of introduction and conversations. Carillon watched people react to Lizzie, taking in who was curious, who was catty, who was polite. And one or two were decidedly not polite.

It was clear that the last, at least, hit close to home, but she hid it quite well. Just a flicker of her steadiness before she dove back into the conversation. She had a knack for drawing people out, too.

She'd listen to them for a sentence or two, then find something they were passionate about, or interested in sharing, and encourage that. Devorah Levy on architectural magics. Espiridion Biggs on a matter of current law. Asenath Sibley on a history of jewellery. A most useful trait, and one he hadn't often seen in someone not in his line of work.

After that hour, she disappeared into the withdrawing room. While she was gone, no less than four men inquired about her.

"I don't suppose she's a paid companion, Carillon? You don't go in for that sort, but I wondered."

Carillon stiffened. "I'd not do that kind of thing. Not to a large party like this." Nothing wrong with a paid companion, but he'd not mix business and pleasure.

The man moved away, and another inquired how they met, which was easily answered. He was glad she was up for telling the truth, it always made things much simpler to keep track of. And, for that matter, you never knew when someone had a bracelet or necklace or some such that would tell them you were lying.

He noticed that it was the men who were more curious about her, trying to figure out what to do with her. The third was curious what he knew about her family, which got Carillon murmuring, "We're still getting to know each other, I haven't pressed her. I know what was in the papers, the ship disappearing, the firm going bankrupt. Just Elspeth and her sister, now."

That got the man cheerfully talking about Laura, apparently he'd met her at Tibbie's office or some function. He was already deep in his cups and it wasn't quite clear.

The last was a rather blunt inquiry, asking what Elspeth did now, and Carillon waved a hand. "Some office job. Ministry. Steady work, I gather."

That got someone overhearing and laughing. "Well, if she's setting her cap for you, she won't need to work much longer, will she?"

It was awkward, because Lizzie came back just after the man finished speaking, and Carillon could not decide if she'd heard it or not. He immediately turned, offering his arm again. "I was just thinking we've not explored the dancing, Elspeth. Would you do me the honour?" All quite courtly and proper.

She inclined her head and let him lead her off to the dancing. Once they were properly settled into a partner dance that would keep them together, she murmured, "Rather a lot while I was there - too much to talk about here."

He nodded. "Supper, afterwards? I was thinking we'd stay another hour or two and then fade away."

That limit helped her relax, he could feel it in her back. He considered, then murmured, "Anyone give you trouble?"

"Not more than usual." That was quite clipped.

"You let me know if anyone's particularly difficult."

"So you can be gallant? Not the usual thing for an Owl, gallantry."

Again, he couldn't figure out how to take that. He spun her, in lieu of saying something immediately, then managed, "A verray, parfit, gentil knyght, that's me."

This made her laugh suddenly, loudly enough others noticed, and then she leaned in to murmur, "Well, it goes with your pavo, I suppose."

He smiled back at her, and a "Man has a reputation." She was, he was quite sure, sharp enough to realise that he was playing up the public image. And perhaps she was wondering what was under that reputation. He rather hoped she was, just as he was wondering what was under her quite pleasant public face.

Mind, he had also noticed that she hadn't answered him about people being more than usually difficult.

Another dance, then another, and they could retire to seats and a drink. They were settled amicably, watching people, when he realised there were fewer there than there had been earlier. He was about to lean over and murmur something about that to Lizzie, when a dark-haired man, maybe in his late twenties, stumbled in the middle of the foyer floor.

"Oh, hey." And he blinked at Lizzie. "D'I know you?" His voice was decidedly slurred, and Carillon straightened.

Lizzie peered at him and said "Tristam Dyer." she said. "Elspeth Penhallow. You were a few years behind me, in the Stream."

This earned her a charming, drunken smile from the man. "Oh, yes. Remember you now. Turned out right pretty, oh. D'you want a drink, pretty lady? Makes you dream and dream and imagine such things and places."

He held up a bottle, which shimmered. Shimmered two ways. Carillon saw the magic a hair before the gleam of gold flakes and inhaled sharply. He was about to murmur to Lizzie, when she said, "Oh what have you got there, then?"

"Gold. Gold. Gold water. No, that's not quite right. Drink of the gods, though. Ambrosia, nectar, amrita, honey wine, all sweet like peaches, oh, glorious elixir of life, the aquae vitae of the great alchemists." He raised the bottle, which let Carillon get a better look at it, the shape and size of it.

They needed some, but how to get a sample without drinking it.

Dyer came closer, holding out the bottle. "Oh, you want a glass, where's a glass, where's a..." He raised his voice, and that attracted more attention. Three people, no, four, converging on him from several directions. They clearly hadn't seen Dyer offering, but Carillon turned his head.

"Beg pardon, we need to not be obvious to them. Do you... may I kiss you?"

His arm was still politely around her shoulder, and he could feel her initial shiver. Then a stronger shudder, but as she was turning to him it was neither an argument nor a refusal. He shifted, leaning to cover her face, hide whatever expressions snuck out, with the angle of his, and kissed her.

He had expected resistance here, now it was hidden. Instead, she moved into the kissing as neatly as she had stepped into the dancing on their first night out together. It was not a perfect kiss, a kiss for the ages, no first kiss ever is except in stories. But it would do brilliantly to hide their interest in that bottle.

Carillon felt her shift a little, slipped his arm lower, toward her waist, to let her brace against something, without venturing too much of an intimacy. They paused, here and there, for breath. And for his part at least, to focus on what sounds he could hear from Dyer behind him, letting her lean into the back of the sofa.

The fourth round of that, she shifted to brush her lips against his ear, and murmur, "They've hurried him off. No luck on the bottle, quite sure someone took it."

He exhaled sharply and pulled back, taking care to make it not abrupt. "I am thinking we might want to take our leave sooner than later? Discuss next steps?"

Lizzie nodded. He could not help noticing that she was a little flushed, her eyes a little wider. He could not tell if that was the kiss, or the situation, or something else she had seen. She was superb at not giving much away. Practised.

And then, after a moment, he said, "Salmon House? I'd not have thought that for you."

She shrugged, and it at least let her ease into something she was more at home with. "I don't normally wear my stone where people can see it. I'd rather keep them guessing. Plenty think me an Owl."

"You've seen mine." He turned his hand, showing the ring.

She shrugged. "Also, it's in your profile in the Gold Book." The book that laid out all the Great Families, their children and descendants. He made a face.

"You have an unfair advantage, m'lady."

She snorted. "I use the tools available to me. I'd have thought you'd have realised that by now."

There was nothing sensible he could say to that, so he did not try. Instead, he rose and said, "Let us make our excuses properly, and go to supper. My club or yours, or somewhere else?"

Her lips were a bit tight. "Mine, I think."

He could only bow, and escort her to make the necessary pleasantries, and to reclaim their cloaks.

# THIRTEEN

## TRELLECH

Lizzie had to stop herself shivering. She wanted nothing more than to retreat, back to the house on the cliff that was dented and too empty, but at least familiar. But no, she would do her duty. Lizzie had said she would go to supper, so she would go to supper.

She let Carillon escort her through the streets, from the triangle of the Portals. They walked through the older Tudor era homes, all plaster and wooden beams dark with age, not that one could see much in the lamplight. Then a right, so they walked with the looming Ministry buildings in more insistent grey stone, along the left. And finally, the sharp turn to the neighbourhood where all the clubs stood.

He knew the way, she noticed, but he let her precede him once they got to the low steps. She slipped a hand into the strap of her dress, drawing out the chain with her stone on it, and held it for the doorman at The Stream to see.

He bowed slightly. "Miss Penhallow and guest?"

"And guest. We'd like supper, Myron."

"Small dining room, Miss Penhallow, or there are private booths in the Guest Dining Room if you prefer."

Lizzie nodded. "The latter, please." She leaned to murmur to her escort, "There are privacy protections built into the booths, I don't know if you've been a guest there before?"

This made him smile, for some reason he didn't explain, but he nodded. "Quite suitable. Also, I find the curtains in the Small Dining Room a bit distracting."

Lizzie blinked, and said, "They are a rather - yes, that pattern." Which was of a school of swimming fish in a baffling design. It had one set of fish swimming one way in shades of gold, and another set swimming the opposite direction in shades of blue, tiled in such a way to make the head spin.

It was at this point that they were inside, and someone was coming along to show them to the Guest Dining Room. Lizzie knew perfectly well that there were ways the staff communicated with each other, but it bothered her, still, not to be able to figure out how they did it.

They were escorted to a pleasant and comfortable booth, a table between them, and plenty of space, presented with late-night supper menus and a drinks list, and left promptly alone.

Lizzie let out a long breath and glanced at the items, then at her companion. "That was - I'm not quite sure what I expected, but it wasn't that."

Carillon snorted. "No, it wasn't. But that's for after we've ordered. How does one trigger the privacy here?"

"It takes someone with a house stone, or one of the staff." She paused for a moment, unpinning and shrugging out of the shawl, then slipping a pendant on a chain out of her dress. She unlatched it from the strap it was looped around.

Finally, she extracted a small bracelet cuff from her

cloak, slipped it on her wrist, and slotted the pendant into it. The small click made her relax, quite visibly, she was sure.Only then did she touch it to the panel on the wall, to set the privacy protections, that would prevent anyone from overhearing unless they were right at the table.

"That's how you usually wear it?"

She nodded. "Safer than a chain if you're doing some kinds of things." Lizzie paused, then said, carefully, weighing her words. "I did a lot of sailing with Papa and Uncle Kenver." She watched him, across the table, try to decide what to say to that. When he spoke, it wasn't what she'd expected.

"It must be very hard, not knowing what happened." It wasn't a question at all.

Lizzie nodded quietly, looking down for a moment.

"I didn't invest with them. I was overseas. But it seemed a sensible plan, from what I heard. And there is tremendous potential in some of the Amazon plants. Risky, but a reasonable sort of risk. Well-communicated."

Lizzie made a small noise and had to take a deep breath, wishing for rather more alcohol on the table than was currently the case. Even if she needed all her wits about her with this man.

"Thank you for saying so," was what she managed, quietly after what felt like a year-long pause.

It was at this point that the waiter appeared for the fortuitously timed and necessary interruption of ordering. Lizzie asked for a glass of hard cider and Carillon ordered wine from the middle of the list. The waiter glanced at him, for her order, and Carillon shook his head minutely, not even attempting to order for her.

Once that was done, he asked, "Cider?"

"I don't mind wine, but we always had local cider at

home. My family preferred it. It's a staple drink, in Corn-wall, has been for ages." That, at least, was a safer topic than her father.

"Where in Cornwall, do you mind me asking?"

"The house is off a little magical village, maybe... four hundred people, total? Lanyon, way out on the tip." She pronounced it properly, the old way, la-nine.

He tilted his head. "Hence the sailing?"

That made her smile, despite herself. "The sailing. Though we mostly went up into the Celtic Sea rather than the Channel or the ocean. I mean, for pleasure. Uncle Kenver would take people across to Wales, sometimes, for the weekend."

Carillon watched her, and said, "That seems like a good memory."

She looked up, and nodded, then coughed, and said, "We're not here to talk about my family, though."

He settled back and said. "We have business. Shall we take it in sequence, then? What of the early part before you split off?"

Lizzie tapped her fingers on the table for a moment, thinking back. "I've - it's been a while since I was at a house party. Since 1915 or so. Other than our earlier one. I'm not sure if or how the customs have changed."

He leaned forward a little. "Tell me what you noticed, please."

"Everyone seemed rather - separate. Like it was lashings of luxury, spread out, but people were doing their own things. Their own little circles. I..." She paused, trying to find words. "Some parties I went to before, they were - symphonies, people bringing together different guests, making something larger and better? Oh, it didn't always work, but there was a sense of trying?"

Carillon lit up, she could see that. "That's it, that was the thing I was trying to pin down. Oh, you're a clever lady, spotting that. Mind, I think it's a bit more common now."

"Than before?"

"Than before. The War shook up the usual layers of society. And yet, young people still want to marry, and their parents want to find them matches that are suitable some way. Whether that's land or titles or money or magic."

"Or all of them?" Her voice was a little sharp, and she coughed. "Sorry."

"You've nothing to apologise for."

Lizzie shrugged. "Well. More than one person, when I was on my own, pointed out you were all four. And - neither unattractive nor with distressing tastes in bed."

His expression was entirely worth framing just like that, a sort of combination of stunned ox migrating to uncertainty, finally settling on a sort of amused distance. "Oh, is that what they said?"

She nodded, now a little more sure of herself. "You have a pleasant reputation. Though I rather suspected you didn't let most of them see some of you? Kept yourself cloaked, even in more intimate engagements?"

He blinked at her, and oh, that was a delightful thing, to see him set back on his heels again, and so quickly. She felt a little guilty about it, he'd been nothing but pleasant all evening. Even the liberties he'd taken were as careful and limited as the situation allowed.

But something about him made her unsettled like the universe was waiting for her to throw herself into his arms or that he should sweep her away. She was having none of that, thank you.

Fortunately, he diverted the discussion himself, saving her the difficulty. "Leaving aside my personal life." About which he hadn't talked much, actually, she realised. "What did you hear among the women on other topics?"

She wiggled her hand. "An analysis of who was invited and who wasn't. I scribbled down some notes, enough to work with, I hope, for you and Madam Porter. Vivian." She coughed. "But more than one person implied that some guests were a cover for the others. Respectable, but known to like a good party, that kind of thing. Who'd keep things going, bubbling, while others did things they would prefer not be noticed."

"Like dangerous drinks?"

"Possibly." Lizzie paused. "Probably, well, almost certainly, other drugs, too. The usual range, from what I understand, most of that didn't startle the other people listening."

"Not your thing, then?"

"I prefer a clear head, thank you. Cider's one thing, but -" She grimaced. "I have enough herbalism to know most people who make illegal concoctions don't necessarily know how to make them well or safely or of a consistent strength."

Carillon blinked at her. "That's not the usual take on them. I'd have thought you more likely to say you don't like giving up control."

Lizzie snorted. "Well, I should have thought that that was obvious, sir, from first principles."

It made him laugh, which was a good thing, she'd seen his shoulders getting tighter about something. It wasn't clear if it was the drugs or the implied commentary about his usual social set. If that was his usual social set. She wasn't sure, for all he'd known, known and bedded, more than a few there. It was possible he'd had a past history with a bottle or the needle, but it wasn't quite like others she'd seen like that.

The food came, then. Salmon cakes for her, which she admitted a fondness for, even though it was rather a stereotype of the house. He'd ordered something easy to eat, a mix of small finger foods. Neither of them were terribly hungry.

He took a few bites, then said, "What else, then?"

She laid out the rest of what she'd heard, as evenly as she could. A few signs of who was included in which social circle, who was not. Several of them were known to him, she could see that, but two were a surprise, and he asked her for more detail. Then, "How well did you know Dyer?"

She looked pensive. "We weren't close. He was a few years behind. Gather he wasn't a bad bohort player, the house team. Not the best, but not bad?"

"That might give an in for me, maybe. Nothing on your end?"

Lizzie considered. "I'd have to think about it. Check some notes. See what he's been up to," she finally demurred.

Carillon nodded, and from there they dissected the rest, the little bits and pieces and shards until she was tired past yawning. He murmured, finally, "I should see you back to the portal, or are you staying here?"

"Here, I think. I've a case in storage, in case I have to stay over."

So he left her, in the front foyer, to go up to the little cheap rooms in the fourth floor. It meant bed that wasn't her own, and a little washbasin to clean up in. She'd not have risked it, but she was on expenses. And yet, she couldn't make use of one of the slightly nicer rooms, with a tub, not without attracting comment.

It wasn't until she was getting into bed that she realised he'd shared only the most general details of what he'd heard when she hadn't been there.

# FOURTEEN

## TRELLECH

Monday morning, Lizzie went into the office and knocked on the door. "Ap Rhys?"

"Meeting at ten." He didn't look up.

"I have an update on the goldwasser. And a thought."

He leaned back in his chair, eyeing her thoughtfully. One of those looks where if she got this wrong, she knew it would affect things. She'd reported the initial information, after the first party, but he'd waved it off as not relevant to his interests unless she had something a little more solid.

"Sir." Very polite, though he was usually not terribly formal. "I attended a party on Saturday night. We got a glimpse of the goldwasser, but no sample."

"That's not much use, then." His tone was dry and sharp.

"Sir." And then she swallowed. "We got a look at it, though. And it was - shining. Not just the gold in it, though there was that, flakes of it."

"Flakes." He leaned forward. "Not shavings?"

She shook her head. " I was perhaps three yards away. They were little flashes of - flat pieces. Maybe the size of... a quarter of my fingernail, the bigger ones? Like you'd apply to a manuscript."

Ap Rhys tapped his fingers irritably on the table, thinking. "You said that wasn't the only thing."

She shook her head. "The bottle was shimmering. A golden light. We were in a well-lit hallway, he was standing in the middle, under the chandelier, but it was still a distinct light source."

"How bright?"

Lizzie frowned, considering. "Less than one of the wall sconces? Not much less."

"And you're sure it was the liquid glowing?"

"Certain, sir. About a quarter of the bottle was gone, we could see the glass clearly, and it wasn't."

"That's something." He considered, thinking for a beat, and then said, "What did you do in the War?"

She stopped, uncertain what to answer, and he raised an eyebrow. "Come on."

Lizzie swallowed then said "Hospital administration, sir. Under Master Groton." She was baffled he hadn't found out earlier.

"Indeed. What did you think of the work?" His voice was dry and precise.

That took a moment's thought. "I liked the challenge of figuring out how to manage the different aspects smoothly, and with optimal outcomes for patients and staff. I appreciated Master Groton's standards, even when they could be frustrating on a practical level." She felt she needed to be honest.

Ap Rhys looked at her for a good half-dozen breaths and then flicked his fingers at her. "Go away, then. Meeting at ten. May have an assignment for you later."

Lizzie went back to her desk, fidgeting with moving

things around and aligning stacks of paper between the various small tasks that came in.

At two minutes to ten, everyone swept into the little cramped conference room that was all scarred wooden table and barely enough room for chairs. Precisely on time, ap Rhys strode in, nudged the door closed with his toe and set the extra privacy enchantments going. She could feel the hum of them at the base of her neck.

He gestured at Halwyn Jones, the junior of the two cultural specialists. "Go through the proper approaches to arrange a meeting with the Belin. It won't be sooner than next week, but soonest is best. You know the protocols?"

"No direct reference, but say 'the matter in which we have a shared interest', the proper offerings for…" Halwyn considered. "We want the summer ones, yes? Even if it's a trifle early yet?"

"The question is better suited for the liminal offerings, but there's no way we'll have a meeting by then. The early summer ones, yes. Arrange your journey plans, and I'll push through the expenses and item requests."

Tilly, one of the two researchers, said, "I have the requisition notes from last time, I think we can get the paperwork through promptly."

"Show her how to do it." Ap Rhys gestured at Lizzie. "All the details."

"All? Yes, sir." Lizzie got the sense that was not what was expected.

"I'll be wanting a full write up on what to plan for, as soon as the arrangements are made. Details on related projects, the cousins, all of that." He gestured at the specialists, Halwyn and Grwn Morgan, who both nodded in unison. Ap Rhys considered, then said, "We'll take Verch Hendrek for administrative support."

Ap Rhys went on, detailing a list of things for the materia experts to have ready, testing potions, examination kits, reagents, to thoroughly clean and prepare the lab. Lizzie thought Warin Burke looked a little unsettled by something. He was the junior of the two materia staff. He'd only been there nine months, and Lizzie thought he'd be far happier in a job with fewer odd requests and surprises in it.

Just because there was a particular query didn't mean that was the end of the meeting. There were the usual questions about ongoing projects, how to set them aside or wrap them up. The staff nodded and made notes about their particular tasks and asked tightly phrased and particular questions.

Lizzie took minutes, making notes for things she needed clarification about. She kept glancing from person to person, becoming certain something was odd here. The process was a well-oiled machine and yet something about this was odd for the rest of them. If they all looked confused, this was not something she was going to sort out on her own.

The meeting wrapped up, with a "Verch Hendrek. Well spotted," before he went stomping back to his office. No one else left the table, and they inhaled, and then leaned forward, almost as one.

"What did you tell him?"

"Come on, he never does things like this."

"It is rather urgent, sorting out the Belin." That was Halwyn.

Tilly tsked at him. "Still."

Lizzie blinked at them and then considered what she could share. "I was at a party, this weekend. I got a look at... something seemed odd. New kind of drink, it had gold in it. I told him about it this morning, and then this." Best to keep the fact she'd been with someone entirely out of it.

That got a snort. "Something in there. He hoards information, fit to be a dragon."

"We don't actually know that dragons hoard things, you know the research is unclear."

"Oh, shush, Halwyn."

It was a chaos of commentary, all at that pitched sound of polite voices in urgent conversation, that never rose to anything that might be considered an objectionable volume.

Lizzie let them talk it out before she said, "Could do a drink after work, but Tilly, would you show me the paperwork? So I can understand it?" Tilly was the senior of the researchers, a woman in her early fifties. Her dark hair was perpetually coming down, and her cuffs were often smudged with ink or graphite or chalk, but she could be relied on to both understand which things mattered, and explain them to others.

More importantly, Tilly could be relied on not to talk down about things she knew, which was more than Grwn or Warin could manage. Grwn had some excuse, he came from a family who'd been negotiating with the Belin for at least a thousand years, handling gold and copper.

That was an agreeable alternative. All of them put their noses down, working more or less through lunch. Lizzie had a snatched half sandwich at her desk while waiting for a new copy of a particular form to be duplicated and ready for pickup.

Warin came by her desk while she was waiting for Tilly to review a different form and leaned his hip on it. "I don't know why he wants you on the trip. It ought to be me or Amberton, properly."

She blinked up. "I'm not sure either, Warin. Have you gone before?"

He narrowed his eyes, then huffed a little. "Ought to be

me. Or Amberton." The latter was a little grudging. He pushed off the desk, adjusting it, making her grab for a pen about to roll off, and then have to rearrange three stacks of papers.

Tilly was another ten minutes, then came over, and said "Let's take the notes to the conference room, spread out a little." Lizzie wasn't sure what to make of this. She nodded, and brought tea in the spill-proof cups when Tilly indicated it, and waited while Tilly closed the door and nudged the privacy charms.

"Is that..." Lizzie gestured. "Expected?"

"No. But they can cope. Or they won't." Tilly was very blunt. "I saw Warin earlier but didn't hear what he said. Was he being an arse?"

Exceedingly blunt. Lizzie waved a hand. "He thinks he ought to be going. Or, if not him, Amberton."

Tilly snorted. "Look, you know... actually, what do you know about the Belin?"

Lizzie took a deep breath. "They're what some people would call dwarves, but that's not accurate, and certainly not polite. They live in the deep lands, in the Welsh mountains, and they have cousins under the mountain in other places. Slightly different customs, but it's important to get the differences right."

Tilly nodded, making an encouraging noise, as she sorted a stack of fifty-odd pages into five distinct and unequal piles. "Go on."

Lizzie continued. "The customs are very important. There are different offerings that change based on where you are asking to do the meeting - so it's different in Gwynedd than in here in Sir Fynwy."

Tilly nodded her approval at the proper Welsh name for the area Trellech was in. "Quite right," she said. "That's what Halwyn's sorting out. You'll have a shopping list for it, for tomorrow. You can get all of it here, except for what has to be selected fresh at the site."

"At the site?"

"Oh, some of the list is always local, a rock from the nearest stream to the meeting site, a flower that's just past peak bloom, or a cup of snow melted from the peak. Depending on the season and the place. Some of them are standard, but sometimes they'll add something, based on - well, actually, we've no clue why they add things. But sometimes they do."

"So why are you the one doing the fussing over the lists? Not that I don't appreciate it."

"Research is research. It ought to be Halwyn and Grwn, I suppose, but they're both lousy with details and much better with the language."

"And Amberton and Warin?"

"They're needed for, well." Tilly settled back, having sorted the papers. "I'll explain those in a moment. In the usual course of things, we'd have a meeting twice a year, on the equinoxes. We take a certain small amount of material with us, from the agreed upon mining, and they pass back a small amount. And both sets are tested. It's like weighing things on a scale at the market, to make sure it's the trade that's expected. And that's why we need materia experts."

"Do they look for anything in specific?"

"We don't know, honestly. If you ask Grwn on a good day, he'll tell you it's about a quality of the gold or the silver. Something they look for that isn't about weight or ore precisely, but about something we don't have a word for in English, don't even have a sense for. Not that Welsh is better on that front, it's just that the Belin will speak a dialect you can get to from Welsh if you ask nicely enough."

"Did Audrey go to these meetings?"

"Audrey didn't care for travel. And honestly, she was sweet, and she was grand at talking to people in other offices and getting them to sort things out for us. But she wasn't very good with the specific things we do here. I think the Belin unsettle her, and I know the selkies do."

Lizzie considered that then quietly said, "Oh. So. How do I do what I need to?"

Tilly waved a hand. "That's the pile for Ap Rhys. That's for Grwn, that's for Halwyn. That's the forms we file with the Ministry outside this office. The big stack is for you, to keep track of everything. Pull it over, and I'll talk you through all of it."

It took the rest of the afternoon, but by the time they left, Lizzie was feeling confident she'd manage the needed forms and permissions. Eventually.

# FIFTEEN

## TRELLECH

The next few days, Carillon was busy with the stable, three more mares in heat, and all the fussing over them that required. It was not until Thursday that he made it back to Trellech, to check in with Vivian.

That itself went smoothly, a pleasant hour of tea and commentary, only some of which was about the project.

Having a profusion of clubs to choose from, he wandered along to stop in at Bourne's. He planned to go down the street to the Explorer's Club after a brief check. The former was higher status, but far more tedious, on the whole. Men only, whose places must be inherited. Only certain families.

What he found, however, was a surprise.

"Letter for you, my lord."

Carillon blinked. "Letter?"

"Left Monday, my lord. With instructions not to forward." The man's voice was rather insistent. "We inquired, my lord. Knowing your preferences."

Carillon frowned and reached to take it before he forced himself to stop and take a breath and think. Personal correspondence would have gone to Ytene. Stable business, the same. Someone who wanted to catch him the same day or the next day might have left a note here. He was in several times a week, usually.

But why was there no name? He turned the envelope over in his hands. Plain ivory paper, good quality, nice thickness. There was a wax seal, in a deep red, but the seal itself was blurred, unreadable. He passed his hand over it, and there was the faint shimmer of colour from his ring, a brush of materia in the wax, perhaps.

He flipped the envelope over to look at the writing on the front. It was utterly uninformative. Plain black ink, the handwriting the formal precise hand so many people his age had been forced to master early.

It was aggressively unidentifying, like someone had copied it from a penmanship book. The writing was without a hint of the personality or quirks of the writer. No little extra flourishes, no narrowing of the curves.

"Can you bring down the kit in storage for me? The one in the grey box. And may I use one of the small workrooms?" The footman bowed.

He was glad, yet again, for the rigorous expectations of his family that meant he kept a small kit at each club. Never knew when you'd need one.

The magical work rooms were a feature of most clubs. The ones at Bourne's were rarely used, the kind of place that would have a few cobwebs in a less diligent establishment. Someone went ahead of him to light the lamps.

They showed Carillon to one, and the staff brought out a marble-topped table for him, at his request. Not terribly reactive, and therefore useful. Also, less likely to go up in smoke or shatter if he guessed wrong. Then a table for the working kit. He waited for them to bring a basin of water, a pitcher, another table for his notes, before locking the door behind the departing staff.

He then settled in for the tedious part, cleansing the table thoroughly, pouring a tube of salts in the basin and then dipping his hands up to the wrists. He had no idea how people did any kind of complex magic without a small staff on hand. The cleansing precautions alone for anything like this were rather a lot of work.

Wash his hands. Dry his hands. Undo the case, which was only ever opened with clean hands. Apply drops of oil to both palms and smooth it over in a pattern that had been drilled into him relentlessly since he was thirteen. It was not prayer, not meditation, not anything like that, and yet it was very like that, at the same time.

He thought about drawing out the fine silk gloves, for the protections sewn into them, but it was always a toss-up between protection and decreased sensitivity of touch. Even fine silk confused things too much, for most work.

Carillon drew out the silk mask, however, to keep anything away from his nose and mouth, checking the magical barriers were still in place. He did not know all of how they worked, but he'd trusted such masks with his life before, in the War.

He went through the proper motions, finally reaching for the toolkit, drawing out the small brazier and pot, setting it to burn. While he waited for the pot to make steam, he checked the other tools.

The knife for opening the seal without touching it went to one side. One set of tongs for the seal, another for the letter inside. A non-reactive weight to hold the letter inside when he set it on the table. Then the silk case to place it in afterwards, insulated and protected. Finally, he set out the stone plate for small pieces.

If it was what he thought it was, he'd need that. Something felt wrong in this, a little shiver of unnameable perception.

Part of him felt he was making a fuss over nothing, that what he'd find inside would be some casual invitation, hoping to catch him. A party, a dance, a frolic, a pavo match.

The pot whistled, and he shifted to let the knife heat in the brazier, getting it warm enough to peel the wax back. Then, he settled in to do so, working carefully, taking his time. He eased the seal off, dropping it on a separate stone plate for later examination. The next step was sliding the letter out with tongs.

It wasn't until he had levered the pages open that he felt the brunt of it. A burst of magic, something that might be a powder, there was no canister for gas. He had to hold the table for a moment, gripping hard enough to leave aches in his wrist later. Then he forced himself to let go, to stand, to not act until he was ready.

Everything now had to go in its proper sequence. He collected the powder, something fine and glistening, a gold, he thought, though it was hard to tell in the golden lamplight. First, he poured what dusted the letter into a vial and set the paper aside. He extracted his wand for a cleansing charm after he braced the letter firmly enough it would not blow or shift. Then he sealed the vial, with a strip of adhesive tape from the kit.

Only then did he turn his attention to the content of the words.

It was a threat, in word and deed, but the threat was to Lizzie, not to him. Or at least, not directly. There were hints here and there, for all the text was blunt, in undistinguished block letters.

STOP STICKING YOUR NOSE IN

P IS SURETY FOR GOOD BEHAVIOUR.
WE HAVE FRIENDS IN HIGH PLACES.
AND LOW.
BACK OFF.

It was, at least, he thought, evidence that they had stumbled on something worthwhile. P was, presumably, 'Penhallow' and Lizzie. At least, he could not imagine any other plausible expansion for the initial.

High places, though, that was worrisome. Low places, well, there were protections for those, if one needed. Mostly. He'd have to talk to a few contacts, and to Lizzie and Vivian. It was perhaps a slight reassurance there was no mention of her.

High places, though, implied the Ministry, the courts, or something else of the kind. People who could leverage not only political power but magic and a staff of dozens, at least, if they put their mind to it.

Carillon considered. He would have to get the powder analysed. It might have evidence of who created it, or where it was created, that would let them narrow down the sender, and open up options for investigation and assistance.

For now, he frowned. Then, he reminded himself of what they had taught him, the attention to detail, the importance of cleaning up one's work as precisely as one had begun it. His Master, during his apprenticeship, had said, over and over, that that was the difference between a middling magician and a great one.

Also, he had pointed out rather often, also the difference between a dead magician and a living one, if one were inclined toward experimental magics. As Carillon was.

So he checked the vial with the powder one more time and slid it into a lead-lined box in a quilted silk pouch. The letter went into another, the wax into a third. Finally, they were all bundled up together in a small flat case he drew out of the lid of the toolbox.

Once they were tucked away securely he could begin the rituals to burn away all specks of dust and powder from the table, cleansing it thoroughly. He repeated the same process for the stone floor. It took three passes for him to be satisfied. Only then did he close up his tool case and go to the door, setting the light that would tell the staff that the room needed special attention.

# SIXTEEN

## LANYON, CORNWALL

Thursday evening, Lizzie had settled into the library after she'd had her evening meal. She was still puzzling over something she'd heard referenced at work and hadn't asked about, and she thought one of her uncle's books might be a help. She had a half-memory of a story he'd told, about the banking families, some tidbit from the Italian city-states, how Venice differed from Florence, and it was taunting her.

It was still light out, though she could see the gradual progress toward sunset from the window. This room had once been a dining room before her parents rearranged things. Her father never had enough space for books.

She heard the noise, then the sound of the kitchen door, with the precise high squeak she kept meaning to fix. Lizzie startled, wondering what to do about it, then she heard her name.

"Lizzie?"

It was Laura. Laura, entirely unexpected. Especially on a Thursday.

"In the library," she called out. "What - what brings you out here?"

Then Laura got to the door, and Lizzie couldn't help the gasp. "Come sit down, please. Or do you want to go upstairs?"

Laura was pale, and she had that brittle brightness in her eyes that Lizzie remembered from the rare visits they had permitted her at the sanatorium. Laura brushed the offer off, and then she stopped and closed her eyes, her balance clearly unreliable.

"The housekeeper's room. Down here. It's already made up." Lizzie could be decisive.

There were a series of tasks, then. Getting Laura tucked into bed and fetching an extra blanket from the wardrobe. Checking the fireplace was behaving. Rummaging in the henhouse for more eggs, finding none, and putting up a note to the milkman for an extra pint. Making another pot of tea.

Tea was never a bad idea.

It was a good twenty minutes before Lizzie could sit down next to the bed. The room hadn't been used in years, not since the War, but she'd kept it in decent repair. Impersonal, but tidy and aired out.

This was a distraction. "Laura, are you feeling any better?"

Laura waved her hand. "I'm fine. You're fussing." There was an edge to her words. She didn't look fine, however. She was still drawn and pale, and her breath was shallow.

"You look awful. Shall I send a note, to your work?"

Laura made a sharp noise, clearly wanting to protest, then said, "Please. Just for the day, tell Mr Morland I'll be back on Monday." She added after a little pause, "I told Mrs Mackenzie I was coming here. My landlady."

Lizzie nodded. "Are you all right for half an hour? I can take the note down now, so it goes first thing."

That led to rather more fuss and bother, bringing a lap desk and paper for Laura and the house seal, and waiting while Laura figured out what to say. Then she had to get the bike out to ride down to the village so she could drop the note in the mail slot by the portal. Then she peddled back up the hill, certain she felt someone watching her.

Lizzie looked over her shoulder, several times. It was past twilight, she was managing the road by habit as much as eyesight, and there was no way she could spot anyone who didn't want to be seen. Or someone who was standing in a shadow, for that matter. Shadows were decidedly in abundance.

When she got back into the kitchen, she heard Laura's voice. "That you, Lizzie?"

"It is. Making another pot of tea. Want some mint?"

Laura made a non-committal noise, and Lizzie measured out enough for them both. Mint wasn't the best herb for lungs, but it wasn't bad. More to the point, there was plenty in the tin.

She considered, puttering around the kitchen and making her lunch. Basic brown bread with a bit of butter from the crock on the table. She added a hard-boiled egg, the last small ends of the cheese, and a rather pitiful salad made from spring greens. Nothing fancy. She'd leave the soup and the other egg she'd meant to bring for lunch tomorrow for Laura. All that went into the keeping cupboard until morning.

She brought the tea in when it was ready with the last scone she'd been keeping, cut in half. "Only the one scone, but it's currant, I know you like that."

Laura blinked, distractedly, and didn't respond.

"Is this something coming on then?" Lizzie paused, trying to figure out how to ask what she did and didn't want to know. Was this tuberculosis again? Was it something else like that? A slow death or a fast one or not a death at all?

Laura blinked, and then she laughed, high and pure and the sound shifted into something brittle.

"Oh, nothing like that, Lizzie. I feel a bit queer, that's all. You fuss and fuss. Worse than Mama."

Lizzie barely kept herself from flinching. Their mother had spent a decade and more doing her best for Laura. Getting her into the best care. Arguing for her care. Reading the latest research, what they could find. Giving up all her other interests to follow Laura where Laura needed to be, away from her husband, and away from Lizzie.

She busied herself with her teacup instead. "No honey, sorry. I need to trade a bit of help to Mrs Tregallan, for some of last year's batch, but it's been so busy at work."

Lizzie knew it was a mistake, saying that, because Laura leapt on it, out of her daze. "You don't talk much about work, do tell."

"Oh, nothing that interesting. A lot of filing and filling out forms, very precisely. But they've got to be done just right, or they send the forms back."

"And that's what they need you for?"

"Well, I needed a position, it's steady work and Ministry pay scale. And the people are pleasant."

"Does your boss still do that thing where he calls you by Papa's name?"

"He does, but I've sort of got used to it. And he does it to everyone. Sometimes it's informative when he's talking about other people in the Ministry. Connecting them up."

Laura waved a hand. "Wouldn't know about that.

Though I am meeting more people. Is that what apprentice-ship would have been like?"

Lizzie settled back. This was delicate but much less so. "A bit, yes. The apprenticeships, partly you're learning the skills, but they also want people to meet other people. Enough older, if you're young, that you'd not have known them in school. Or maybe who went to different schools, or went straight into apprenticing."

"You went to lots of parties." Laura's tone was contemplative, not accusing. Or at least, not very accusing.

"Quite a few. And that's how I met Leander. I wrote about it. Meeting him at an apprentice ball, and then he invited me to other things."

This got Laura settling back against the pillows that were propping her up. "I'm getting that now. People are inviting me to such glorious parties."

"Oh?" Lizzie tried to keep her voice even. "I'd love to hear." Keeping Laura talking, maybe she'd learn something.

"There was that pairs party, that was fun. I spent most of it in the garden with this lovely young man. Didn't know who he was, he had a mask on. But oh, he was fun."

Lizzie murmured "What kind of fun, then?"

"Oh, there were people dancing, but you know I'm not for that. Though I guess a couple made a stir? Dressed as something Italian, or was it French? A harlequin, someone said. No one knew who they were, not even good guesses."

"That's got to be part of the fun, figuring out who's under the masks."

Laura purred. "Mmm, yes. And Tourney - that's the nice young man - he said how to leave a note at his club if I wanted."

"Which club?"

"Not Bourne's, the other posh one. Wishton's."

"And you wrote him?"

"Oh, yes." That purring voice again. "And he's taken me to other parties. Some bigger, some smaller? The one last weekend that was a smaller party. Him and a dozen friends."

"Had fun?" Lizzie felt like she had to hear more about this. Not just as Laura's sister, but it felt like there was something drawing her in.

"Oh, yes. They had this new drink - well, I'd heard about it at work, too, the office, they know some people working on making it? Goldwasser. It's got little bits of gold in it. And it tastes like..."

Laura paused, sipped a bit of her tea, and coughed. It wasn't the racking horrible cough she'd had for so many years, that made it a relief to hear. But what Laura was saying wasn't a relief at all. Lizzie waited until she was done, then murmured "What does it taste like?"

"It tastes like Papa's stories. All the places he and Uncle Kenver went, like seeing amazing things, and meeting people, and trying different foods, and sleeping in strange beds. That story he told, about getting stuck in a cave in Nepal, and the yak? Like that. All jumbled together. Flashes, like a dream. All amazing colours and people and all kinds of magic."

Lizzie tilted her head. "And - how'd it make you feel?"

"Oh, made me feel wonderful, while I was drinking it. While I was getting all those images. Like floating, like dreaming, only much more vivid. And I slept a lot, after, deeply. Each time I had some, it was bigger. Grander. Better. Only, I'd like more, and it's hard to get. There's this wonderful sort of lassitude, after, not the bad kind, but like drifting."

Lizzie made a non-committal noise. "Wonder what's in

it, then. Maybe something they'd planned to get from America, and now they can't? You said there was real gold in it? What was that like?"

"Oh, it sort of glowed. And you'd think you'd feel it, swallowing? But it wasn't like that, it was so fine that as soon as you poured it, it would shimmer into dust. Something magic, maybe? That glow, made me feel all warm, all the way through."

Lizzie nodded, and murmured, "If you get your hands on a little, I'd be interested in seeing it."

"Oh, do try it, Lizzie, if you can. It's... I haven't felt that good since I was tiny. That week when Papa took us over to France, in the boat, and it was all sun and flowers, as far as we could see and further, the cottage? Before I got sick." There was something so wistful in her voice, then.

Lizzie swallowed. "Made you feel wonderful, then. Well, if you get your hands on some, I'll see."

That said, she made sure Laura had what she needed for the night. Finally, she made her excuses, that she had to finish reading something so she'd understand a report she was working on at work.

# SEVENTEEN

## TRELLECH

Lizzie left Cornwall extra early the next morning, setting out a tray for Laura with the last of the soup she'd been saving in the keeping cupboard. She added a note that the milk had to last until Monday.

She had been up since dawn, working on a note for Madam Porter, and one for Carillon. Once she came through the portal in Trellech, she deposited one at Madam Porter's office. Then she had to take the long walk to leave a note at the Explorer's Club, as Carillon had suggested.

She had to force herself up the stairs at the entrance. The Explorer's Club had been Papa's and Uncle Kenver's club, and now it was like walking a gantlet, people whispering and turning away. Leaving a note wasn't too bad, but only because it was still early.

She almost didn't think to stop in at the Stream, but did just on the off-chance Dyer had responded to the note she'd sent him. Nothing from him, but there was a message from Carillon, asking if she could meet for lunch, as his guest at the Explorer's.

Lizzie went back and wrote him a new note agreeing, naming the time. She asked the porter to drop it off before she finally went along to her office. Despite all the errands, she was on time, which would make taking a reasonable lunch easier.

By lunchtime, she was both cranky and starving. Warin had spent all morning coming over to ask her questions, always at the absolute worst moment. Sometimes she'd been in the middle of counting forms, other times checking her maths, or doing a little confirmation magic that all the forms required. It had meant that she'd got through only a third of what she'd hoped to.

Tilly had leaned over, around eleven, and said, "He's not usually like that."

Lizzie, doing her best not to be irritable, said, "Well, I wish he'd stop." And after that, Tilly had run a bit of intervention.

It all meant that she arrived at the Explorer's Club later than she'd wanted to, out of breath, and feeling at odds and ends. It wasn't the kind of place that cared overmuch how you dressed. All the same, she knew her hair was sticking out and her dress was rumpled, and she looked down at her hands to see splotches of ink she hadn't noticed before she left the office.

The staff were kind enough not to even blink, and she was shown immediately up to a private room on the first floor, overlooking the street, with a high window. She barely had time to feel uncomfortable at being there. The wooden table was big enough for a meal, a substantial mix of sandwiches and finger foods, but Carillon had also set out several books and a sheaf of papers.

He had been sitting, but he stood immediately. "Miss

Penhallow, thank you for your consultation. Adams, thank you, we'll ring if we need anything." The man bowed and withdrew, and Carillon went to touch a panel by the door. "There, now we're quite private."

Lizzie took a deep breath, then said, "Pardon. I wanted to see you, I have a piece of news, but it was a..." She paused. He knew Madam Porter, quite well. "I was juggling several things at work, a bit more hectic than I'd hoped today."

Carillon nodded and gestured. "I've something important to tell you as well. I'd left the letter yesterday. Pardon, but I hope nothing unusual happened to you?"

"What sort of unusual?" Lizzie took off her coat, and settled in the chair, with a "Do you mind if I eat? I'm famished, I'm sorry."

Carillon blinked and waved at the food. "Not at all, that's what it's here for. Tea in the pot, a green you might like." He waited until she'd had half a sandwich, a bit of tea. Finally, he said, when she paused in the meal to consider what else, "I received a rather nasty threat."

She set down the cup with a rattle of the saucer. "What kind of threat?"

"A letter left at Bourne's with instructions not to forward it. I examined it, something seemed off about it. It had a powder in it that is being tested by a materia expert friend of mine, quite private."

He sounded almost dismissive, and it took her a moment to realise it had been more serious. Lizzie was not at all sure what to do with this. "And you wanted to meet with me because?"

"First, because threats often mean you are closer to discovering things than you might have thought. And second, because there's a fair likelihood you're mentioned. I had to leave the note with him, but I copied over what it said."

She looked up at that. "Do you have much experience of threats, then?"

"Enough." His voice was quiet. He passed a slip of workroom paper over to her, the little grids for precise note-taking and records. She read it, then read it again.

"And I'm the P, you think?"

Carillon spread his hands. "You are the person with that letter prominent in their name who makes much sense. I mean, Mistress Popple, in the village near Ytene, asked me to see about a fox that keeps getting into her chickens. One of those lord of the local manor things, but that note seemed unlikely to threaten her, or be about a fox."

Lizzie snorted. "Well, could still be a Fox by house."

He considered that leaning back for a moment, then he reached to take a sandwich or two to fill his own plate. "Have more, please. There's plenty."

She took another sandwich and then thought while she ate before she said, "Why didn't you tell me sooner? And why you?"

"I didn't have a way to reach you quickly. Though if you don't mind, I think it might be good if I did. As to why me, I'm not sure. Rather insufficient information, this note. So far."

Lizzie grimaced but nodded. "I'll - let me finish eating, and I'll write up directions from the portal, to home. Or I can check for messages regularly."

"You don't have a journal, I assume?"

She shook her head. "They came out - well, they're quite dear yet." She stumbled over the explanation. If they'd come out before her father left, she'd have had one, and she'd have known what happened to him, or at least more.

Carillon paused, almost said something, then said, "What's the best way to get a note to you?"

She nodded, eating the sandwich, a very pleasant salmon and cream cheese, then said "It'd be easiest if you left them at the Stream. I'm checking there to see if Dyer gets in touch."

That got a nod. "Quite easy. Sorry for insisting on here, but I prefer their precautions over Bourne's, and the Owlery is, well, its own place."

"I suppose." She considered. "There are two things I should tell you. The one I'd planned on, and something else."

He settled back in his chair, listening in that laid-back, relaxed way that hid the fact he was paying quite close attention.

"My sister came back to the house last night. She was feeling very poorly. I'm not - now I think about it, not even sure how she got up the hill. I'll ask. But - pale and faint and breathing shallowly."

"Is your sister prone to being unwell?"

"She had tuberculosis. Left school at sixteen, she was in and out of sanitariums. Switzerland. Austria and up north after the War. They said she was cured, though."

Carillon nodded. "That must be difficult."

Lizzie nodded. "I wasn't sure about her - stamina, the job she's got. And I know she's going out, parties and such on her days off, rather than resting. But when I tried to ask about it." She made a little shrug with one shoulder.

"Was that the only thing, her turning up? Do you need to check on her?"

"Oh, I left food, she's in the downstairs bedroom. And

I've an afternoon of work to do, besides." She paused, then added, "It's a chronic thing, not an acute thing. If I panicked over everything, nothing else would ever happen. It's been like this since she was fifteen."

He nodded, considering what she said, and gestured for her to go on.

"Anyway, she was talking, last night," Lizzie paused. "First, I took a note down to the portal to go through first thing to her employer, so it would get delivered in the first mail." The one that went out at half-six. "But biking back, I couldn't get over the feeling someone was watching me. I couldn't see anything, it was past twilight, just the lamps, and they don't give much light."

Carillon made a displeased sound. "How - pardon, how protected is your property?"

That got a laugh. "Better than you'd think. Papa and Uncle Kenver brought home a wide range of things. They always worried someone might get an idea to come prowling. Good stone walls with protections built in, warding magics at the corners, and I walk the boundaries at least once a week, check on them. It's the one thing we've never skimped on."

Carillon let out a breath. "Well, that's a sensible family for you. Though I suppose you don't have so much land walking the bounds is a challenge. I have to do Ytene in several passes."

She shook her head. "It doesn't include some of the pastures, no need to. We do the two fields by the house, so we can move stores or animals there if we need to. And these days, I just have the chickens. I'm leasing the other pastures to someone who's taken our couple of sheep into his flock. Our cow died last year."

Which is why she had to spend too much money on the milkman, not that she'd tell Lord Carillon that.

Carillon nodded, and then said, "What else, then?"

She paused, frowning. "Laura, my sister, she told me that she'd had goldwasser. She was dreamy over it."

That got him. He leaned forward, now, eagerly, "What did she say about it? Vivian will want to hear, I'm quite sure."

"She said it was like our father's stories. All the places he'd gone with Uncle Kenver. A couple of specific ones - trying all sorts of different foods, she remembered one he told about getting stuck in a cave in Nepal. It - it made her feel healthy, I think. A way she hasn't felt since she was little. But it was more than that."

Carillon considered quite carefully. "Any chance she has some? Can get some?"

Lizzie shook her head. "I said if she got some, I'd be interested in seeing it, but I'm not sure she can. And she didn't say anything about where she got it, other than she was at a party."

That made her remember, and she had to smile. Carillon caught it, of course. "Something else?"

"Oh, only we made quite a stir at the pairs party. People couldn't figure out who the harlequin was, or the woman with him."

That earned her one of those glorious grins. The one where the foolish socialite lord and the clever man met in perfect harmony for a moment, the face he showed the world and the one she'd seen in private. "Gossip's rarely a bad thing."

He then brushed his hands together. "Back to business. Madam Porter's, after work? Or do you have to get home?"

"I could manage half an hour, but much later than that and Laura will wonder."

They made the arrangements. He encouraged her to have another half sandwich. Then when she was ready, she was presented with the rest wrapped up to take with her in a keep-fresh box, a clever little thing folded out of waxed paper.

# EIGHTEEN

## TRELLECH

"Vivian, someone sent me the most curious letter bomb."

Carillon had been shown into the sitting room, and Vivian was already waiting with Lizzie. He had been held up in two of his errands, so he was perhaps five minutes late. All right, ten.

On the other hand, it did permit a certain entrance.

He was rewarded by Vivian's expression, which was full of a startlement she rarely let anyone see. He had flat-footed her twice in all the years he'd known her. Three times, now.

He swept a slight bow. "Pardon my tardiness, dear ladies, but I have been a very busy man around town."

Vivian gathered herself and looked him up and down. "Obviously, yes." He glanced down and saw the inch of mud on the hem of his over-robe.

Carillon grinned. "It will wash." He settled down.

Vivian waited just a moment, then said, "I presume the letter did not actually explode."

"It was sufficiently suspicious I took precautions, yes."

"Do you know what they intended?"

"I am waiting on a full report, but Cephus said that, among other things, it has gold dust in it. Of a kind that comes from the Dolaucothi mine."

Vivian made a thoughtful noise, nodding at the name of the researcher.

Lizzie ventured, as if she were cautious about breaking her silence in his company. "That's where they get the gold for coins, isn't it?"

"Highly secret, yes." Carillon agreed. "And they don't use much for anything else."

Vivian frowned, considering the implications, and Carillon settled back, reaching for the wine glass she'd set out.

"What was is supposed to do?" That was Lizzie, pressing.

Carillon gestured with his other hand. "Nothing pleasant, we're sure. They designed it, we believe, to explode in my face. So I'd inhale the powder or something of the kind. But my... associate wasn't sure what it they meant it do."

"Do you think it's like the goldwasser?"

"The dreaminess, you mean? Disconnectedness?"

Lizzie's voice got sharp. "The addictiveness, from what I've heard."

Carillon winced. "That too, yes."

Vivian was blinking, flat-footed again. "Wait, did you get more information about the goldwasser?"

Carillon nodded at Lizzie, and she said, "My sister's been given some. Not a bottle, just tastes. She turned up last night at our family home, in Cornwall, looking horrible. She couldn't stop talking about it."

Vivian swallowed, reaching for her tea for the bit of fussing that would keep her from answering. They waited until she said, "How do you intend to proceed?"

Carillon leaned back. "Ah. That's where my other errands come in."

Lizzie raised an eyebrow. He reached into his pocket and drew out a small velvet-covered box. "Would you do me the honour of accepting a token of my esteem?"

That earned him a glorious face, dubiousness and curiosity tangled together. "What sort of token?"

"Protection." He opened the case, revealing a piece of amber, in a silver setting, elegant and eye-catching, bringing out some of the highlights in her hair.

"Amber?" Vivian leaned forward. "Why amber for this? I'd have thought you'd go for jet or obsidian."

"For a few particular properties. Once attuned, it will offer protection from attempts to confuse the mind. It can alert the carrier of a matched piece to problems, and I had suitable paired amber on hand. It provides a modicum of ability to track, though I'd prefer a few drops of blood. That would be much more reliable."

"And you think I need this." Lizzie's voice was flat. "I am not accustomed to gifts of this kind."

"I believe it would be a sensible idea." Carillon was careful. "Oh, there are other precautions one could suggest. A dog collar if one were concerned about a garotte in the dark. A bodice dagger if one expected to be accosted from dark corners. Escape items tucked into one's clothing, sewn in if one expected to be kidnapped. On that note, people I respect recommend the usefulness of a pocket knife, hidden somewhere less than obvious."

Lizzie waved a hand. "Pocket knife is covered, thank you." Not that she explained further, for all Carillon leaned forward a little. "And do you suggest other precautions?" She was frowning, he could see her thinking through all of the variables.

"That is where the other errand comes in. I was...
mmm. Offered an invitation to a party, with you as my
guest, specifically. Two weeks from now, on the Saturday. It
has some specific dress requirements, and if you permit, the
seamstress you used before would be delighted to make
something that suits. If it goes well, I suspect we might have
a house party invitation in the offing."

Lizzie considered. "What sort of requirements?"

"I expect the party will be more on the risque side. The
request is for clothing that shows skin or at least teases about
it. You're welcome to check with her, about the design, or I
brought sketches." He waved a hand. "That was why I was
late."

"And what's your role in that?" Her voice was sharper.

"To treat you as my partner, my respected partner, and
not touch you more than you agree. Though there may be
something like last time, again. We should discuss our
respective limits in advance, but that is for a - different
conversation." He coughed softly. "I know you need to get
home."

Lizzie glanced at the time and grimaced. "I do, yes."

"Do take the box." He held it out.

"And if people ask questions about it?"

He gestured. "Oh, it will fit in your little cuff, as well, or
should. If it doesn't, they can fit it on Monday. That is the
other reason for the amber."

She blinked and then reached to take out the citrine's
chain from where it was tucked behind the fasteners, then
looped her house mark over her head. It took just a bit of
working her fingers to press the new amber piece in its
place. It settled with a satisfying click and a little bubble of
golden light.

"And the... other things you wanted?"

"Your club, on Monday, for lunch? Can you arrange a private workroom?"

She frowned but nodded. "I can. I'll send a message from the portal."

He nodded and stood. "Let me walk you out? Vivian, I'll fill you in on the other details in a moment."

Lizzie made a small noise but gathered her things. Carillon escorted her to the door, murmuring, "I won't share the personal pieces, but she needs to know about the threat."

That got him a nod of agreement. "Let me know when to meet you. Monday or later."

He came back from the door, brushing his hands together for a moment, and Vivian looked up at him sharply. "Talk."

Carillon settled into his chair, took a sip of his tea, and said, "You've heard most of it. Her sister. The party invitation. The current meagre state of our research knowledge."

Vivian snorted. "There are other things. Several of those injured by the drink have died. Five, to date." Carillon winced, and she went on quickly "They had declined steadily, from the beginning. Others are slowly recovering. We're not sure why."

There was quiet for several minutes, then Carillon said "So we need a solution to the problem, as soon as can be arranged."

"Quite."

Circling back, Carillon said, "I am concerned about why I received the note in the first place."

That made her pause, consider, and then say, "That is a point. I suppose I'd assumed there was something from the party."

"I don't believe there was. And if she'd been... careless,

while she was in the withdrawing room, I'd have assumed the letter would come to her. I'll discuss precautions with her."

"How did you spot it?"

Carillon tilted his head back, trying to recall his chain of thought. "Part of it was the instructions about not forwarding it. Which is curious, because normally that would have ensured I'd read it."

Vivian considered. "Forwarding would have meant it was moved. Moved by portal, most likely, unless you were staying at the townhouse."

Carillon head jerked up. "Point. An indisputable point." He considered, then said "Which implies moving it by portal is a problem, somehow. Is it possible that's true for the goldwasser, too?"

"The sources we know got it at private parties. Two, no, three here in Trellech, the others at private homes. Though I think all in south England or in Wales. Easy enough to take by land, the slower route."

Carillon made a disgruntled noise. "Cephus here in Trellech, at least. But I'll see if he can take a small portion elsewhere and test it. I had considered David, but it's not quite his line of work, and he's on the Isle of Man these days."

Vivian nodded, then she said, "You consider Miss Penhallow reliable?"

Carillon looked up and nodded. "Quite. I've seen no signs she might not be, and I was - attentive to that."

Vivian nodded again, then slowly said, "So how did someone know to approach you? If she did not tell someone, not directly, how would that someone know?"

"Ap Rhys knows about this, yes?"

A nod. "He does. His department had to because of the implications for the Belin."

"Is it possible there's someone in that office working with the goldwasser people? Goodness, we need better terms for our parties in play."

Vivian contemplated this at some length. "I think we should keep an eye on that possibility. Will you discuss that with Lizzie next you see her? She would take it better from you. Perhaps we should consider planting a little inaccurate information, see where it takes us?"

Carillon nodded and then said, "I should go see my researcher. I half-remember there's a class of preparations that alter when in strong magical fields, like a portal."

# NINETEEN

## YTENE

The week dragged on. Carillon spent Friday night, after he got back to Ytene, pacing in the library, trying to settle his head. Benton, his valet, fussed at him.

Saturday he gave over to checking the property, riding the bounds and checking the protections, fussing with the warding stones, before doing a thorough review of the portal's wellbeing.

They were a curious thing, half-shaped, half-grown. Rather like magical topiaries, he thought whimsically. Whatever the image, keeping a portal in proper order took a bit of doing. He'd been using it rather more than usual with all this back and forth to Trellech.

None of it occupied his mind, except for a few of the more technical checks. By the time he'd had supper, he was half-vibrating.

Benton helped him change into his night things, and then withdrew with a slight, "Sir, a choice of books on the table." It was the tone of someone who knew what was needed better than Carillon himself did. Which Benton did, of course.

The books on the table were varied. Nothing of pavo, nothing of magical theory, but instead a recent biography of the first Minister of Materia. Another a mystery by one of his favourite authors, with a clever sleuth and plots he didn't figure out until most of the way through.

He fell asleep reading it, and sometime later, rolled over to realise that Benton had put the light out. Carillon dozed again, that middle of the night stretch of time that seemed endless, then slid more deeply into sleep.

It wasn't clear at first he was dreaming. There was something intensely vivid about it, a tint of the light, a clarity of the sound, that was impossible to ignore.

The first thing he noticed was the sound of a party, people talking and laughing. There was the clink of glasses, the pouring of something from a long-necked bottle. Even in the dream, he half-thought that maybe it was just this case, getting the better of him.

Then he felt a touch on his hand, and he turned, seeing a figure beside him. Rather like Lizzie, only her hair was different, and her manner. It wasn't a costume, but rather like something fundamental had changed for her.

Given their time so far, it didn't surprise him that they swung into dancing. She was a lovely dancer, he'd known that from the first, with a light step. Not showy, not a diva who wanted all eyes on her. Rather, she was someone who enjoyed finding how to fit herself into the music, into the swirl of dancers and partners, how to interweave what she was doing into her partner's movements.

Then something changed, one of those moments in dreams where the scenery shifts and it's not clear why or how. And oh, that shook him. He could feel himself, stretched out on top of her on a bed, his hips rocking into her, how hot and tight she was around him.

That was a dream of a kind he hadn't had in years. Since early in the War.

It wasn't just that, though, the kind of dream that might have been written off to close contact with a woman he didn't know. It was her reactions. The little breaths and gasps she was making, the way he could see her eyes open wider, at something that clearly felt fantastic to her. The way he paused in the dream, and then rolled them over, so he could sprawl on his back, and encourage her to ride him.

He had to coax her, even in the dream, to sit up, to move as she wished. All the little guidance of hands on her thighs, the murmur he couldn't quite hear in his mind's ear of his voice encouraging her. Not the foolish praises some women might want, but specifics, details, until he said something that lit her up and broke her open. Until his hands shifted just enough, and she shuddered on top of him, and he pushed up into her.

He woke, suddenly, with his hand gripping his cock, in the aftermath of his climax. He was gasping for breath, damp with sweat and with seed and the sheets tangled around his knees. Then the gasp turned into a whimper, and he had to coil himself on his side, hugging a pillow against his chest.

He waited, willing his breath to slow, his heart to stop racing. Before he'd managed it, there was the knock at the door he knew would come, Benton's voice.

"Sir?"

"Fine, Benton."

For a moment there, he'd felt real, and now it was all shattered, slipping away from him again, lost into the darkness and the distance.

Carillon heard the door close and shivered, now chilled. He knew that in five minutes, there would be hot chocolate outside his door, with a slug of brandy. Benton was utterly reliable, even when woken out of a sound sleep by his charge's sounds.

Usually, it was nightmares. That's why they had the sound carrying devices in place. More than once, he'd been so lost in the nightmares that he couldn't drag himself out. Stuck in a space between sleeping and waking filled with terror and knowing he'd failed.

Knowing he'd always fail. Never live up to the expectations. He closed his eyes, trying not to see the memories, but they were inside his head, crowding his thoughts. Men dying in the mud who he might have saved, if things had been different. Recognising the slow spread of a cloud of sickly green gas, hearing the sounds of men suffocating, as he tried desperately to get as many as he could out of the trenches to somewhere safer. Knowing there was nowhere safe for miles and miles. He shivered, clutching his hands into his sheets, unable to do anything but wait for them to ebb again.

As the rush of memory finally faded enough, he took a deep breath, and another, trying to will himself to some sense of ease. When he felt he could stand, he got up to look out the window. The moon had set, there was just a little light to see by. Enough to remind himself he was in England, not back in the War.

There were no signs of anyone moving outside, nothing that might have triggered a sense of alarm. Benton slept at the head of the stairs, there was no other way into his rooms.

He went to the bath and washed his hands, then the rest of him, rummaging for a clean pair of pyjamas. Right on cue, he heard the knock and a "Chocolate, sir."

"Come."

Benton brought the tray in, a mug for him, and then

went to busy himself with the cleaning magics he knew that would leave the sheets clean and fresh. Benton would make no comment about how they were dirty, he knew, just as he knew his valet would notice it wasn't just sweat. Carillon had no idea how he did it, nor the magics that worked so well for him.

Silence was a blessing, and a great gift, really. And it allowed him to retreat to the easy chair that looked out the window, and sip the chocolate, and cup his hands around the warmth. He was two-thirds done with the mug when Benton murmured, "When you're ready, sir." and excused himself.

Carillon nodded, murmured, "Thank you." to Benton's back. He sat in silence with the dregs of his drink for a good while, looking at the dark outside. Eventually, he closed his eyes, set the mug aside, and went back to curl up in bed, drawing the covers around him. He tried not to think of those last moments before he woke up, but he couldn't stop himself from thinking about what Lizzie might be like if she felt free to show what she felt. Were trusting enough to do it with him.

# TWENTY

## A COUNTRY HOUSE, DEVON

Lizzie was not at all sure about this party. It was quite different this time.

Oh, there were the same clumps of people standing around and talking, but something about the laughter was sharper, the comments a little wilder. Some of the same people, even.

First out of the corner of her eye, then more obviously, she saw people leaning and then touching. A man's hand coming down to cup a woman's hip. One woman draping herself along another woman's back, the back of her hand brushing against one breast. Women still wore the light shawls, but now they were draping down to the elbows, exposing bare skin, a sign of trust or foolishness, depending how you counted. She moved to settle her own shawl over her back and upper arms more securely. She was not alone in that, at least.

Carillon escorted her around, murmuring in her ear a little about this person, or that. More than one person looked her up and down, not sure what to make of her, or turned away to offer a tidbit to others, and not to them.

Once they were between groups, Carillon leaned over to murmur, "Various additives and such being shared around. I assume you'd rather not."

She shook her head. "I don't mind some of the milder drinkables, but nothing strong."

Carillon nodded. "You know how to spot them?"

Lizzie looked at him, and her stare made him step back for a moment, in startlement. It had come out more edged than she meant, and she held out a hand to him, to gesture to everyone else that they had misread it. Nothing to see here.

"Pardon, m'lady." Carillon was watching her closely now.

"A bit on edge. Not just the party, but - other things."

He drew her around, to an open set of French doors and a terrace, with no one nearby. He scanned the space, then murmured, "Your sister?"

Lizzie frowned. "Her too." She was quiet for a moment, then said. "Laura's drifting in and out. She's been staying in town, but she wasn't at work when I stopped in on Thursday. Mr Morland wasn't worried, he clearly knew where she was. But."

Carillon almost said something, she could hear him inhale, and then he shook his head, just watching her in the glow from the windows.

"What, then?"

She grimaced and said, "Not here. Something related to work. A meeting." She had no idea how to explain the upcoming interview with the Belin to him.

She felt Carillon step closer to her, and murmur. "More skin. More show. As my source said." Lizzie nodded, feeling her shoulders tighten for a moment, and then he leaned in as if he were nuzzling at her ear. "We'll make it look good. Not more than you're willing."

Lizzie took a moment to consider the situation. "Perhaps now is the time for me to go get the gossip? And you?"

Carillon went still and quiet for a moment, then let his breath out. "That's sensible." As if he didn't entirely trust his own sense, which worried her. He raised his voice, "Oh, if you must, darling, but do come back soon."

That got a smile from her, and she managed a teasing, "Don't you get into trouble now," before she turned, feeling the flow of the silk against her skin, the folds of her dress flaring behind her. Part way to the withdrawing room, someone handed her a glass of a sparkling cordial. It was like a sunrise, shading from blues at the top to gorgeous reds and golds and corals.

"The drink?"

"A sparkling cordial, miss. To make the party brighter." That was neither informative nor helpful.

She considered it, knowing there must be magic in it, then she sniffed it, and knew what it was, that sharp citrus note mixed with a berry. She'd had it before, at the parties before the War, one of those drinks that would make everything feel good and easy. She passed her hand over it to confirm, murmuring the magic her uncle had taught her.

It shimmered pale white for a moment, then a golden glow. Safe enough to drink, by her standards. Having it in hand would discourage people offering her stronger things. Taking the glass, she nodded, and then went on her way, taking a sip as she pressed the door open.

They needed her sewing skills. Three different people had come up with clothing ideas not well suited to the way a body actually moved. One bodice was torn, another straining and threatening to give way until she adjusted the lacing and tacked a fastener into a better location. One hem was utterly snagged and requiring an entirely different approach to the question of hemlines. She handled it with a bit of gathering and making an impromptu rosette out of the material that had torn off to cover the tear and stitch it securely.

By the time she had done that, she'd gathered plenty of gossip. Who had come with which partner, and might go home with another. A few people speculating about her, assuming that Carillon was considering her as a long-term mistress. She did her best to be unobtrusive until that set were back out in the party.

Most intriguing were the bits about the goldwasser. No one had a bottle, but several people mentioned names - different names - who did. How to indicate you were interested, the code involved mentioning that you wanted to travel to somewhere exotic and luxurious. She filed it all away, without making much sense of it.

It was amazing what you heard when you were sewing around at someone's hemline.

When the rush of repairs finally ebbed, she'd drunk a good half of her glass. The edges were not gone but blunted, she could manage to relax a little more. Carillon had been right, about her being cautious about a lack of control, but she reminded herself that if she didn't ease back, she'd spoil the whole plot. Another three sips and she could leave the glass somewhere as she went back to the party.

She'd been gone thirty minutes, perhaps more, and in that time, Carillon had got misplaced. Or wandered off. She tsked a little, looking around for him, first where they'd been, near the buffet, then in the dancing room. Then, finally, in a room they'd not gone to yet, set out with couches.

Lizzie found Carillon draped across a sofa, his eyes closed. His expression was almost painful, a kind of stored up and reflected joy, deep and solid. He had not appeared to notice neither her, nor notice the footman who came by with a tray of drinks. He just lay there, reclining.

She wasn't at all sure whether to disturb him. She watched for a good minute or two with no sign of him stirring then cleared her throat.

He didn't move. Well, much. A little twitch of the head.

"Carillon?" She tried for it not to sound like nagging, but there are only so many tones of worry mixed with mild annoyance you can use that aren't nagging. She had little practice with most of them.

That got more of a movement, his eyes open at least, and he looked at her. His eyes were intense, the blue-grey of a storm rolling in, and he reached out a hand to her.

"Oh, Lizzie, come here. I feel so terribly good."

It was not at all clear what he meant. He reached up an arm and gestured at his lap, in a relaxed way she'd never seen out of him.

"You found something nice to drink, then?" Lizzie meant it as a teasing line, but as she said the last few words, she saw him shudder. Something in her knew it was a lot more than that. She let him draw her into settling on his lap, feeling his arm tighter around her.

"May I kiss you?"

They'd talked about kissing, as their plots needed. This, though, this wasn't a thing they'd talked about. But he wanted, she could see that in him. And besides, she wanted to as well. All the fluid pleasure of her own drink was bubbling in her, making the world glow and resonate.

She nodded, and then shifted a little herself, to make the angle better. The kiss was far better this time, like a barrier between them had dissolved away. The angle was less awkward, he had his head well tilted to avoid them bumping noses. His arm on her back was steady, holding her so she had no worry about slipping.

He pulled back for a moment, whispering, "Oh, yes. That feels, that feels... oh, mmm, yes," that was all purring sleek contentment, like a panther uncoiling. Before she could reply, before she could think of anything to say, he was kissing her again, intently. His tongue against her lips, slipping into her mouth. All the things he was hinting at that she suddenly wanted, intensely, so much so it made her shudder and clutch at him.

She wasn't sure how long they were at it, but it was not brief, not fleeting. It was time and space and active desire, tumbling together over and over. She wanted so much more, to touch him, to touch skin. She found herself running fingers at the neck of his collar, trying to reach under his coat before the fit completely foiled her.

Her reaction delighted him, and there was a laugh. "Oh, I want to take you off. Do you have people to see, things to do?"

Lizzie's head was spinning. She had tasks, she must have tasks, but no, she'd got the gossip she expected to get. And the party around them was getting more intense, more heated. They'd get no useful gossip here if the people near them were any sign. People in the laps of their partners, skin being bared, skirts lifted, trousers and shirts opened, the sounds of people laughing or crying out in pleasure, in needy desire. Something had changed, rapidly, here, and she couldn't catch up.

She managed to nod. "Let's. Let's go somewhere private."

He nodded, and laughed, and said, "I have a home, in

Trellech. Short carriage ride from the portals. May I take you there?"

Lizzie shuddered again, but then she nodded. "May. Please. Would you? We -" They should talk. They should get this out of their systems. They should a lot of things.

Carillon laughed, and said "Oh, indeed," and then he was nudging her. "Cloaks. Portal. Private." He was earnest and intense, still with that barely contained joy in him, like he was a schoolboy again, taken with the wonder of the magic he made.

She remembered almost nothing of standing, getting their cloaks, doing them up. She'd have remembered nothing of the walk to the portal except for one thing.

The shadow, just off the path, what seemed like a pile of rock one moment. Then it was suddenly unfolding itself, in a shift of shadows, then a murmured series of words that caught in her brain, for all she couldn't make sense of them.

Carillon didn't appear to notice it, whatever it was, and it didn't seem to be a threat. He just swept her on, all courtly attention in a cheerful uncoordinated way.

# TWENTY-ONE

## TRELLECH

Carillon couldn't bear to let go of her. He tucked her hand into the crook of his elbow, escorting her back to and through the portal. There was a carriage waiting for passengers on the street, and he helped her into it.

He didn't want to make her walk a mile in dress shoes, and more to the point, he was not at all sure he could walk that far. He was dizzy with the memories of the drink and how good it was to feel things again. If he'd been alone, he'd have been ridiculous, marvelling at wriggling his toes or his fingers or dancing in the street.

As it was, he suspected he was babbling as the carriage rolled through the streets. She was quiet, though he didn't think he'd offended her. She was responding warmly when he asked her a question, but there was something different, and he couldn't figure out what it was.

When the carriage rolled up, Benton was right there to meet the carriage, and tip the driver. Carillon was amused to see his valet was surprised by the presence of a woman.

"This is Miss Penhallow, Benton. Can you see if we

have something more comfortable for her to change into? We have some of those frocks from..." He waved a hand.

"Do you keep women's clothing around, then?" Lizzie's voice was edged.

Benton bowed, sparing Carillon the difficulty of trying to answer. "We wish to make our guests comfortable, miss. If you'd come this way? Sir?"

Carillon waved a hand. "I can see to loosening my own tie and jacket, Benton, you know that. But if you'd hunt up some food after you've seen to the lady, that would be good. I'll be in the library once I'm changed."

This got a tsk, a hint of Benton near silently pointing out that Carillon's ability to hang up his clothing was not, perhaps, as reliable as he thought, before he led Lizzie off up the stairs. Carillon waited at the top of the stairs for them to disappear into the guest room and then walked down the hallway to the master bedroom. He slipped into a loose silk jacket and more comfortable shirt and trousers, old linen worn smooth.

The library in this house was upstairs, between the two main bedrooms, a familial space rather than a nominally public one. He slipped through the door between his suite and the library proper, considering the difference in his homes.

The small townhouse had been his mother's originally, rather than the more ornate home that had come down through his father's side. That one was all marble and gilt and carved plants that bore little resemblance to the things they depicted. Even the idea of opening the place up gave him a headache. And Ytene was on a different scale entirely.

This, though, was warm wood and comfortable sofas

and an eclectic library. Also, just big enough for the core of the family. No ballroom, no dining room that would seat two dozen with room to spare.

He was standing at the decanter, trying to decide whether to pour a brandy, when he heard the door open, and a "The library, miss." And then a cough and a "Sir, I'll be bringing along something less alcoholic in a moment." It was not quite a scolding, even by Benton's standards.

He turned and blinked. Lizzie was now in something much different from her earlier outfit, a deep green linen dress to match his own choice. He thought it had been his aunt's once, a loose timeless style that made it hard to place but seemed rather Pre-Raphaelite in inspiration. She'd done something to her hair, pinning it up in a loose bun that he found much more flattering than the tight one she wore for work or the sharp pinned curls she'd worn to the parties.

"I hope you're more comfortable, Lizzie?"

She glanced down and at her dress. "If you're sure this is all right?"

"Quite, please. You were gorgeous tonight, but I'm certain that kind of thing can't be comfortable to wear."

She flushed as she came in. "Your man - Benton, is that the name? He asked if I wanted anything to eat, and I said I'd not mind something. He sounded very pleased."

"I'm afraid I don't keep Benton near busy enough. He's been with me since early in the War." It came out flat, too full of ghosts, and he added after a moment. "He's insistent on providing excellent service."

That got a small nod, and after a moment's hesitation, she settled herself on the couch. "We should talk about the party."

He nodded, and coughed, and said, "Someone, they offered me a taste of the goldwasser."

Lizzie's chin came up sharply. "What did you do?"

"Tasted it. I couldn't keep a sample. A few sips."

She inhaled, audibly, but said nothing. The silence grew, then became uncomfortable. He wanted to speak, but he was becoming trapped in the memory, all golden around him like being caught in amber.

A man had asked him if he'd been at the front. Carillon never dissembled about that, it was too easy for people to find out where he'd been. There was a new drink, the man said. Something that took those dreams away.

The man went on about dreams of being other places, under flowering cherry trees in Japan in the spring, or the spice market of Constantinople, or a temple in India. All his comments full of smells and colours and all sorts of things so different than that deadly mud.

Carillon almost hadn't realised it was the goldwasser. He never saw the bottle, only small shot glasses. The glow was a bare shimmer, a hint of light. By then he was near enough committed, and he drank it.

Instantly, he understood why this thing was so power-ful, even before it flowed into his body. It was an encom-passing warmth. It filled him with a sense of everything being good, being excellent, cradling him and cocooning him. He'd been out in the cold air for so long, and suddenly this was warmth and pressure and touch.

It was all he could do to lean back on the couch and let it take him. To close his eyes, do his best to mark the sensa-tions, let the moments shift in him. He visited no temples, no markets, no blossoming trees. There were visions, but his were something more complex. The hut in the Amazon where he'd spent a month finding plants, enjoying the simplicity of each day, nothing but his task.

The trip to Egypt, before the War, and his memory

supplied the tour they'd had of immense ruins in the desert, then only recently unearthed. Supper, that night and the joy of sharing new ideas and asking questions about what different aspects meant in the hotel at night with others, listening to the archaeologists.

There were other memories from his travels, times he'd felt engaged, delighted, enveloped by what he was doing. He remembered sharing Anna's bed after she'd sung in the opera in Vienna, while he was on what he liked to call his Grand Tour. Or the elderly woman in the Austrian Tirol who'd taken him in after an avalanche closed the roads and seen to his bruises and his fears with equal attention. He missed Frau Faber a great deal, she had died during the War, and he'd never seen her again.

There were other things, too, that he didn't understand, like glimpses of someone else's life, laid on top of his own. They pushed at his senses, expanding him, but his mind kept coming back to those memories. They changed quickly, like they were snatches of moments, never long enough.

The effects had faded somewhat by the time Lizzie came back to find him at the party. A sip was not so very much. It would not do him harm, he hoped. It felt so good, so wonderful, he could see why people wanted more and more.

As the memory released him, he was startled to realise she was leaning forward. Benton was there, he'd brought in a tray. Not just a few seconds lost but a long time, then. He reached for a handkerchief and said "Pardon," before wiping his face.

"May I bring a suitable pickmeup, sir?"

He shook his head. "This isn't an ordinary drink," he said.

"Ah, sir. An investigation."

He nodded. Benton at least understood that such things should not be meddled with.

Lizzie was not so phlegmatic about it. She stood, moving to look to the side window for a moment, then back over her shoulder. "I can't leave you alone for twenty minutes without..." Her voice trailed off.

He had no idea what to say to that and sensibly kept his mouth shut.

Finally, she said, "You took a very great risk. You know what it does to people."

"I only had a sip or two," he pointed out, weakly. It was a lousy argument, and they both knew it.

"And you were drunk on - whatever it did. Half an hour then. A good five minutes now, just in memory. Do you normally drink things that people present you? You were cautious enough about an unexpected letter."

He started. "Oh! I got results back this afternoon, just before I left. Benton, the letter, please, it's on my desk downstairs."

Benton disappeared, and Lizzie tapped her foot. Which was a tad ridiculous, since Benton had found her some wool slippers. It was more of a soft thumping sound like a kitten or puppy rolling onto the floor to be petted.

Why would his mind not settle? This was fae-touched of him. That sparked something in his thoughts, he tried to track down, which meant that he missed the next thing she said. Possibly, he missed the thing after that, too.

"... and really, I would have thought you'd have better sense than that. I did look up your exam results, and your apprenticeship, you've far more of a sense of Materia than you let on. What were you looking for at the auction, anyway? It certainly wasn't just the books you bought."

That was easy enough to answer, so he did. "I keep an eye out for the Ministry, things that shouldn't circulate back out into private hands if it can be avoided."

It brought Lizzie up short. She wasn't shouting at him, he found that fascinating, but instead laying out his irrationalities quite precisely. Or so he thought. "Oh," she said, finally. "Well, I suppose someone ought to."

It was at this point that Benton reappeared, with the letter, and Carillon waved it over to Lizzie. She took it, and peered at it, a little closer to her face. She wasn't wearing her glasses, but could clearly read without them. "Intended to entrance and enchant. Do you have the references handy for this?"

He waved a hand. "In the library, where we are, yes. There and there." He indicated the two volumes, one on the desk, one on the bookstand. "They're bookmarked from when I looked at them earlier."

Carillon watched her read, how she scanned through once, then went back and read more closely. She wanted the arc of what was discussed before she let herself linger on the details. It was a fascinating glimpse at how she went through the world.

Her reading took her an hour, at least, as those two books lead her to half a dozen others. Carillon sat silently, other than directing her to the works she requested. He ate a sandwich and drank tea, slowly coming to feel rather more himself.

Finally, she turned and said. "Someone didn't intend to kill you, but they wanted to make a specific point."

He nodded. "Exactly."

"But they still want to hurt me."

"That is implied in the note, yes."

A moment later, she was in his arms, and he was not at all sure how she'd got there. But clearly she wanted someone to hold her, and so he did, hoping this was not too much of an assumption.

# TWENTY-TWO

## TRELLECH

Lizzie wasn't at all sure her knees would support her. She tried to understand what had led her to want to be holding someone. Here Carillon was, and here she was, and he was holding her as insistently as she was holding him.

He was saying something terribly earnest in her ear she couldn't make sense out of for a long moment. It resolved into a, "Please do tell me, Lizzie, how I might, what would be of help?"

There was a sturdy arm around her - whatever had hurt his left shoulder in the past, it did not affect that. She made a small noise against his loose jacket, and then lifted her head, and suddenly, desperately, needed to kiss him.

Lizzie knew she wasn't actually drunk, despite the giddy, uninhibited feeling that was so like intoxication. It wasn't the remains of the magic in the drinks at the party, that had worn off, it was something else. She could feel his arms, settling around her, turning her, then a more urgent whisper in her ear:

"May I kiss you again? Please?"

There was something needy in it, a tone she'd never expected to hear from this polished, controlled lordling. She had not minded the earlier kisses, he was certainly both skilled and practised, but this was more. Not about who was watching, or playing a role, but about her.

Surprisingly about her. She took a deep breath, and then nodded, turning her face to look at him better, pulling back just enough to focus on him. "Please."

He shifted all his honed focus, coming to settle on her, a hand coming up to cup the back of her head like he couldn't bear to have her move too much. Then he was kissing her urgently, like she held the secrets he wanted to know.

They were like that for a stretch of time she couldn't count, but by the time she noticed the world around her again, she had somehow settled into his lap, her arms around his shoulders, and she was kissing him quite as energetically as he was kissing her. She shifted in his lap and could feel how much he wanted other things. Probably wanted other things.

The shift made him grunt, a sound she'd also never have expected from him, and then he leaned, to murmur in her ear. "I'd not venture more, without your wishing."

It placed the choice firmly in her hands, and she had no idea what to do with it. Her thoughts were rushing, but they were both grown, they had no other partners, they could if they wanted to.

And it had been such a long time since she had.

Carillon inhaled, burying his face in her neck, where her hair was coming down. She was not at all sure what to answer him for a long pause, before she said, "What did you have in mind?"

It made him laugh before he answered. "You are ever cautious, domina. I like that about you."

She blinked at the title, but the rest of it was promising. Confusing, but promising.

"If you permit, my bedroom is just through the door. Broad bed and space to explore. Will you, with me?"

"Do you take all your ladies to bed?" It came out sharp and barbed, and she flinched as soon as it was out of her mouth.

He settled a hand on her shoulder and pressed her back so he could look at her, more steadily than he'd managed since they left the party. There was a complex pause, something she could not read at all in his face, before he said, amused. "Not all, domina. Not so many as gossip suggests. Have you, before?"

She looked away, suddenly shy. "Not recently. Some years" She wasn't sure what the right answer was here, but she was sure that wasn't it.

Carillon nodded, and then said, "Will you, domina? With me?" There was something earnest in his tone, an emotion she had no idea how to interpret, intensely vulnerable for a moment.

Lizzie didn't understand what she was feeling, or how she could want him. What to do with the insistent thoughts of him and what he'd be like in bed if all the ease of his dancing translated into lovemaking. She took a deep breath and remembered what her father had taught her when caught in a storm, about not letting it shake her sense of where she was and what she needed to do.

It did not entirely serve here, but it did enough. It brought her face to face with her desire to not be alone tonight, and that she found him an interesting partner in other ways, in investigation and in dancing. She thought he'd be sensible about it afterwards, the gossip she'd managed to gather was that he knew how to be easy in the departure as well as the courting.

Lizzie inhaled, and then watched him, observing his fixed attention on her every move, before she said, "I will. With you." And then a shakier. "Where?"

He nudged her to stand, before slipping an arm around her, and murmuring, "This way." He led her not out into the hallway, as she expected, but through a door in the side of the library, drawing her into a large bedroom.

It was an excessively large bed, the kind you found in storybooks, a great four poster with carved pillars at each corner. It had neither the eccentric carvings of something properly mediaeval, nor the stark curves of something modern. If it were metal, it had what might be a patina or a softening, a sense of age without being easy to place.

"Sit, domina, on the bed. Let me see to the lights, a few small things." He did something to a bell pull by the door. She heard no noise from it at all, but he seemed satisfied with the result. As she kicked off the slippers, he went to the lights, dimming most of them, leaving one by the bed to light him as he came back.

"Do you mind the light? Are you shy of it?"

She inhaled sharply, and then said, doing her best to be honest in speech, at least. "I'd like to see you."

"Mmmm. I've a scar or two." Giving her the information, letting her decide.

She shook her head. "I'd... will you let me?" There was something suddenly sharp between them, it felt like, and she said, "Please?"

Carillon was watching her, and his interest had honed into something much sharper for a moment, a falcon about to stoop on prey. Then he closed his eyes for a long moment, breaking the enchantment, and nodding. "As you wish, domina."

The undressing was awkward, she'd never had a time when it wasn't. Despite his uncertainty, he was not fastidiously modest. She saw, quickly, why he'd favoured clothing that kept his arms covered. There was a line of healed skin down from left shoulder to elbow, long faded but slightly off the colour of the rest of his skin, coming from a knot of scar where his arm met his shoulder. "Sniper," he murmured. "Ricochet."

Lizzie nodded and reached to touch it for a moment, letting her fingers linger on the ridge of skin. It was not what she'd expected, seeing the controlled and polished presentation he offered the world. This was a hint his War had not been as simple as it had seemed when she first saw him. Rather like the rest of him, complicated under the pleasant surface.

She'd have thought about it longer, but he took advantage of the pause in movement to settle his hands on her hips. "I would like to undress you, domina. Unwrap you." But he hesitated. "There's... I should tell you something."

This was not, she thought, usually a thing he told people at this point, the way he switched from easy flirtation to something much more uneven and raw.

Lizzie shifted to settle her hips, leaning against the high bed, running a hand along the bared skin at his ribs. He arched with it, instinctively.

"It isn't just women I've taken to bed." His words were so quiet she almost couldn't make them out. She made sense of them just as he opened his mouth to say something else.

"Recent?"

"A few."

"Who were at the parties?" She cared about tonight, what mattered tonight. And during their investigation.

He blinked at her several times, then shook his head. "Not that I saw. Generally - chose men from different circles than those. For several reasons."

She considered this. "Good."

Carillon looked entirely unsure what to do, searching her face for her reaction. "Are you upset?" He looked like he might say more, but then stopped again.

She considered. "I don't like to be made a fool of, as I said. Since you didn't, there's no trouble."

He shivered at that and then reached up to touch her cheek. "Who did that to you, domina? Hurt you so?"

Lizzie flinched and half turned away, the feeling still too raw, even a decade later. Time was supposed to heal, and yet here it was, as jagged and bright and loud a memory as seeing him had been then. She paused and said, "Someone I was close to. Almost engaged to, I'd thought. And then I was somewhere he didn't expect me to be, and he was with someone else, and... a lot of people had known."

Carillon was quiet, watching her, for a long pause, then he leaned forward and kissed her. It was not fervent or intense, like the kiss in the library had been, but something much more tender. "I may favour Arlecchino, but I will make no fool of you, domina." His voice was gentle in her ear. "May I, please? Treat you as a queen?"

It was like there was a cup she was holding, and it was overflowing with magic, transforming her and the world around her without ceasing. She moved, settling her arms loosely around his waist and then nodding, giving herself over to it entirely. "You may."

# TWENTY-THREE

## TRELLECH

Carillon tried to still his heart and his head and the room's spinning, and none of them were remotely obedient to his desires. He felt like a breeze could knock him over, and like he could climb the highest mountain and taunt the strongest winds, all at once.

Here he was, and here she was, and oh, she was glowing and glorious. He was sure she had no idea how much, no idea how he wanted to press her back against the bed. No, undress her first, revel in that skin and the glow of her hair, explore what curves and shapes were under the linen.

Lizzie was watching him, and he tried to think. He wanted to make it clear she was in control and that he'd not press her more than she chose. He hoped he'd live up to that and feared he wouldn't.

Carillon looked back at her, willing her to understand like she'd understood so many other things without words. That having failed him, he took a deep breath and said, "I want this to be - what you choose." And then, "I'm saying this badly."

She considered, and then said, "What do you like, in bed?" It was inquisitive.

"A wide range." Carillon would be honest. She deserved it.

He took a breath and continued. "A wider range than most. But I take pleasure in all of it. If what you want is - mmm. Me on top of you in bed, in the sole approved position of *Mistress Moreley's Advice For Young Wives*, then I will gladly oblige. If what you wish is something more along the lines of the *Gifts of the Lotus,* or the *Nine Magical Feats*, or any of the other pillow books.... In that case, I will do my best to balance on one foot and make the appropriate gestures while murmuring the correct incantations."

Then he offered an amused, "I admit, I would prefer to bone up before attempting those. Given the chance." That made her smile, at his earnestness. Possibly also the pun. He hoped she didn't mind the occasional pun.

Lizzie considered, leaning forward before she said. "I think I would like you to help me undress. And then..." She had a considering expression. "Do you know much about sensation magics? In this..." She paused, a perfect hesitation "In this particular application?"

He inhaled, his trousers now achingly tight, and managed a nod a fraction too late for ease. "I do, yes. Made a bit of a study of it, actually."

That earned him a nod. "That, please." It was clipped, clear.

It was a decision, and he was very glad she'd made one. Even more glad she was not the sort of woman to dither about asking for what she'd like in bed. "Any sensation in particular? Warmth, or tingling, or pleasure, or - some like a hint of pain or ache, like salt in a biscuit dough." As he spoke, he reached to undo the buttons fastening her dress.

Lizzie let her eyes close, and she was letting him do this without interfering. She was listening, though, because she said, quite promptly, "More complex than simple warmth, but I've a taste for sensation tonight, not pain. Your creativity. Your skills." The last words came out more hesitantly, breathy.

He busied himself then in baring her skin, helping ease the line of buttons open, then separating the fabric, finding her entirely naked. It took him aback for a moment, then she said, "Nothing suited under the gown."

The idea that she'd been naked all evening, under those layers of silk, overwhelmed him. But for a fold of cloth he could have pressed up into her. Thinking of it, even so briefly, made him draw her into his arms again.

The kissing was grand. Even more so, when she lifted one leg, bracing her thigh against his, her foot angling behind him and holding him closer. She leaned back against the bed, that was better. He arched, moving against her, letting her feel him. It would be difficult to miss how hard he was, with how his cock had got arranged in the trousers.

He heard her make a noise, not quite a moan, not so open as that. He ventured to run his hands down, cup her body and pull her tighter, before he shifted, and murmured. "Do stretch out on the bed, domina. Explore your realm." With that, he reached to undo his trousers, suddenly very much wanting to be rid of them.

She moved awkwardly to the centre of the bed before propping herself up on one elbow and watching him. The intensity of her attention made him blush, but he undid his fly, lowered the trousers, and stepped out.

He was not sure at all what she made of him. He knew he had a reasonable sort of body. Pavo had been good to him but adventuring had been better. It had broadened his shoulders and left muscle in the wake of the gangly adolescent he still remembered being. He climbed onto the bed, to settle more or less beside her. He propped himself on his left arm, so he could contemplate what magics to call up with his right hand.

Lizzie leaned back, and she shivered, so he leaned in to kiss her again, reassuring her. Whatever else was complicated, the kissing was not, she responded to him just as willingly as she had each time so far. He pulled away to breathe, and murmured, "There, we'll do more of that."

He shifted, just enough to free his hand, closing his eyes as he gathered his thoughts, the particular gesture for this magic. It meant moving his ring finger to touch his thumb, exhaling and pushing all the swirling magic into his hand as he murmured the incantation.

She moaned when he reached to touch her side, something utterly delightful, and he settled into stroking her, palm against skin. Long stretches first, down her hip, her ribs, nothing too sensitive, to let her get used to it.

"It feels..." There was a dreamy tone in her voice now, that made him realise the edge that was always there, the slight wall between her and the world. "Warm. Like distilled sunlight."

"That was the idea. Pleasure and the dance of the magic within you, responding to mine."

That made her shiver, visibly, but she didn't pull away. He watched her, let her ease through it. Then he bent again to kiss her, stroking and touching her more, letting his hand wander to her hip, the curves of her body, then up to cup one breast. She arched, more fiercely, and he breathed, "Oh, you're going to come apart in my hands, aren't you?"

She murmured something he couldn't understand, and he didn't press, because she wanted more, her tone made that abundantly clear. He bent his head to nuzzle at her chest and felt her hand come up around his shoulders, holding lightly but feeling where he was. There was a moment where she reached to touch the scar. He wondered what she made of it, but then she settled her hand to cup his arm a little below, where the ridge down his arm was most obvious.

Feeling impish, he inhaled, made the gesture with his other hand, and gathered the magic there. He shifted to stretch himself out between her legs, his hips fit against hers.

It encouraged her to settle on her back, one hand going to his hip, barely brushing, the other lingering around his bad shoulder. He lifted his head to watch her, balancing on his right hand, moving to caress her with his left. It was all about letting her shift and enjoy it like a cat demanding its due praise and petting.

He was considering what next, when she opened her eyes again, letting her hips rock, and said, "Can you - that feeling, somewhere else?" She let her glance shift to where his cock was pressed against her stomach, and the mere thought made him moan, on the edge of it being far too much.

"I might not last long."

She considered, and then said, "Do you mind?" in such a thoughtful, contemplative tone, one that encouraged him to hurl himself utterly into fulfilling all her desires.

"As you wish, domina." His voice was quiet, and he felt a curious sanctity at the moment. He had given up all but the minimally necessary offerings to the gods, but it was a time he wished he could call out to whatever Venus dwelled here.

He took the time to shift and get a hand against her, to

tease and touch and warm her fully, to have her ready for him. She moved and arched and reacted so beautifully, making it clear there was nothing in the world for her right now but what he was doing with her.

It took him five breaths to gather the magic, to will it to his cock, to breathe and resist the urge to plunge forward. Only then did he permit himself to find his proper place and begin to push inside her.

He had just enough time to think it was far better than his dream had been, and then any comparison was impossible. Smooth and tight, and so gloriously herself. Her hips scooped against his, and his desire to go slowly and fill her fled with her movement. She would not be still, she would not let him be measured, she always pressed him forward somehow.

His thoughts fled, and he found himself moving, bracing on one elbow, then kissing her hungrily, needy, as he let his hips move in and out. He felt her follow his lead as tidily in bed as she had in the dance. In and out, seeking out their perfect rhythm to music only they heard.

It lasted longer than he'd feared he might, but in entirely too short a time he could feel his control begin to fray, and he had to thrust more strongly. He could hear his pulse pounding in his ear, a drumbeat he couldn't ignore. The more he moved against her, the more sounds she made, the more she responded.

The last few strokes had her crying out, pure and high, louder each time, until he could not hold back, and held deep inside her. He felt himself explode into light and a glorious silence, free from fear. He shuddered, he wanted to bury himself in her. Only as his climax faded could he get his fingers against her, rubbing with one thumb for a few strokes. Then, glory of glories, he felt her tighten around him, and her orgasm almost drove him to madness.

Her pleasure seen to, he finally allowed himself to collapse to one side and let the magic flow out into his body, now exhausted. One arm draped over her, comfortable rather than possessive, leaving her space to move if she wished.

# TWENTY-FOUR

## TRELLECH

Lizzie woke up a little after dawn, judging by the light through the curtains. She shifted, not sure what to expect. Carillon was stretched on his back, but something about the angle suggested he'd had an arm around her for a fair bit of the night before he had rolled.

He didn't snore, which went nicely with the polished and considerate image he insisted on projecting. His position made it easier for her to ease her way out of bed, to go find her discarded dress. She considered using the lavish bathing room she could see off his bedroom but worried it might wake him. Instead, she retreated through the still-open door to the library, back to the guest room she'd used to change, and the sink in the bathroom there.

Once she'd washed up, she felt a good bit better. Her face was clean, her hands were clean, she'd sponged between her legs. She wanted a full bath rather desperately, but that was for later. She settled her hands over her lower stomach, and gathered her magic, murmuring the words she'd learned more than a decade ago. She repeated the chant her aunt had taught her to remind her body she wanted no child, not today. The family chant that they'd all sworn by.

That done, she combed her fingers through her hair. She pinned it up with the hair pins she had left from the previous evening before going back to the library to find a couch to sit on. She didn't want to wake Carillon. Besides, she was sure if she tried to sneak out of the house, some ward or magical guard dog or sphinx or trap door would capture her. Or else Benton would look at her sternly.

At least in the library she could occupy herself with books. She had to restrain herself from prying. She'd had sex - excellent sex - with the man, but looking for his pillow books seemed a step too far. Several steps too far, in fact.

His shoulder kept popping into her thoughts. She'd assumed the face she'd seen, the smooth aristocratic face, belonged to a man with no cares but the latest society foibles and perhaps the nuances of pavo. But there was that scar. And he'd known precisely what to do with a suspicious letter, a level of ritual magical theory and skill with specialised tools far beyond the ordinary.

That brought her face to face with the discomforting realisation that Carillon expected people to try to kill him. That he'd had it happen enough that it was no great surprise, though the particular method might be a trifle unusual.

Lizzie closed her eyes, trying to make sense of it all. It wasn't just that he was clearly familiar with that level of threat, but how he approached it. How he kept the genial affability he talked about pavo or planning for a party or, she was sure, managing his estate or discussing a particular vintage of wine.

It was a puzzle, and she felt like she'd tumbled deep into a labyrinth without a useful ball of twine to find her way out. She had no idea if the man she saw was really like that. Perhaps the man she'd gone to bed with was a mirror, reflecting back what he thought people should see of him. It made her head ache.

In the end, she retreated to the safety of books. She settled on a recent title she'd been wanting to read, a biography she'd not be embarrassed to be caught with. She was a good quarter of the way into it when she heard a murmur of noise from the bedroom. The clock read half eight. There were two voices, one clearly Carillon, the other must be Benton.

In two or three minutes, she heard the door from the bedroom move, how it squeaked very slightly. There was Carillon in a deep purple dressing gown and pyjama pants running his hand through his hair and looking delightfully rumpled.

"Lizzie." He said her name, and then he stopped talking like he wasn't sure what to say.

"Carillon." Two could play at that. And honestly, she wasn't sure what to say either. Thank you for the glorious sex, I'll be taking myself back to the chickens now? That was a stunning orgasm, but I'd not want to expect it will be repeated. The sex was great, can I lounge in your extravagant bathroom which probably has plentiful hot water, mine doesn't.

What she finally said was, "I hope I didn't wake you?"

He shook his head. "Not at all. Benton thought you'd been up for an hour or two. He'll be bringing breakfast if you'll stay for it. Do you need to get home? I'm sorry, I should have asked."

She shook her head. "The chickens will keep." And then she felt so stupid. "Did I - um. Did you have plans?"

Benton saved Carillon from saying anything by

appearing with a small cart and plates of food. It was nothing fancy, toast and poached eggs and jam and butter and sausage, but it was filling. Far more than the party food last night, she realised, which had been rather illusionary. It had been the kind of meal that looked like it was far more substantial than it was.

She thought they were both glad of the excuse not to try to talk. But when they'd had a bit to eat, and most importantly had a bit of tea, she had to say, "This doesn't change the investigation, of course."

He blinked at her, and then said evenly, "Of course not. I hope I didn't overstep?"

She shook her head. "Oh, no. Just." She gestured. "This - I can't afford to mess it up."

Carillon leaned back slightly. "I take it seriously too." His tone was neutral and impossible to read.

Lizzie swallowed, tasting bile rising in the back of her throat, trying to figure out how to explain the gaping chasm between their experiences. Ideally, without insulting the very complicated man sitting across from her, a man clearly well acquainted with both violence and complex magic.

Finally, she said, "I don't have much left, but this job. Both, the office, and for Madam Porter."

He leaned forward. "You, I beg pardon. You haven't wanted to talk about it, so I didn't want to press. But I'd like to understand."

Something in his tone made her shiver. She forced herself to reach for the teacup and take a sip, doing her best to mask the emotions she couldn't make sense of.

"It's just me and my sister, and not much money. If she needs treatment again, if." She gestured in a little circular motion, the endless potential of the future.

"My house, our house, it's ancient. And not the good

kind of ancient, like this. The kind of ancient that has a leak in the ceiling, and bricks coming out of the chimney. There's a nest of mice who insist on taking up residence in the pantry, and chickens who get egg-bound. Half the village isn't sure what to make of me, and the other half is quite sure and wants nothing to do with us. Polite, no one will turn up with pitchforks to run us out, but nothing more than that."

He made a noise deep in his throat but didn't interrupt her.

"And the office, I'm there on trial. I like some of them very much, but there are others, where I'm sure I'll never measure up to their standards. I'm not at all sure I want to, in at least one case."

That got a "May I ask?"

"Someone else fairly new. And a couple of the others are dubious about me."

Carillon frowned. "And Madam Porter?"

Lizzie shrugged, a careful tight gesture. "She's the only one would give me a trial, after everything. But she made it quite clear if I didn't meet her standards, I wouldn't get a second chance. And I don't know what I'll do if...."

Carillon sounded puzzled. "But surely other people would..."

Lizzie shook her head and counted it out. "Leave out the people who invested with Papa and Uncle Kenver and lost their money. Leave out the people related to those who did, who'd have difficulty at home or in their club or their bohort team if they hired me. Leave out the jobs I'm not actually suited for. Leave out the ones that want references."

"Surely you've got references."

"I worked for Master Groton during the War. He

won't." Her voice was flat. The reason given was that
Master Groton was a fiend for medical privacy, extending it
even to his staff. He'd give his approval or his disapproval,
but no details at all. The real reason was more complicated,
that Master Groton had his fierce defenders, but there were
far more people he'd offended, insulted, or argued with over
the years.

Carillon clearly knew him, though his, "I see, quite,"
didn't give her any real data for interpretation.

"Not very many people left." She was quiet, then. "And
I quite like working, thank you. Even if we had money, not
that we do, I'd want to be. The classic answer for someone
in my distressed position would be to retreat to the colonies
or a post in the Empire, but I don't want that."

He leaned forward, and said, "If I offered help, you
wouldn't take it."

She looked up, met his eyes for a moment, then looked
away. "No." A pause, then, "We don't have - that particular
kind of relationship, do we?"

He recoiled, sharply, for just a moment before she saw
him gather the polished image and present it to her. "As you
wish." His voice, even those few words, sounded suddenly
distant and clipped. He almost said something else, but cut
it off. It was not rude, it was as if there was now a wall
between them.

She closed her eyes and more gently said, "I'm sorry. I
must be overtired, still. I've meetings at work this week, I
won't be able to see you easily. Will you write if there's
something else about the investigation?"

Carillon nodded and then said, "Benton can show you
out. I should wash up before wandering downstairs."
Benton had clearly been hovering, since the first ring of the

bell brought him at once to the library door. Carillon stood. "I will let you know of any further happenings, as you ask."

She nodded, then was utterly unsure how to leave, so she settled for, "Thank you for a..." She stopped, trying to find the right adjective. "Thank you for an unforgettable evening."

He made an indescribable face at that, but then the smooth courtesy took over, and he bowed. "Entirely my pleasure." Again, she got the sense of a missing word, something entirely excised.

She let Benton show her out, trying not to think about the expression on Carillon's face. Or the one on Benton's face, the suppressed disapproval.

# TWENTY-FIVE

## TRELLECH

Carillon slept badly all week. Benton fussed about it, but it was the kind of bad sleep that could not be cured by hot chocolate or by brandy, or even by a sleeping potion. He had tried all of that.

Some part of his mind knew it was a lost cause. He could feel himself back in that desolate icy wasteland of the War and the year or two after where nothing broke through. He could be terribly efficient in this state, nothing to get in the way of his chosen tasks.

That would have been a comfort if there were space in his head for comfort, and there wasn't.

He was aware of Benton fussing over him, of Ytene's housekeeper debating meal choices and presenting the choicest dishes. He knew they had warned Rufus, by the way Rufus was careful to ask only the most interesting questions, to try to draw him out.

Inside his head, though, everything was chess pieces, moving them about for his long-term strategy. A bohort match rather than pavo. This breeding choice, so that in the next generation from now, they might do that. A particular fix to Ytene's foundation, so that they might avert further damage in case of a wet winter. Reviewing the stocks of potions and powders and other sundries, so they would not be at the mercy of trading prices. Discussing improving the roads around True Eyeworth so carts would stick less.

Carillon went through it all point by point, with Benton always within the sound of his raised voice. He read his papers; he perused the journals and reports he always reviewed; he rode out on one or the other of the horses; he practised the pavo drills and trained up the new black mare he'd been working with. He had always found the training the most satisfying part of pavo. The strategy of bohort was much more his intellectual fancy. There were so many puzzles that weren't safe with horses on the field, that required deep attention and both hands.

But the sharp intelligence that set the best bohort players above the rest did not fit the face he chose to show the world. Pavo's nuances did. Those who were not serious riders found it utterly mysterious, and those who were riders themselves tended to favour horse-craft over politics or subterfuge.

The mare, at least, was an interesting project. She was an intelligent and curious mount who would consider her rider's guidance into how to meet different challenges of the sport without automatically doing as she was told. Intelligent cooperation was what he wanted. He could lose himself in that when he was with her, at least a little.

Carillon did not write to Lizzie. He had nothing that was urgent to convey, and she had been so very clear about several things. He reported to Vivian, noting that he'd had a chance to taste the goldwasser but not get a sample. And that he did not know their next opportunity yet, he would be in touch when they did.

Lizzie did not write to him. He was in Trellech on the following Friday, to check for any messages, at all three clubs, on the off chance something had gone astray. He had left Bourne's for last, near lunchtime, in case someone offered lunch who might have information of interest.

The club was quiet, so he spent half an hour reading the London papers in the library. Nothing very notable in them, other than a number of hints of financial instability, and reports on the ongoing Paris Olympics. It was not enough to distract him, so he was almost pleased when he heard a "Lord Carillon." from someone whose voice he did not immediately recognise.

He looked up, and inclined his head, setting the paper aside.

"You may not remember my name, sir. Warin Burke." It was a young man.

Carillon considered him and said, "The young man with the interesting drink at the last party."

Warin nodded. "Just so, sir. May I have a moment of your time?"

Carillon paused. "A private conversation?"

Burke nodded. Carillon sized him up. The man was younger, of an age where he might have fought in the War, though possibly not, and wearing a fairly formal set of business robes. Working entirely in the magical world rather than a mixed community, then.

"Regarding what?"

"The bottle in question and some related plans. Mr Morland mentioned you might be interested in learning more."

"Tibbie knows how to reach me, rather than send someone else." Carillon's voice was dry, dispassionate.

Burke flinched, for just a moment. "Since I had met you

at the party, sir, Mr Morland thought I might be better able to answer some questions."

Carillon nodded, then looked up and caught the glance of one of the staff. "A private room. And lunch. Make your order, Burke, on my account." It caught the younger man off-guard, but after a moment ordered something unobjectionable, and Carillon added his own order for chicken and asparagus. "And the house white," he added.

The man went off, and by the time Carillon had gathered his things, there was someone else to show them to a private dining room.

"What is so important as to need privacy, then?"

Burke settled on the edge of the chair facing him across the table. "You were with a - woman, yes?"

Carillon nodded. "I was."

"She's not tried the goldwasser, has she?"

Carillon raised an eyebrow, and said, "I do not believe so, no."

"It's assumed, sir - beg pardon for bringing it up - that she is your mistress, or will be. Given her family and status."

Carillon paused, retreating into the icy depths so that the few flickers of what he felt wouldn't show.

"Do I whisper confidences in her ear in bed, is that what you're asking?"

Burke had the decency to flush at least. "The partners involved in the project need to know, my lord."

"And they sent you to find out." Carillon's voice was dry.

"My lord, yes."

"What made them think I'd tell you?" He was, in some distant realm of his soul, deeply insulted. He'd had mistresses before, that was well known. But the idea that he'd parade one of them so, in those circles besides, was painful. And the idea that a stripling young man, barely out of apprenticeship, would be the one pressing him on what he did in private was outside enough.

Burke stammered something and was saved from further embarrassment by the arrival of the food. Carillon let him dangle in it, not offering a way out until he was halfway through his own meal. Mind, he couldn't have told anyone a thing about what it tasted like. Competent, he was sure.

Eventually, he took a small amount of pity, in part so he could learn more, and said, "I gather her sister has had some experience with your bottle. She's curious about it, of course. And has some reason to want an escape, however temporary, as so many of us do."

This got Burke lighting up, and an immediate, "Oh, yes, my lord. That's what got me so interested to begin with. How it was, how I felt when I was drinking it." He was a tumbling colt about it, entirely unpolished.

Carillon could only feel a sort of gentle amusement at it. He had not lied, but that is what they got for sending a stripling in to question him. His reputation as a pavo-obsessed gentleman traveller was serving him well again.

"If you'd like to learn more, my lord, the partners would be glad to extend an invitation to another party. A chance to get to know you better. With the - ahem, woman in ques-tion. If the weekend goes well, they would be willing to discuss the provision of bottles, even a chance to become a sponsor of the production."

Carillon made a non-committal noise. "What would be involved?"

"A Saturday to Monday, full formal dress for the evenings, on the weekend following this one. A grand ball on the Saturday, outdoor activities, riding and shooting. You know the sort of thing. Those about your age and older, there'll be another gathering for the younger set elsewhere."

That got a nod. "I would be most intrigued, yes. You will not name the people involved, I presume."

"No, my lord. They prefer to be judged on the quality of their work rather than the history of their names."

Carillon scoffed at that, somewhere deep inside his head. That meant they didn't have much name or reputation to trade on, or at least not a good one. Any fool knew that. He wondered if they were war profiteers like Tibbie, or something else.

"Send the details along. And some method of contact if I have questions about the arrangements. I will make sure my companion knows what is expected."

Burke nodded and then gestured. "I will not take your time further, my lord. You can expect the invitation in the afternoon's mail, I suspect, here, or should we send it elsewhere?"

Carillon considered. He intended to attend an auction in London by portal in the evening, then return to Ytene, but he did not want to advertise where he would be. "Here will do, thank you."

The younger man nodded, and stood, and took his leave, and that meant Carillon was alone with his thoughts again.

It was easy for him, in this state, to look at this purely analytically. Progress toward their goal of finding out who was behind the goldwasser was being made. He and Lizzie simply had to attend the party, make a good enough show, and by Monday enough details would likely be revealed that the Ministry could take action. Perhaps even enough to treat those who had become addicted.

Nothing they had not already done. Nothing, in fact, they had not already done before they shared a bed. They could be entirely professional about it. He could, and he was quite sure she could.

And yet, part of him, some distant part he was trying not to listen to, did not want that. He wanted to tell her about this new opportunity, rush to explain to her, to plan clothing and mood and how they might divide up people to talk to.

There would be none of that. She had made it clear there was no hope there. If he hung onto that hope, he would be back where he had been a year or two after the War, lost in things that were not good for him, and certainly not good for his responsibilities. Far better to be here, where he was, where things were far away, but manageable, and he could keep his commitments.

# TWENTY-SIX

## TRELLECH

Lizzie was impatient. Laura was five minutes late, already. It had been a hectic and complicated week.

There had been the train to the magical town outside of Bangor, then a series of increasingly rickety trains and carriages to a tiny village perched on the side of a mountain. She was not clear why they had to go to Eryri, but she was increasingly sure that it was deliberately as remote and difficult to get to as possible.

The whole thing had given her a headache, above and beyond being three and a half days of travel in the company of ap Rhys, Grwn, and Halwyn. By virtue of being the only woman along, she got her own room. That was small mercy since she could easily hear ap Rhys snoring through the shared wall. Her room was small and cramped and the roof angled so steeply that she cracked her head on the plaster twice.

Which might also explain some of the headache.

She had not even had the satisfaction of seeing the Belin. She had been left behind to watch the assembled items they had brought with them, the spares everyone hoped they wouldn't need. Her small hoard included a bottle of honey, a selection of crystals all shades of the rainbow, a mess of thin chain and rusted nails, half a dozen teeth she tried not to think about too closely, and a trunk that had yet more in it.

On the way up, they'd had to collect a bottle of water from a stream, five pure white pebbles, and one rock to represent each of them. How did one pick a rock to represent oneself? She had chosen one that had the beginning of a crack through it, for the competing demands on her.

The men had gone up over the hill, and for about ten minutes, she had had the definite sensation of being watched. Her logical mind knew there was nothing there - they were above the tree line, there were no large rocks, she could not see anything nearby. Her mind, though, persisted in feeling there was something there, something vaguely familiar, undeniably present. Eventually, the sensation disappeared and there was only the waiting to do. It was, she had been told, rude to read, all she was to do was sit and listen and observe.

She began by chewing on the reading she'd been doing on the train, working with one of the dictionaries and two of the more practical translation lexicons, to see if she could make any sense of what she'd heard in the dark when they left the last party.

She had not been sure what to make of it, only something Grwn had said made her wonder if it had been the language the Belin used. If so, it either meant that the bees would make good honey this summer, or that there was some kind of taint she didn't have. It was not at all clear. Possibly, it meant that the water was sweet and not brackish.

This also gave her a headache. It was one of those

languages that were fascinating in theory, and where she was quite clear she was missing all the cultural context that would help it make any sense.

Which brought her, eventually, back to observing. What she observed involved a few birds, a raven and a peregrine she could identify, a small flock of very annoying goats who wanted to try and eat all the supplies, and she thought a pine marten or something of the kind. She had not been able to tell, because of the goats.

Hours later, in the late afternoon, the men came back, all looking rather drawn and exceedingly baffled. She almost asked what they'd learned, and ap Rhys waved a hand. "Take this jar of honey to that rock and leave it, verch Hendrek. We'll pack up."

By the time she came back from the rock a fair bit up the hill, they had everything bundled and all three men were resolutely quiet. The hike back down the uneven path kept them all busy, and then everyone disappeared to their respective rooms. Lizzie arranged for sandwiches to be sent up, and for breakfast in the morning, before finding her own room. She did get a brief thank you the next day for it when they were waiting for the train back to the portal.

The meeting in the office on Friday morning had been slightly more informative. That was to say that Ap Rhys and Grwn and Halwyn all had mysterious pronouncements in obscure dialects to try and decipher. They thought the Belin were irritated but not precisely at them. Exactly what they were irritated at, however, seemed to be phrased in riddles they couldn't work out.

To make things even more annoying, she got back to Trellech to discover no message from Carillon anywhere. She had told him she would be busy, but still, she had expected something by now. They did, after all, have a serious task they had not yet begun to resolve.

It had been another five minutes, and still no Laura. Lizzie was about to give up and go back to the office when her sister came in. Laura looked a little better than she had in some ways, but her skin was still quite pale, and there was the worrisome brightness in her eyes.

Lizzie swallowed what she wanted to say, and instead said, "I wasn't sure you'd make it. How's the office?"

That got Laura off on a cheerful babble about meeting new people, and also about a new scarf she'd found in a second-hand shop and fixed up with the help of someone in her rooming house. It kept her busy until they'd placed their order for food, and then Laura tilted her head and said, "You've come up a few times, actually."

"Me?"

"Mmhm. You didn't tell me you'd been to parties with Lord Carillon. He's quite the interesting man."

Lizzie shrugged slightly. "A few parties. I was actually hoping to hear from him now I'm back in town. I'd rather like his advice on something."

"Advice, is it?" Laura was teasing, leaning forward.

"He's got a good sense about how to ask people things. The meeting I was at, it was very curious, the bits I was around for." Lizzie made a face, then said, carefully. "Do I want to ask what the gossip is?"

Laura settled back, looking delighted. "Do you know much about him? I mean, people said you've been at a couple of parties, but there's no gossip about you being seen with him other places."

Lizzie waved a hand. "I'm curious what you know about the gossip. And we've had lunch at one of the clubs, a few times. As far back as you like, then?"

Giving Laura her head might fill up the lunch with cheerful amusement, and save her from making other conversation. And possibly Laura had heard something useful.

"Well, you know of course, that he's the lord of Ytene, and lord over the north half of the New Forest, all the magic. He was the younger son. He'd served in the War, earned a couple of medals, then he got a mysterious posting away from the front after something happened. No one talks about that part at all, but it must have been unpleasant."

"Very little was at all pleasant, Laura." Her voice came out more stern than she'd meant to.

Laura made a face, more bafflement than discomfort. "Well, I suppose not."

Lizzie closed her eyes for a moment, at her sister's innocence about it. Lizzie had not been anywhere near the front, but she'd worked with enough people who had been to never be able to keep that distance from what it was like. She ventured, to break the silence, "What about his people?"

"Oh, they go far back. First or Second families, both sides. His brother was married to one of the Penningtons, and something happened. No one talks about that. And his parents were on one of those great ships, that went down in the Atlantic. I forget which one."

Lizzie nodded slowly. That much she'd gathered from her research. Good thing, too, since Laura was not the queen of details, as a rule. She gestured a little with one hand. "What about him and women?"

Laura beamed. "He's been associated with all sorts of people. Several mistresses." Then her expression sobered for a moment. "People are wondering. Um. If you were."

Lizzie had to look away for a moment, then said carefully, "Is that the gossip, then?"

"Well, some of it. Some people insist he must prefer men, I mean, in bed. They giggle about it. And they won't tell me details of what men do, they say I'm far too innocent for that. But he's been known to escort women around, quite in public."

Lizzie paused, and then said, with a little more amusement. "He's, oh, he's a very pleasant companion. He's a fine dancer. I could see benefits to being his mistress. But he's not asked me that."

Laura tilted her head, clearly not sure how to take some of that. "And you're sure he's not that way?"

Lizzie had to laugh at that, something in the tone of it, and then leaned forward, and said, "Oh, quite, quite sure. As it turns out."

"You are sly!" Laura sounded delighted. "When, do tell?"

Lizzie had to blush. "After the last party. And no, I won't kiss and tell, that's not kind. But it was quite pleasant. More than pleasant. I mean. If he wanted, I'd do it again." Then she flushed, and said, "Do keep it to yourself, though?"

It sounded decidedly pale and flat compared to what she'd felt. The gossip, was that why he'd been clear with her that he'd been with men, then? But if it was a known gossip, why pause in the middle of things to reassure her about it? He'd been nervous, she had seen that.

Lizzie was entirely tangled in her thoughts, and she didn't hear Laura until she caught an "Elspeth Penhallow, are you listening to me at all?" that was so like their mother's tone she had to look up.

Laura stuck out her tongue. "You weren't listening. Just

like Papa, sailing away in your head. I didn't get to the other bit of the gossip."

"Other bit?" Lizzie was not entirely sure she wanted to know. Except of course she wanted to know, needed to know. Everything, ideally.

"Of course, he's such an eligible bachelor. It's not just the title. Or the fact he's a champion pavo player, and I do think that does lovely things for a man's legs, don't you? And his shoulders. Mmm."

Lizzie coughed, and Laura laughed. "Oh, you do fancy him. Anyway, it's not just that, they have the estate in the New Forest, Ytene, and two townhouses here in Trellech, and an estate up in Cumbria, and someone said something about an island, but I think that is actually pure gossip. Anyway, after his parents, well, that was very sad, but people were throwing their eligible daughters at him, one after another, and he was very polite but didn't ever take them anywhere more than once. Well, not a party more than once."

Lizzie tried to figure out what that meant. Though of course, he was taking her places because of their task. That didn't count. And neither of them had, strictly speaking, been entirely their usual selves when they went to bed.

"When are you seeing him again?"

Laura wouldn't let her leave lunch until Lizzie had, in fact, promised to go take a note around to his club and to let Laura consult on her clothing. Feeling entirely scolded into something she mostly wanted anyway, it was easier to oblige than argue. Or so Lizzie tried to reassure herself.

# TWENTY-SEVEN

## TRELLECH

C arillon had arranged things on Monday so that no one would comment on his meeting Lizzie at the dressmaker. Benton expected him to be out and about until at least supper. Rufus knew not to expect him at Ytene until sometime on Tuesday. Various other people who'd asked for his time had been put off, more or less gently.

It was entirely necessary for Lizzie to be dressed properly for the weekend, and otherwise prepared, and that was what Carillon would do.

He had arranged for a private room at his preferred dressmakers, her sole attention for the necessary fitting. Mistress Castalia had a fine touch with her needle, but more than that she was discreet and clever. They would have privacy thereafter for conversation.

"Carillon." She was all politeness, and he thought maybe just a hint of puzzlement. "You said bring other things with me, so I brought one of my mother's cases."

He nodded, and Castalia bundled Lizzie behind a changing screen. When she came out, she was wearing a rather conservative set of underthings of well-made older silk and was carrying the indicated case.

It was a solid and magical travelling trunk, designed to have drawers of clothing that pulled out and packed away into something the size and weight of a lightly filled carpet bag. He let the dressmaker fuss with it, hanging things up, tsking over various minor details.

"There is not enough time for new things all round, but a few new items and some tailoring or refinements should do well."

Lizzie watched him, and he wasn't sure what she was looking at, though she nodded to acknowledge the dressmaker. "What should I expect, or is that a conversation for later?"

Carillon considered the dressmaker, and then said, "Some of it for later, mmm?" and then he said, "The outline - have you done a Saturday to Monday recently?"

"Not since early in the War. I know things are often less formal now, that's why I wasn't sure about the clothing. Or the shoes and accessories, especially." There was a tiny pause, and she added, "I've arranged things with ap Rhys, to be away from work on Monday as needed."

Carillon tapped his fingers and gestured. "We will arrive Saturday just after luncheon, by portal. There will be a man to see to your bag. Do you need help to bring it from home?"

Lizzie blinked, something in this confusing her, he thought, then said, "If that isn't a bother, it would be a kindness."

"I will arrange it with Benton, I have the directions to your home you gave me earlier. Make whatever adjustments to the warding you need." His voice was a bit clipped, even to his own ear, and he took a breath.

"We will arrive, there will be a light luncheon, and then various activities. Lawn or party games, cards. We'll likely be separate for much of the afternoon. I have made sure a maid will be available to help you change for the evening and arrange your hair. I presume we will gather for cocktails and then a formal dinner rather than a buffet, but I am not entirely sure what to expect there myself."

"So I should prepare for a variety of conversations, and for unknown conversational companions." Lizzie paused. "I realise a maid is expected, of course. I have a little experience."

Carillon nodded, then discarded what he had been about to say for later in the conversation and more privacy. "There will be some sort of festivity on Saturday evening, dancing or some such. Again, I am not quite sure what to expect."

Lizzie nodded. "And on Sunday?"

"A more leisurely morning then a similar pattern in the afternoon. At other gatherings, I would expect croquet or lawn tennis or a lawn game of bohort, but again, this is not my usual crowd."

She made a face at that he could not decipher at all, then she said, "So I do not get to see your skills?"

Carillon had no idea how to read that or respond, so he went on as if he'd not heard it. "And another social evening, though probably slightly less formal." He gestured at the dress she was being pinned into, a modern short thing of silk and ribbon. "Like that, rather than a formal gown, I suspect."

Lizzie nodded, and then said, "And the clothing for the daytime?"

The dressmaker tutted over that, and took over, sparing Carillon from having to speak further. He murmured a

"Back soon." and left them to a discussion of fashionable cuts for necklines and hemlines. He walked in small circles around the front room to try to settle the little anxious prickling he was feeling, like something was terribly wrong. Nothing was wrong, he had a role, he was doing the necessary things.

Twenty minutes later, Castalia came back into the front room, brushing her hands on her apron. "The lady is dressing. I'll be going out now for my lunch, your lordship, it will be quite private for another hour."

Carillon nodded. "Benton will be along to tend to the bill in the morning, thank you."

That earned him a snort. "She's not at all extravagantly minded, but she sees the value in doing the thing right. So you're aware. I'll have everything ready on Thursday for her to pick up, and we're arranging shoes to be picked up at the same time. You mentioned you had some suitable jewellery?"

Carillon nodded, then let the dressmaker go out for her lunch. Once she was gone and the door shut behind her, he made his way into the back again. "May I join you?"

Lizzie had finished changing back into her suit. "You wanted to speak more privately?" Again, there was something exceedingly cautious about her.

He made a slight bow toward her. "There is a couch, please sit if you would be more comfortable."

She hesitated but then moved to settle on the front of the sofa, perched rather than relaxed. "Is something wrong, Carillon?"

He waved his hand. "I wanted to be very clear with you. We have a task we are attending to, an important one. Once we are done with that task, you may be quite sure I will not intrude on you again. And, of course, I will give my highest recommendation to Vivian and to ap Rhys about the quality of your work, which has been impeccable."

Lizzie opened her mouth, closed it, and opened it again, before saying, very carefully, "I appreciate the clarity, thank you."

He nodded, briskly. "I don't know what rooms they will put us in this weekend, but you may also be assured I will not press you."

Again, she opened her mouth and closed it. There was more of a snap this time, and then another clear precise, "I appreciate that as well."

There was a long silence, and then she said, "I would like to tell you about my trip north this week, if I may?"

It was not what he was expecting, and he murmured, "I had an interesting conversation myself, but yours sounds more so. North?"

"Ap Rhys wanted me to go to the conversation with the Belin. Well, not into the actual conversation, as it turns out, but to sit on the hillside they were having it on."

Carillon blinked. "Do tell. Please." He found a stool, and set it down about five feet from the sofa, sitting and leaning forward to listen.

Lizzie explained the trip north, and the amount of sitting around, and the range of items she was watching over. "I thought I heard something when we left the last party."

Carillon shook his head. "Did you mention it?"

Lizzie shook her head. "No. It was only later that it stuck with me. Taking the train up, listening to Grwn talk about the language, I realised some of it sounded similar to what he was saying. I couldn't ask them about it, of course, but I had a look at the reference materials."

He nodded. "And what did the reference say?"

Lizzie paused, gathering her words carefully. "You understand I couldn't actually ask Grwn about it, or Halwyn, not directly. It would reveal what we were up to."

He nodded. "Taken as given, yes."

Lizzie took a deep breath and continued, "One interpretation is about bees making good honey. One is about water being sweet and not brackish. And one is about there being some kind of taint I - or some being, feminine - does not have."

That made him blink several times. "Indeed." He contemplated. "And you're not sure which?"

"That would be the part where I am decidedly not even barely competent in the language. And it is based on allusions, associations, and an approach to grammar that approaches sympathetic magic theory."

Carillon frowned at that, then pondered for a minute, finally venturing, "I am wondering if it is something about the nature of liquid. Honey and water."

Lizzie made an entirely non-committal noise, then said, more sharply, "As I said, I was working off a lexicon. I'd not trust my own work on anything with nuance, and you shouldn't either."

Carillon waved a hand and said, "Let me pursue the theory. If there is a link to liquids, we know the Belin are upset about something. We know they spoke to you, and not to me, that I did not hear a thing. We also know that I have had some of the goldwasser, and you did not. The connection seems plausible."

"Do you think?" Lizzie had to consider this, and she chewed on her lip in concentration.

"It seems a working hypothesis. I think we had better make sure you continue to avoid it." He tried to avoid it coming out like a sharp order but was only somewhat successful.

She looked up, and just nodded, with a softer, "Quite." before she continued, "You said you had something?"

"A young man invited me to this party, as I mentioned in my note. The same one who gave me the drink last time."

Lizzie nodded. "And?"

"He gave me his name this time. Warin Burke."

Lizzie shot straight up, standing. "He what? That little twerp."

It startled Carillon so much so he overbalanced on the stool and slipped, tumbling onto the floor. He landed hard and had to pause to catch his breath.

She immediately said, "Oh, I'm so sorry," and offered him a hand.

He was entirely hesitant to touch her, but she held it there, waiting, and after a moment, he put his hand in hers and let her help him up. She knew how to brace for pulling someone up without thinking about it. Once he was standing, he brushed off his trousers and coat, and then said, "You know him, then?"

"He's the one I mentioned, who was being difficult at work."

Carillon winced, suddenly unsure what to make of this. "Oh. That does complicate things."

Lizzie nodded. "We have to go through with it. As you said, it's the task in front of us."

He considered, then said, "Let me see if I can find anything else about the family that might be of help." He was about to say something else, then a series of things hit him, near enough like shells.

"Burke is being difficult with you. We know he knows about the goldwasser, between him giving it to you and the invitation. And we know the Belin seem very likely upset about the goldwasser." Carillon paused, then said "Vivian and I wondered if there might be a mole in your department."

Lizzie had shifted to try to straighten her hair and cut off. "I don't like that combination one bit."

Carillon shook his head. "Nor I. And I've not forgotten that inventive letter with the nasty threat."

She grimaced then said, "I can see what he does at work?"

He sucked in a breath, then watched her, and said, "You know the risks. It is true it would be a help."

That got her standing and saying, "I'll stop by the bakery on the way back. Food is always a good lure."

He wanted to say a dozen things, and none of them would come out. He settled on the exceedingly pragmatic. "You need to get back to the office, yes? I will see you Saturday morning. I'll have Benton call at noon, they're expecting us through the portal for the party by one."

Lizzie nodded, and packed up her things, pausing at the door to say, "Do take care until Saturday. No conversations in dark corners, mmm?"

He stood at the window, watching her go down the street away from him for quite a long time.

# TWENTY-EIGHT

## TRELLECH

Thursday at lunch, Lizzie felt even more confused than she had been on Monday.

Warin had been spectacularly boring at work, so much so that she was sure he was doing his best not to attract attention.

It would have worked better if he had been doing it all along. His demonstration of manners, work ethic, and ability to avoid scowling at Lizzie if he put his mind to it all earned comments from the others as soon as he was out of the room.

Lizzie couldn't explain. She made pleasant replies to various people, mentioned that someone had invited her to a party this weekend, maybe with people he respected? She had no idea.

Lizzie thought she saw ap Rhys smirk at overhearing a part of that explanation to Tilly, but it was hard to tell, especially with the beard. Lizzie's job was to be pleasant and organised, and by Thursday morning, every piece of paper near her desk or filing cabinets had been firmly put into proper place. Often several times.

Since she was now sitting at a cafe, there were no papers to file. She could not organise the bag of clothing she'd picked up, there was no space. She could make lists, but she already had all the lists she actually needed. And the little round table was suitable for delicate sandwiches and a pot of tea, not for a decently sized notebook.

She let out a sigh and was saved from further difficulty by her sister's arrival.

"Sorry, Lizzie. Were you waiting long?"

"Rather a lot on my mind." It was rather brusque, and Lizzie corrected it, after a moment, with "Sorry. I didn't mean for it to come out like that. I seem to keep doing that."

Laura raised an eyebrow and made the little adjustments to scarf and bag and umbrella that coming in from outside involved.

"The party, this weekend. I'm nervous about it."

"What does Lord Carillon say?"

"We've not had much time to talk - work's been busy, and he's been back at his estate, the one in the New Forest, Ytene, since Monday, anyway. I've had a note or two, but all very short and to the point."

"You said he was charming." Laura looked just like their mother, trying to figure out how to inject sense and a grain of practicality into the latest scheme of their father and uncle.

"He is charming!" Lizzie objected and then sobered. "Something was different on Monday."

"What sort of different?"

Lizzie considered. "He was... extra polite. Sort of clipped about it. Precise." She opened her hand, and closed it, trying to find words. "He made a point of saying I'd done nothing wrong?"

Laura blinked at her, and then said, very carefully, "You really are Papa's daughter."

Lizzie was entirely unsure what to do with that, so she folded her hands, and watched her sister, now wary and cautious.

That was exactly when the woman turned up to take their order, and convince them they wanted to try the special. It took several minutes to get her to go away. That was enough time that Lizzie had to admit that perhaps her sense of equilibrium and patience were not at all what they ought to be.

When they were alone at the table again, she said, "What do you mean, Laura?"

Laura settled back, watching her sister. "Lizzie, love. When people say that, it usually means you've hurt them, badly, but they don't dare say so."

This made Lizzie blink and say, "But...." before her voice trailed off.

"Mama said it fairly often to Papa, yes."

Lizzie closed her eyes. It did not make the world stop spinning around her head. It did at least mean she wasn't dealing with the disconnect between her metaphorical world spinning and the physical world sticking resolutely in place.

She was quiet for a minute, maybe two, before she said, "Can you explain it?" And then, more urgently, "Please?"

Laura shifted, and said, "You've never..." She stopped, and it was the tone of a younger sister utterly exasperated with the elder. "I'm not sure I should."

Lizzie shivered. "I don't want to make things worse." Her voice was decidedly plaintive, and she had to hug herself.

"Tea." Laura's voice was firm. "Tea first."

Lizzie obediently took a sip of tea, which helped a little, and another. It was only after she'd had half a cup and Laura had refilled it that her sister spoke.

"It's not safe to let people who can hurt you know they have." Her voice was a bit flat but so insistent, so solid, so certain.

Lizzie wanted to say a dozen things. To insist she hadn't hurt him like that, she couldn't hurt him like that, it was ridiculous. He had all the power and all the options. Then she wanted to demand how Laura was so sure of this, how could she possibly know. She'd spent most of the last decade either in sanitariums or quietly at home in a country cottage with their mother for company. Even if Laura had a point, it didn't make sense here.

Laura just looked at her, waiting, sipping her own tea, and smiling pleasantly at the woman who brought their sandwiches.

"Eat, Lizzie. You need to get back to work soon. You've always had an appetite at lunch." She took half a sandwich herself, and Lizzie was struck, as always, by the differences between them.

It was only after Lizzie had taken two halves of different types, had a bite or two of the egg salad, and set it down, that she spoke. "He's the one with all the power."

Laura looked at her, not saying anything. Just waiting.

Lizzie knew trying to explain was the wrong thing, and she couldn't stop herself. "He's - he's got the country estate, and I don't know, dozens of horses, and two townhouses. And I don't know what else, and an amazing library, and all sorts of options. How could I possibly hurt him?"

Laura asked, still quiet, still so very much controlled, "How did you meet him? You hadn't told me."

Lizzie sucked in a breath. "You know the pairs party?"

She wasn't sure she could confide, she wasn't sure she trusted her sister not to spread it, and yet she felt Laura slipping further and further away. "Promise me you won't tell anyone?"

"Promise." That part was very clear and easy.

"We were both trying to get in, both in costume, stumbled into each other in the bushes."

"Now, that's a story. What were you?"

That made Lizzie smile, with the memory of the party, and the memory of Laura having heard about them. "Arlecchino and Colombina."

She was briefly rewarded by seeing Laura's jaw drop, her calmness shift. And then she gathered herself. "You got all the gossip. You know that. I told you. And you didn't let on."

There was something quietly hurt in how she said it. This one, Lizzie could spot.

She closed her eyes and said, "Sorry. Some of it's - related to a thing I can't talk about at work. Not to anyone who isn't directly involved."

It did not make anything better, but Laura at least moved on. "A thing he knows about?"

Lizzie nodded. "Yes."

"And then what happened?"

"The - thing we're not talking about, it made sense for us to work on it together. Which got us invited to a party, and then another one."

"And then the one on Saturday?"

"Yes. And, he's a grand dancer."

"And grand in more horizontal forms, you said."

Lizzie blushed, and shivered again, but said, "Yes." It was barely more than a whisper.

Laura watched her, letting the silence go on and on

until she decided something. "Let me try to explain. Do you promise to listen until I'm done?"

Lizzie sucked in a breath and then did her best to match Laura's promise from earlier. "Promise."

There was a nod, and a sense of Laura summoning a hundred things, small experiences, into her hands, bringing them to her like bees returning to a hive. "I know you think I know nothing about the world. Don't say anything, you're listening now."

Lizzie could only nod. Because it was true.

"I don't know about your world. But I do know about being in places where people can hurt you, over and over again, and smile while they're doing it. Where being the right kind of patient, the right kind of woman, the right kind of person, is the only way to avoid that. And even then, it doesn't work all the time." There was something decidedly haunted there.

Lizzie made a small noise in her throat, gesturing a little with one hand, but Laura went on with a sort of utterly unanticipatable relentlessness.

"You hurt him. I don't know exactly how you hurt him. I don't think it's in anything you've actually told me. But you hurt him, and badly, and he doesn't dare admit it. You dance very well together and he apparently thinks highly of you. And yet, despite all the things you're insisting get in the way of him treating you decently, you've gone entirely off the map on a foggy day."

Laura watched her for a long moment and finally said, "I don't know how you fix it. But I'm sure you need to." And then she added, "You can stop looking at me like that. I'm done with the talking for right now."

It was more than that, Laura had a fit of coughing that was only helped by a long pause and more tea. Lizzie did her best not to fuss further since that wouldn't help anything at all either.

"I didn't know." Lizzie finally found enough words for that. "About him. About you either. I'm sorry."

That got a wave of the hand, and a very soft, "Telling you how you can hurt me, that's not an easy thing."

It made Lizzie wince and then say, "We should talk more. Not today." She took several moments to gather her thoughts, and a sip of her tea, before speaking again. "Can I ask you a thing? A very hard thing, and I can't explain it, not yet."

Laura blinked at her, slowly.

"Don't drink more of the goldwasser. Go to the parties if you like. Do whatever you want, besides that. You're right, I'm not Mama, and even if I were, you're a grown woman. But please, for me, don't drink more."

Laura tilted her head. "Why that, in particular?"

"I can't say - truly not. Not yet. Sometime soon, I hope. And I know it feels so good to you. But please, it's not..." She stopped, trying to find the words. "It's false gold. Goblin fruit. Leading you to something that looks so good and seems so wonderful, but destroys you."

Laura closed her eyes. There was utter silence for half a minute, and then she said, "Because you asked, I'll do my best. If you promise to find me and explain when you can."

"Promise. On Papa's compass."

That got a little quirk of a smile, a moment where Laura was weighing it before she nodded. "That will do."

Lizzie let out a long breath. "Thank you. Can I walk you back to your office?"

"What are you going to do?"

"What's needed. Go back to my office. Go to the party.

Do my best not to make things worse. I'll probably fail, but that doesn't mean I shouldn't try."

This made Laura smile, and there was an even "Ah, you needn't be quite that fatalistic. While there's life, there's hope."

Lizzie looked up, hearing that sentiment, then nodded. "I'll trust you on that."

# TWENTY-NINE

## TRELLECH

It had not been the best morning.

Carillon had said he was fine with the public waiting room by the portals, but Benton had stiffly insisted on arranging for one of the private rooms. His back was to Carillon now as he prodded the controls on the heating grate.

"I will not be here that long, Benton."

"Sir."

Carillon was quiet for half a minute. Long enough for Benton to stop tinkering with the grate, and start fussing with tea and a tea warmer, and a plate of biscuits. Finally, Carillon said, "I know you disapprove."

That was blunt enough that Benton's head came up. Any other man might have grunted or had the tea spill minutely, but Benton kept going with his self-assigned tasks in impeccable form. Finally, he straightened, and said, "Sir, it is not my place to approve or disapprove."

"Still." Carillon's voice was quieter.

"I should be seeing to you, sir."

"They were quite clear about not bringing my own man, Benton."

Benton sniffed slightly. "It is not the done thing, sir. And you are bringing her." If he hadn't known better, he would think Benton was actively objecting.

That got a cough. "They requested her presence. Also, needed."

"Sir." He was back to the unyielding wall.

Carillon considered, and then said, "Do you have time before you need to meet her?"

"Eight minutes, sir."

"And do we have privacy charms?"

That got a slightly warmer "Sir," as Benton set about testing them. He set the standard ones in the room going, then withdrew a small folding device from his pocket, and walked once around the room, turning precisely in the corners. "Secure, sir."

That got a nod. "Mine is packed?"

"Sir."

Carillon had to smile for a moment at that, then realised he did not have much time. "You know I am working on a significant investigation. One you are not well positioned to assist with."

"Sir." That was grudging, but at least he was listening.

"You are entirely too well known as forthright, sober, and unimpeachably honest for a plot involving intoxicating and possibly poisonous liquids, Benton."

That made Benton's lips twitch, which Carillon considered a decided improvement. And then he ventured, "Sir, but her?"

Carillon took a breath and then said, carefully. "I am setting out the pieces, Benton. It is a long game."

Benton shifted, a slight movement in the set of his

shoulders that Carillon recognised as the expansion of thought.

"Sir, you have not been your preferred self, since the last time you went to a party with her."

Carillon closed his eyes for a long moment, and then said, "That makes no difference to the match strategy, Benton."

Benton was silent, then said, "I wish they permitted my presence, sir." It was far more emotion than Benton usually admitted to.

Carillon nodded. "I do too. But I will be more free to act without you there. And I suspect even you could not work your usual charms in that house. I need you well away, both in case we need to call in outside reinforcements, and so that I can make use of the entire field."

Benton considered, and then said, "Like that match in 1919, sir?" He paused, remembering, before he said, "May it end as well."

Carillon couldn't help but remember as well, sharp and cold like it was yesterday. It had been an unpleasantness, after the War, tracking someone who had stolen one of the more nightmare-inducing poison gases. He had posed as a potential buyer, and Benton would have given the game away at first glance.

"Much like that, yes. You understand?"

"Yes, sir. I will go fetch the lady and her case."

He pivoted, his heels almost snapping together, and then he made his way out of the waiting room. Carillon watched him go, and then picked up a book and the teacup. Time to look like anyone who passed by the window like he had not a care in the world.

He was entirely lost in thought when there was a precise knock on the door, Benton with Lizzie behind him.

The door opened, with a quiet, "M'lord, when convenient."

He stood and extended his hand. "Lizzie," he said, and then took in her outfit. It was quite proper for this stage in the day, in a rich sea blue, jacket and blouse and skirt. It looked older, with a few tailoring touches to bring it into the current mode, and included a hat he remembered seeing her glance at several times on Monday.

Old or not, it suited her. There was something in the saturated blues that brought out her eyes, and the blush in her cheeks, even though she looked very serious.

"Carillon." She glanced at his valet with a tight little smile. "Benton has been very helpful, thank you."

That got a nod at Benton. "Benton is entirely reliable that way. Do you need to pause, a cup of tea? Or shall we make our way to the portal?"

"I'd rather go on through if you don't mind?" She stopped, then said, "Unless there's... no, I suppose we'd better keep on."

He tilted his head at that, but tucked the book he had been ignoring into his smaller case, and offered Lizzie his arm. "Benton will see our cases stowed, of course."

That earned him a nod, and then, "I hope your week went well?"

He could tell she was trying to ease things, and he wasn't entirely sure how to take it. "I was at Ytene most of the week. The horses take a bit of attention."

"You'd mentioned, in your note. You take it seriously." And then she was more hesitant, but offered, "I'd like to hear more about it, if you're willing?"

He paused for a second, enough to break stride, to look at her. Entirely ungraceful, and it almost upset Benton, who was behind them with the handcart. "You would?"

She was not doing what he expected. He could deal with her if he thought of her the queen on his chessboard, powerful and flexible and entirely aloof. Making conversation with her, that was an unexpected challenge.

Lizzie nodded, and when she looked up at him, she was rather earnest. "It's not something I've thought much about. Either the breeding or training."

He was about to say something else, try to find words, when Benton coughed and said, "Sir, the portal here is ready?"

They had to spend the next few minutes fussing with setting the portal. Burke had sent along a card with the formal address, using the sigil form rather than the name. The sigils were both more precise and more private, since it was impossible to tell where you were going.

That was part of why Benton was coming through with the luggage. That way, he could figure out where they were.

The portal keeper finished setting the sigils, then murmured, "Three, sir, ready on the mark." The portal flared into activity, and he added, "Now."

Carillon let Lizzie drop his arm, and proceeded her through, in the proper etiquette so as to make sure the other side was clear. He came out in an area that felt like further north in Wales, but Lizzie's arrival interrupted any thought of the specifics. She stumbled slightly, and he reached out a hand automatically, before escorting her to the side.

"Do you know where we are?" It was clearly also the first thing on her mind.

He shook his head, moving to peer at the portal on this side, running his fingers over the carving on the arch. "Benton will have to look up the sigils later." Now they were here, he had the final two that showed the portal's distance from Trellech and compass orientation.

Benton arrived with their luggage and Carillon passed the direction card over to him with their practiced sleight of hand. Benton murmured a precise "Sir," before moving off to speak to a liveried footman with a carriage. "Sir, this man will take you to the manor. I will ride with the luggage cart and see your things set out."

Carillon nodded. He and Lizzie were shown into a closed carriage, and driven a modest distance, perhaps a mile. He thought, based on the distance, that they used the portal for shipping or business rather than for the manor alone, unlike the one at Ytene. He had not had time enough to look around, never mind explore the geography.

They rode in silence. Carillon was quiet because he was not at all what to say, and besides, someone might overhear them. Lizzie was quiet for reasons he could not begin to sort out. As they pulled up the drive, he commented, "It seems the grounds are quite extensive. I know you enjoy a walk now and then."

She looked up at him and nodded, but then they were pulling up to a grand manor. The footman let him out first, and Carillon came around to offer his arm to Lizzie. The manor's butler was waiting, with a "Lord Carillon, Miss Penhallow, welcome." Notably without any name, either of the manor or their host.

"Sir, if you would care for a drink, your host is in the red room and has been looking forward to your arrival. Miss Penhallow, perhaps you would like to refresh yourself before meeting the other lady guests?"

Lizzie took in a deep breath and glanced at Carillon. He nodded slightly at her. He did not like they were being separated so quickly, but neither of them could make a fuss about it. "I will go make my introductions to our host, Elspeth. Do take your time, and I'm sure they will let you know where you can find other guests when you are ready."

Lizzie managed a pretty smile, and, "Of course. And thank you, yes, I'd love the chance to straighten my hair." She spoke to the butler with precisely the right degree of politeness, accepting the offer as her due.

The butler gestured, and one maid came forward to lead Lizzie off. Carillon could just see the luggage cart starting up the drive and circling to the back of the house. Benton was sitting on the back with his legs hanging off, looking rather mortified. Not the done thing at all.

He got no chance to look around further before the butler led him off and into the house. They went down to the right, into a large room with deep red furnishings and dark wood. Georgian, he thought, though the glimpse he'd got of the outside of the house suggested some Victorian additions.

The man who greeted him was perhaps fifty-five, all hail-fellow-well-met, and introduced himself as Ambrose Thirke. That was not a name that went with any house like this. Carillon became more certain that those behind this plot were either using pseudonyms or were entirely new money.

He knew quite many people with no titles, but most of them had better manners and less destructive hobbies than his host likely did. Based on the current evidence, at least.

But he smiled, and said, "Grand for you to have us, thank you kindly."

"Pleasure to have you. And your friend, my people will take good care of her."

Carillon wished he could read that as less threatening than he was, but there was no way out of it now.

It opened the way for a particular bit of conversation,

but before he could say anything, the man continued. "Mind, there's quite a bit of gossip, my wife said, about why you're keeping company with her. Given her family situation. But more than one person said she was quite a suitable guest for our gathering."

"If I stuck to the people I already knew, I would hardly be here right now, would I?" He left a tiny pause, then continued, "But I say, old man, it is a bit rich, insisting I not bring my valet. Not the done thing at all, the house parties I generally attend."

"Ah, we explained, yes? New staff downstairs, so difficult to find proper people after the War, you must know all about that."

Carillon sniffed, and said, "Well, that's the common complaint." Not one he'd had overmuch difficulty with himself, thank you, he tried not to be that sort of idiot. "Still. That and the dashed secrecy almost put a man off. Not even knowing where I was coming to. One scarcely knows how to pack in preparation."

That got a snort from his host. "Ah, you have your choice of activities, other than a few events. We've planned for a dance this evening, I understand you're quite the dancer. And the usual amusements tomorrow. Monday, when some of the party leave, we can talk about other business, if we like the look of you, and you like the look of us."

He paused for just a moment, letting that sink in. "Only rabbit shooting this time of the year but the grounds are quite pleasant if you're inclined to a little walking or riding. I rather suspect most will sleep in. You might well, if you take proper advantage of our drinks. We get up a bohort match in the afternoon though I gather you're a pavo man?"

"Pavo, yes, these days. The horses do take more planning, really. Still building up my own stable again. Got quite a good man now, doing the day-to-day training."

He thanked his earlier strategising for the ease with which he could natter about pavo with people who didn't appreciate it. Thirke kept the conversation on pavo and a few related topics. No matter how Carillon tried to get it around to the party and the other guests several times, he had no success. About the fourth time he tried, he gave it up as a lost cause and decided he would just have to see what he spotted on his own.

# THIRTY

## A COUNTRY HOUSE, WALES

The afternoon had been difficult in unexpected ways. They'd separated her neatly from Carillon, to lead her up to a shared room, something no proper house party would ever have done even in this more dissolute age.

It was not the risque but private solution of adjoining doors. Nor was it the more common variation of putting them down at the end of a hallway no one else was assigned. She was familiar with those possibilities from her time with Leander, back at the beginning of the War.

This was entirely different. It made her instantly wary, wondering what other rules they would ignore, what pit of adders she might be dropped into.

The maid waited. Lizzie said, "Oh, um. I don't need much help. I'm sure you must have other things to see to." She paused for a second and added, "May I ask your name?"

The woman bobbed. "Mally, miss."

Lizzie considered, then said, confidingly, "I'm not used to having a maid at all, doing for myself. If there's something else you'd rather be at."

That got a startled noise. "My mistress wishes me to escort you to see her when you are settled, miss." Mally paused, and said, offering more information than anyone else had thus far. "Dressing gong is at seven, supper at eight. The ladies gather up here until then."

Lizzie nodded. "Oh, thank you. Of course. I wouldn't want you to get in trouble. As soon as I can get a few things from my case, I'll be ready quite promptly."

Mally had shown her through a large drawing room on the way from the stairs to the bedroom. It had been empty when they went through, but Lizzie thought she could hear voices of other women, someone a bit too drunk for quite this early in the afternoon.

There was a single knock, and Benton entered, with both cases. There was a flash of startlement on his face, then a "Miss Penhallow, may I assist with your case?" The housemaid made as if to help, and he sharply added, "My lord has his own particulars. You may return and help the lady in a quarter hour."

Something in there was quellingly effective, and the maid bobbed and murmured, "Quarter hour, miss."

Benton looked her up and down, and then said, "Miss, perhaps you might wish to wash up, while I unpack? Perhaps you might prefer one of the less formal day dresses? Might I select a scarf? His lordship had a piece of jewellery he thought you might find pleasing."

Lizzie knew when she was entirely outmanoeuvred, and nodded, gathering the necessary things. When she came out ten minutes later, she had changed, washed her face, and applied her cosmetics in a more modern style. Even her hair was behaving as well as it ever did.

Benton was in the midst of unpacking her clothing. She wanted to feel embarrassed, but he clearly did not allow such trifles as handling her underthings to interfere in his duty.

Without pausing, he murmured, "My lord hopes you find that pendant pleasing, miss. And a matching scarf, there." The scarf was a fine silk, and not hers. The cream went beautifully with the deep teal of the dress, and the amber and teal of the embroidery picked up the pendant. His Lordship had an incredible eye.

There was a tiny flick of his fingers, enough to make her examine the wirework pendant with a deep amber stone. She discovered a small note folded and tucked into a hollow at the back. He came around to help fasten it, using the necessary proximity as an excuse to whisper, "If you'd give that to his lordship, he would be obliged," in her ear.

She nodded, and he withdrew, going back to the packing and leaving her to drape the scarf over her dress and arrange the folds.

It was good they'd managed that bit of sleight of hand because the maid came back as he stepped away. "Miss. If you'll wait a minute, the footman will show Lord Carillon's man out, and I can bring you to the other ladies."

Clearly, they were not permitted any meaningful conversation. Lizzie did not resist though she took a moment to check where Benton had put each item. The good hatpin was here, the notebook with her particular shorthand was there.

Nothing terribly suspicious. The notebook was new, and just had a brief series of quotations from the biography she was reading. She fully expected someone would search their room before she and Carillon returned. She'd eat her new hat if they didn't.

The maid bobbed again, and led her back off to the drawing room, where a woman in her early forties, trying to look younger, stood. She was wearing a dress that was a hair too tight in places, and a shade of salmon that was fashionable but not entirely becoming.

"You must be Elspeth, oh do come in, can I call you E, that's so much better, isn't it? Now we're just all dying to hear all about you."

Lizzie took in a deep breath and said, "Thank you so much for having me, but I'm afraid I'm quite at a loss, not knowing you. Entirely my doing, but - please." She did her best to look pleasant and polite. Most of the women were older than she was, only a few around her age.

The flurry of introductions that followed was not as informative as she'd hoped. The names she heard were first names or nicknames, which made it hard to connect them to each other, or to families. She might manage a few with research, and she was sure Vivian could help with others, but it was terribly confusing.

They expected another dozen or so in the evening, making the overall party about fifty all told, quite a large group. "Oh, but some women will just be coming in for the night." The others immediately changed the subject.

Lizzie had managed not to give too much away, she thought. She was working in an office in the Ministry, oh, it wasn't interesting at all, really not, but she liked Trellech, had they seen this shop display? She did her best to chatter along, and certainly to ask questions. She drew people out a few times, but only briefly. It was as if they had no habit of the more usual sort of confidences among women or the small talk she'd heard at other parties.

By the time they broke to change for the evening, she had at least sorted the women into a few rough groups. Four or five seemed to be related to each other, by blood or marriage. Two were clearly younger second wives, which was not the done thing in the better families without an excellent reason.

She found a few of them curious. There was a lull, partway through the afternoon, where Lizzie talked quietly with Gretchen, who had been governess to her husband's children after his first wife had died young. She insisted she was very happy, but Lizzie thought it likely that her love of the children made her so, rather than the husband himself.

It wasn't in anything Gretchen said directly, more in what she didn't say. She talked much more about her former charges, and the few times she smiled were more about being at home with the children than her husband. It was clear she both didn't care for parties like the one they were at, and came solely because she had to.

Another woman was older, reminding Lizzie of Tilly, at work, but this woman was Indian, Lizzie thought. Perhaps second generation in Britain, by her accent and the way she wove idioms together. Whatever her background, she had enough status here that when she laughed openly at ridiculous gossip, no one shushed her or shamed her or ignored her. Another seemed more like a grandmother, half-nodding away in a sunny corner, overlooked.

Then someone noticed Lizzie's lack of participation and the women set about prying again. It was the questions she'd expected. They asked her how long she'd been seeing Carillon, what he was like in private, and got bawdier than Lizzie cared to think about. She had enjoyed their time in bed, but talking about it, like this, that made her squirm.

Finally, the dressing gong rang, and she escaped back to her room. Mally was waiting there, her evening dress set out. She was about to change when she heard a noise from the bathing room and she called out "Carillon?"

"Be a few, darling. Get dressed, do."

Lizzie nodded and turned to Mally. "I'm sure you've other people to see to, a hand with my hair would be grand, but I don't need anything fancy. Just a little help with the back of the dress, too." It was a beautiful silk, deep blue-green, with a fitted bodice and a high hem. Quite fashionable, even if the figure inside it was a bit too curved for the current dress lines.

Mally worked quickly, and when Lizzie's hair was done, she said, "If I may, miss? I'll come see to your night things later."

Lizzie smiled, and said, "Your service is excellent, thank you."

The sounds from the bathing room had got quieter and quieter. After Mally left, there was a pause before she heard footsteps, the tap of leather soles on a stone floor. He came around, half dressed in evening wear, his cuffs undone. He looked gorgeous, the mix of proper evening attire and being not yet pulled together.

"Lizzie." He murmured her name. "Dashed awkward, this." He gestured at the single bed. "Of course I'll..." He gestured at the floor, and then put his fingers to his lips, and gestured at the space.

She mouthed "Listening" to him, and he nodded.

"You're just not used to doing without Benton. Here, come here, let me see to your cuffs. You might need to remind me how you like them done best." Her tone became amused, affectionate, and she could see him shiver once, but he came and sat down obediently on the bed.

"The cufflinks are there, in that tray." There was a note in his voice she didn't know how to answer at all.

She fetched it over, and then picked one up, looking to see how it worked, before she reached for his hand. He almost jerked his hand away when he touched her before he visibly forced himself into patience. She bent to ask him something, and he shook his head, and murmured, "Later."

Chastened, she focused on tending to his cuffs as quickly as she could, fumbling once or twice. That done, he went back to his own toilette and she settled at the table to finish setting her cosmetics. He silently offered her an ornate jewelled necklace in exchange for the pendant. That gave her the opportunity to indicate the note Benton had hidden with a flick of her finger.

He palmed it so expertly she'd never have noticed if she hadn't known it was there, and then offered his arm. "If you're ready, m'lady, may I escort you?"

The supper and dancing that followed seemed to follow the norms for a house party well enough. But she continued to have the sense that many of the guests knew each other slightly but not well, and only a few were closely acquainted.

Almost everyone used first names and nicknames that seemed to have no real connection to their actual names. The usual Bunny and Tibs, Eight and Minx, with a range of others she couldn't even begin to make sense of. She resigned herself to being E, repeatedly, glad it wasn't worse.

The group did not separate after the meal, these women did not segregate themselves in the drawing room. Quite the contrary, in fact. Lizzie realised that at least some she had not met that afternoon were paid escorts, paying close attention to particular men, deliberate about it. They cordially ignored her as no threat at all. That was unlike the other female guests, who alternately talked over her about people she didn't know or treated her with a sharp-edged deliberate exclusion.

They had gathered in a large room, set up with Roman style couches. The whole setting allowed for quite a variety of positioning, depending on how close and personal one wished to be. Quite a few people preferred to be quite up close. One man, drunk on something other than the gold-wasser, spent twenty minutes telling her how she looked like her sister, and how her sister was much prettier. It was not an effective means of flirtation, at all.

Mind, she could see why he was talking to her. Others had paired off. More than one brightly dressed woman was nestled in the lap of a man with wandering hands. Some were kissing, some were undoing clothing.

Gretchen sat uncomfortably on a couch, glancing over at an older man. He had one companion in his lap, his hand pushing her dress up her thigh, nearly to her hip. Lizzie could see Gretchen's hands clench at the fabric, and she determined to do the little she could to help.

She moved over to the nearest chair, leaning to murmur, "Tell me more about your children." Gretchen's face lit up, and there was an oasis of pleasant conversation for them both for twenty minutes. It was only broken by their hostess realising they were ignoring the party and dragging Lizzie off.

There was conversation after conversation where Lizzie was introduced, then ignored. The other guests talked about those she didn't know and things she didn't care for, leaving her to listen and observe.

She kept getting glimpses of Carillon, who had been welcomed into different conversations, more serious ones. She thought that most there would read the way he kept looking at her as affection, or at least lusty interest, but she could tell it was something different there. Distance, and complexity.

The party moved on, dizzying and with a burble of noise that began to wear on her more and more. She passed on half the drinks, not willing to risk an unknown potion at the best of times, and especially not here.

Another man sidled up to her while she was looking out a window, listening to music, and put his hand around her hip, tugging her close and squeezing her. "Can do much better than that stick up his arse, you can. Come along to my room tonight, sweet, and I'll show you a good time." Then he laughed, more loudly, and said, "Or now, shall we?"

Carillon saved her himself. Last she'd seen him, half an hour ago, he'd been sitting on a chair talking to two other men about pavo. They had disappeared, and she caught a moment of Carillon's attention focused on two men kissing on one of the sofas. One was not much older than Carillon, dark-haired, the kind of distinguished nobleman who littered young women's fantasies, the other blonde and younger. He was willing, however, very willing, given how he was straddling his partner's lap.

Carillon had been leaning forward, watching them with the kind of intensity that comes from need or hatred, though he drew back when someone else turned his way. Then he'd melted off into conversations again, or the terrace, and she'd lost track of him in the press of bodies and dim light.

"Here, Elspeth." She heard Carillon's voice behind her. "Come join me." It had just a hint of a command to it, enough to startle the man holding her, to let her say, "Pardon," as she twisted away.

He reached out a hand for her, murmuring "When in Rome, mmm?"

Lizzie had to close her eyes, lightheaded. She hadn't wanted this, not like this, to need to put on the show, when what she wanted to do was apologise, to talk, to be honest. None of this was honest.

But there was his hand, and there was his lap. She took

a breath, smiled, and set her hand in his, letting him draw her down into his lap. His breath tickled her ear as he murmured. "Give them a bit of a show, then we will retreat to the room when we can, mm?"

That got a nod, "I'll follow your lead." It made him shiver again before he moved to adjust his position so he could kiss her.

The next half hour worked them both up rather more than either of them might have chosen. Even with the awkwardness and difficulty between them, her body remembered what his kisses were like, and his body clearly wanted more. She could feel his cock hard between them, the way she was settled in his lap.

As the others around them became more and more caught up in their own erotic moments, he ventured a bit more. His fingers undid a bit of her bodice, he slipped a hand to cup her breast, all the things that made a good show and felt even better. Finally, the noises around them suggested everyone else was distracted, and he murmured into her neck, "Let me pull you up and out and away. Will you trust me?"

She murmured, "Always," before she could think to say anything else.

## THIRTY-ONE

### A COUNTRY HOUSE, WALES

"Do you ride?"

Lizzie blinked at him, and he repeated it. "Do you ride? Well enough for a quiet hack through the grounds?"

They had retreated to their room after an awkward and lonely breakfast, no signs anyone else had been near the food yet, nor sounds from other guests in the house.

Lizzie paused, considering, then said, "I've a skirt that would work for sidesaddle and boots." And then she offered, "I'm not a brilliant rider. I gather you are."

"We will not be doing the sort of riding that calls for my skills." He was firm about that.

Once they had changed, they went to inquire at the stable about a suitable pair of horses. The head groom had obviously heard of him and kept trying to talk up a particular sharp bay, but Carillon shook his head.

"Miss Penhallow has not been on a horse in a while. I want something that will suit a quiet hack, not a challenging ride. I might come back this afternoon for something more energetic."

This ended with Lizzie mounted on a sedate grey mare, sturdy and pleasant, and Carillon himself on a black mare with a bit more spirit, but a steady gait. And it got them a map and directions on a route that would be five or six miles, a pleasant morning's ride.

"You prefer mares?" Lizzie's voice was quiet but interested.

Carillon blinked and nodded. "Yes, but why do you ask?"

"You'd mentioned working with one this week. Also black, if I remember right?"

It had been in his note, he realised, he'd been looking for something harmless to talk about. Harmless, and yet Lizzie had a knack for finding the tender heart and asking about it.

"Mares are the queens of the herd," he said, after a moment. "Learning what they want is a challenge I find especially rewarding."

Lizzie went quiet at that though she offered a little hesitant smile to acknowledge the comment.

They were well out into the fields, near the edge of the property, before Carillon spoke again. "This path goes down onto public lands then curves around into the back side of the grounds. I thought we might pause for a little at the river?"

Lizzie nodded and made a polite comment about the weather.

Carillon swallowed, riding on, managing the same occasional inconsequential comment. A bird here, a pretty view there.

Last night had been torture in several ways. The questions he'd got had been easy enough for someone with his experience to deflect, but then the party had twisted on him. More than one layer of plots unfolding. And more than one set of people being fooled into thinking there was nothing more than intoxicating drink, beautiful women, and the promise of all the luxury one might want.

He'd seen the hints of the undercurrents, two or three men finding a quiet corner, then another set. Several of those groups had withdrawn before the others got wilder. He'd hated watching Lizzie be ignored, and then be treated like a common property. His hands tightened on the reins, his knees clenching, and the mare between his knees threw her head up, uneasy.

Lizzie murmured, "Carillon?"

He took a breath and waved his hand. "Nothing."

They were still entirely too close to the manor to talk freely. He had to stay calm until they were properly away. He hoped this would work. No one seemed to have forbidden them to take horses out.

He had confirmed, before Lizzie returned to change, that there were listening devices in their room. Given time he might have blocked them, but he couldn't risk them taking that out on Lizzie.

When they'd got back to the room, after that single shattering word, she'd clearly assumed they could talk more freely, and he had pulled her close instead, where he could breathe into her ear. "We can't let them suspect. Sweet nothings. No long conversation. Nothing that will worry."

To give her credit, she had nodded, changed into her nightgown, and settled into bed. She'd been exhausted. As soon as it was still and quiet, she'd fallen asleep, trusting. It left him alone with his thoughts for an hour or more until he drifted off, wondering what she'd meant by what she said.

He'd half-woken to find himself leaning against her, one of her arms draped over him. It had surprised him, enough to wake him fully in an instant, and that woke her.

They were coming up on the copse of trees that led to the river, the turn that led them somewhere safe enough to talk.

He gestured. "Let me set a few things out, let the horses be comfortable." She unhooked her knee from the sidesaddle and took his hand to help balance on the way down, tidily enough.

Only then did he draw out the book of days he'd slipped into his pocket and opened it to a particular ribbon book-mark. The left-hand page was illuminated with an image of Mercury Visucius, ravens around him, in shades of black, the deity's robes in shades of rich blue.

Lizzie blinked at it, and Carillon took a breath. He placed his fingers lightly on three particular ravens and murmured a particular set of words under his breath.

He was relieved to find that shimmer of colour around the image did what it was supposed to. There was no one nearby, nothing that could overhear. He let out a long breath and then looked up. "There's no one to overhear."

Lizzie didn't stop looking at the book and murmured "That's, that's..." before she ran out of words.

"A family tradition. Each of us makes one. A little help with the artwork is permissible, but the rest is done by fami-ly." He ran a finger down the edge of the cover. "Few people suspect them."

He had let her see something he normally never revealed, and he looked up at her again, wanting to see how she reacted.

"I was thinking mostly that it's beautiful." Her voice was very low. Lizzie half reached out a hand, and let it drop. "Thank you for letting me see this much."

Carillon had not expected that. She kept doing that, a thing he did not expect. He tried to decide if that meant she wanted to see more, or if she intended to say something else.

Both of them were so focused on that, they jumped when a voice behind them said, "Untainted one. The problem is still."

Carillon wheeled around, to see a form like a small pile of rocks, but with a fuzziness that made him sure magic was at play. That, and a sense of gathering doom, like a fog rolling in. He knew, knew as well as he knew how to sit a horse, that it had not been there three moments before.

Lizzie had taken several steps back, toward the river, but when it spoke, she stopped, and said, cautiously. "Hello?" And then, more hesitant, she shifted into something that had aspects of song to it, a lilt to the words. Carillon could not place it, for all his travels, but it was clearly some formal phrase.

The pile of stone said something back, incomprehensible. Then in English, it continued, "Cave-in coming. Damp and danger." And then it fixed Lizzie with an unyielding regard. "Untainted one, why?"

Lizzie took a step or two back, close enough to reach out and touch Carillon's elbow. "This is one of the Belin, Carillon." And then, "Pardon, but what do you mean by taint? I want to help, that's why we're here, but we - it is a very difficult seam to follow for us."

This got a rolling snort, something that in a man would have been a chortling laugh, Carillon suspected. Something in the gathering discomfort suddenly eased. There was a word, and Carillon rather suspected it was a form of 'foolish humans', the way one would be amused by a cat or dog or small child.

Lizzie waited, entirely focused and patient. When the rocks spoke again, they said, "Did not drink. Can work in harness, yet." And then, as if trying to figure out how to explain something, it settled on "Gold in drink," as if laying out a first principle.

Lizzie nodded. "The goldwasser," she agreed.

The stones made a slight approving noise, and continued, "Makes metal die. No longer phoenix-bright, renewing. Cold and dead forever."

Lizzie blinked, and only then did she turn to glance at Carillon, before she swallowed and said, "Please, I want to have this correct. The way they make the drink, it destroys the gold it is made from? In a way that we humans don't understand."

The approving noise came again, a deeper rumble and longer. "Like so. Coins still in the world. Not given to the dragons to be reborn. Not..." It searched for a word. "Not healthy for dragons. Not healthy for living things."

Carillon breathed out, "It is not the goldwasser itself, but - a coin, maybe something they got in change, or payment. That is killing people."

Lizzie blinked. "Killing people?" It burst out of her.

Carillon nodded, and expanded for her benefit. "Five deaths that Vivian thought related." The comments earned him his own approving noise.

Lizzie nodded and said, "We want to find who is making it. Stop them. We will need help, other humans. We will work as fast as we can."

That got a rumble. "How long?"

Lizzie clearly did complex mental calculations, by the way she tilted her head and chewed on her lip. "By sol..." And then she stopped and said "By the new moon. I hope sooner. But it depends on what we find."

There was a long rumbling noise, like a small earthquake, that made the horses startle. Carillon moved to go calm them, and the stones subsided. "Come to the mountain. Explain. You."

That got Lizzie making a series of faces, and then she said, "Of course. When?"

"High tide."

"I will." And then a cautious, "What offerings are proper?"

This made the stones very amused. "Truth."

Then it was gone, as suddenly as it had arrived. Lizzie went to both knees, with something that looked like overwhelmed relief. Carillon made sure the horses were safe and then bent to touch her shoulder, cautious.

"How long do we have?"

"Full moon is the sixteenth. Maybe the seventeenth. New is July second. I think."

Carillon let out a breath. "So not Monday."

It was that which pushed her over into mild hysterics, a giggling laughter she couldn't stop, even when he set his arm around her shoulders. Before she was quite recovered, there was a groom riding toward them. All chance for a private conversation was gone for the moment.

A COUNTRY HOUSE, WALES

The groom insisted on accompanying them, so Lizzie packed up the blanket with a minimum of conversation. They made a proper show of enjoying their ride along the river.

When they paused to look at a particularly nice view, Lizzie managed to murmur, "We really should find time to talk." Carillon nodded then suggested, "Might manage the bath, for a few minutes. It will take a little magic, but less obvious than in the bedroom."

That was all the time they had, the groom riding close beside along the roads at the back of the property, and back to the stable. By the time they got back, there were people visible on the terrace, and the house was stirring.

Once back, Carillon insisted they should both have baths, which bought them a little more time. Mally set up the bath for Lizzie, first, but while it was running, she said, timidly, "Pardon, miss?"

Lizzie looked up, from where she was choosing a dress for the afternoon. "Yes?"

Mally came over and murmured in her ear. "Would it be very forward to ask you a question, a, a confidential one?"

Lizzie nodded, lifting her hand to get Carillon's attention, then mimed opening a book. "Mally, would you come help me in the bath? I could use a hand with my hair. And Carillon, darling, you wanted to wash that scrape first thing."

They made an awkward trio, what with the bath steaming and the lack of seating. Carillon had brought his book in with him and opened it, moving his fingers in some particular way over the page. Then he said, "We have five minutes, maybe a little longer, without being overheard."

Mally looked terrified, both terrified and overwhelmed, and Lizzie immediately spoke up, "Here, there's a little bench. Sit, please. We promise, we won't hurt you. We want to help."

"You're not like the others, miss. Sir. Your lordship. Oh." She buried her face in her hands.

Carillon gave her about fifteen seconds, before he said, very gently. "There isn't much time. I am sorry."

Mally swallowed and then said, her voice weak. "It sounds silly. One of the gentleman, miss, gave me a coin last night, a thank you for something, and it made me feel awful. All sick to my stomach, and worse today, and I don't know who to ask."

Carillon leaned forward. "Do you have it? With you?" Lizzie was distracted for the moment at how he looked like a hound, finding a trail.

Mally nodded, drawing it out of her pocket, and holding it out, her hand trembling.

He withdrew a handkerchief from his pocket and unfolded it. "Here, this is silk, that's good for magical things." He wrapped the coin up, making a neat little package that wouldn't come undone accidentally. "Who gave it to you?"

"One of the Gordons. The older brother, I think, m'lord."

Lizzie had glimpsed it, and said, "For anything in particular, Mally? That's a fair bit of coin."

Mally blushed, turning quite red. "For, um, helping arrange something with one of the women the master had brought in to entertain. For doing it without Mr Gordon's wife finding out."

Carillon coughed, as if he wanted to say more, but settled on, "I will trade you a safe coin for it. Seems you earned that money."

Mally bobbed her head, scrunching up her apron in her hands, looking from one to the other.

"Why did you ask us, Mally?" Lizzie tried to make her voice calmer and thoughtful.

"I know you went off riding, miss. And you're not like a lot of the others here. You're much nicer, miss, both of you, m'lord." That was very earnest.

Lizzie laughed. "I feel like that's not very hard to do. Who else has been kind?"

"Mrs - I think Gretchen is her first name, miss? And that older lady, the one the others sort of listen to? Mrs Lal? I shouldn't speak ill of the others, miss. Just. I hoped you'd listen."

Lizzie nodded. "Of course. You let us know if you find anything else strange, all right?"

Mally bobbed her head, and then offered, "Miss, can I be of any help to you?"

Carillon was about to say something, but Lizzie was ahead of him. "Yes, actually. Do you know if they're serving the goldwasser tonight?"

Mally nodded. "They were talking about it downstairs. I don't know if I was supposed to hear about it yet."

Lizzie nodded. "It's important I don't drink it. Can you come up with an excuse to get me out of the room when it goes round? Or something else that means it won't look odd? Something wrong with my dress or someone spilling something on me. Nothing that would get you in trouble, I don't want that, but it's all right if the dress gets ruined."

Carillon closed his mouth, biting back a comment.

Mally thought for a moment. "I think so, miss, since I have time to think about it. I don't think some of them want to try it either, but I think it's expected."

"I suspect I must, Lizzie." Carillon's voice was full of something complicated.

Lizzie frowned, trying to figure out how to ask him what was in his head, and not seeing how she could. "Well, we know what you're like when you do, I suppose." She paused, then said "Are you worried about it?"

He pursed his lips, and then said, "It is addictive for good reason."

Lizzie reached out and touched his hand. "I'll take care of you. Best I can."

It was then they all heard the faint chime of something in the book. Carillon said, quite apologetically. "Time, ladies."

Carillon said, "Let me get you the coin, and then you can help the lady with her hair." Lizzie settled into the bath. When Mally came back, she was looking puzzled. She held out several coins in her hand, all gold, several months wages for a maid at least.

"Lord Carillon is very generous, miss."

Lizzie had to smile at this. "He is, isn't he? He helped choose a lot of my clothing and brought jewellery I could wear. I think he appreciates excellent service, don't you?" She settled in the bath, more comfortably. "I got all sorts of dust in my hair, out riding, and that won't do at all."

They drew out the bathing and changing long enough it was nearly luncheon by the time Lizzie and Carillon came downstairs. He was immediately swept off by people who wanted to get up a bohort match and were asking Carillon to come up with the challenges and referee.

Lizzie got pulled into a knot of women, again, and a luncheon outside in the garden. That was pleasant enough, and with the seating was arranged so it was hard to talk to too many people at once. Gretchen was looking strained, and Mrs Lal was with a circle of women who had not been much in evidence as things got wilder last night. Lizzie made particular note of the faces and tried to hear the names as best she could.

Around two in the afternoon, Carillon presented himself to the group of women, and murmured "Elspeth, a walk around the garden, while they're setting up for the match? We've fifteen minutes before they need me."

She stood up, delighted for a little time away from listening ears, even if they would be within sight. "Down to that little bridge, perhaps? I saw a flower that looks interesting, I'd like a closer look, and perhaps your arm to hold me steady."

That earned her a courtly bow, and once they were down at the bridge, he pulled out his book, pressed his fingers to the page. "There's a device up by the women, but nothing here at the moment. In the past, I think. We've a few minutes."

Lizzie immediately set to an excellent impersonation of someone who was interested in the flower which helped turn her body away from the party on the lawn. "We need time to talk properly."

"Monday evening." Carillon agreed. "Until then, we keep on as we can. You let me know if you feel scared, mind. Immediately. Even if it gives the game away."

Lizzie looked up. "You sound quite odd there."

He was about to say something, but Lizzie had more to say, letting it spill out. "I know I hurt you. After the last party. After that lovely night in bed. We do need to talk about it, and we don't have time here, but I'm so sorry, and - my little sister made me feel very stupid about it."

Something in that took him oddly, enough that he took a physical step back. Then she saw a hint of a smile on his face. "Ah, there's a brave thing. We can set it aside, yes. Until we have time and space."

She smiled back at him, shyly. "I - why did you tell me you've been with men? I saw you last night." It hadn't quite been what she'd meant to ask, and yet it was.

He went wide-eyed, she could see something wild in him, before he took a deep breath. He forced himself to say, "That night, I had hope that we might continue to be close. It would be foul to start that closeness with a lie to you, about what I am." His voice sounded small and twisted up.

She had no idea how to respond to that at all, but she knew whatever she did mattered. She swallowed, closing her eyes, then she said, "Thank you for telling me, that. Trusting me. And then I hurt you."

The words came out in a rush. "I pushed you away entirely. I'm sorry. I didn't understand, I didn't understand a lot of things. I still don't." Before he could say anything, she asked, "The men last night, are they men you know?"

Carillon shook his head, and it seemed like this was at least a little easier to answer. "No, not like that. I've seen the dark-haired one at the club a few times. But there was, men together, there is a fierceness in it sometimes that...." His voice trailed off, then he asked very precisely. "Is that a difficulty for you? Now you've had time to think about it?"

Lizzie said, promptly. "Oh, no. Not that. It's not the men that were the problem. Not - in the past. It's other things. Not you, but everything else. Everyone else. People are so hurtful." And then a dry, raw, "I am also people, and I was hurtful."

That made him smile more broadly, something in him relaxing just a hair. He reached for her hand, to pull her into a kiss, long and thorough. This was no kiss about making the proper show, like last night, this was entirely about the two of them and nothing else. When he took a breath, he murmured, "We will see if you can make it up then, when the time is right."

It was then that they heard one of the men coming down the lawn. "Carillon, do come, the field's ready, there's plenty of time for the ladies tonight."

He pulled away, clearly resenting the interruption, but said, "I need to keep up the show."

Lizzie nodded. "We both do." She took a breath. "I promise, I'll take care of you, tonight. All the ways I can."

Carillon nodded, and tucked her arm into his, to escort her silently back up to the others, and then to do his duty as a theoretically neutral observer.

# THIRTY-THREE

## A COUNTRY HOUSE, WALES

The early part of the evening had gone much the same as on Saturday. Mally had helped Lizzie dress, Lizzie had helped him with his cuffs and the last details. The rest, though, became increasingly different.

Many of the other women were in pale colours, champagne silk and cream and silver. From a purely aesthetic point of view, he thought Lizzie looked far more alive, in a rich blue.

They'd been separated at supper, they'd both expected that. She had been alternately ignored and lectured to by her immediate neighbours. Clothing, whether she was leading that nice Lord Carillon on, the deficiencies of her education, not that they knew much about it.

Carillon, on the other hand, had the woman on his left doing her best to get her hand into his lap. The woman on his right kept wanting to talk up the suitability of her daughter as a possible spouse.

The usual protestations of the well-bred gentleman scarcely made a dent. The subtle positioning of his arm to avoid the hand did not work. Nor did, "Goodness, madam, I do not believe a woman of your fine appearance has a daughter of marriageable age."

He was rescued - if rescued was the word - by several of the men who were clearly involved in the goldwasser plot. They were encouraged along to one of the gaming rooms while most of the party went off into one of the larger rooms. As he went by, he saw it had been set again with the long couches from last night, but with a range of pillows strewn on the floor as well. The light was softer and incense wafted out, with hints of spices and scented woods.

Someone called his name, and he turned around, with a "What, then?" that tried to be amiable and did not quite hit the mark, to his ear.

Their host was pouring out generous measures of the goldwasser, into glasses on a tray. A row of larger glasses, then smaller ones. "Take one of those, your lordship." The larger one, of course.

Thirke sounded more than a bit in his cups already, or perhaps on some other substance, and his hand trembled as he poured. "The maids will take the rest around to the ladies and the others." One of the footmen worked on bringing the larger glasses around to the assembled, and a maid came in to take the tray to the other room.

There was no way out, and Carillon nodded. He wondered, with an increasing distance to his thoughts, if Lizzie would come up with some plan to avoid it. He could feel the pull of the drink, from here, the lure of feeling comfortable again, feeling warm, feeling like things mattered beyond the intellectual insistence of his last weeks.

"Right generous shares, if it is as delicate a thing to make as you've implied."

He wondered for a moment if he'd gone too far if that

was a thing he was supposed to comment on, but Thirke looked up, then raised his glass. "Oh, but there's nothing like it in the world. I know you only had a taste last time. Enjoy this. No other cares in the evening."

Carillon could feel his every nerve go afire, like he was back in the trenches. He expected to hear the sound of the artillery change or the sudden silence that promised some lurking magical attack. He had to swallow hard, tasting the bile in the back of his throat, but he nodded, with a "Right generous." It sounded inane, but at least sounding inane went with the mask he was trying to keep up.

Then he managed, "Given last time, I would rather sit down. It would be a shame to have it knock me off my feet and spill."

That got a laugh from about half the men. "Thought you had sea legs. Seeing one of the Penhallows, aren't they required?"

He tried to make sense of that, and he couldn't, so he made a non-committal noise and turned to the door. He couldn't see Lizzie, so he found a couch near the door, off to one side, and settled on it cupping his drink. The other men followed in ones or twos, greeting the men who'd been here already, and the women.

Carillon thought there were fewer of the paid companions tonight, besides the different mood. As he looked around, trying not to be obvious about it, Mally came over to murmur in his ear. "Miss Elspeth had a difficulty with her dress, m'lord, she'll be back down in a few minutes. Should I be letting her know where you are?"

That got a nod, and a wave of his hand, "Please, and whatever help you can give her, much appreciated."

Mally bobbed, not quite a curtsey, and took that as an excuse to flee the room. She looked decidedly uncomfortable. He wondered if the drink made men free with their hands, or if she had some other fear.

It had been clever of Lizzie to think of a way out and to get Mally so willing to help them. And in ways that wouldn't put Mally at risk.

The men were all gathered, and Thirke had gone over to settle next to his wife, who was looking pinched and eager at the same time. "Raise your glasses to the glow of sweet anticipation," he said, coming across as reaching for a joviality that had disappeared into something more greedy and needy.

Carillon could see that others were sitting there, leaning forward, stretching for something just out of arm's reach. It wasn't physical reaching, exactly. He wondered if he looked like that. With the drink. With Lizzie.

And then everyone was drinking, and he couldn't escape. He felt battered again, lost in his own head as he so often had been at the Front, where there was no way forward but through. He took a sip, a modest one. If he had to drink, at least he could nurse it along. Maybe that wouldn't be so bad.

This time, as soon as it touched his mouth, he could feel something. It was not entirely pleasant, either. Oh, of course, part of it was wonderful. Yet there was something underneath, tickling his magic sense, that was like a hint of rotten fruit. Not quite right, not quite wrong. He could taste why the Belin had called it a taint.

Carillon watched the others as carefully as he could. Several had drained their glasses in a few swallows, others were lingering over it, taking a sip and pausing. He wondered, distantly, if they were drawing it out like he was. Then he felt the effects begin to hit properly, the slight glow to the lights and the warmth in his body.

He could feel when the need started to overwhelm him. No matter how good his intentions, he wanted more of what he was feeling, and he had it in his hands. He took a sip, and another sip, almost draining his glass, leaving just enough they might get a sample if they had enough luck. And he was not alone, he could hear the sound of people drinking, of people putting crystal glasses on tables, on the floor by their couches.

He lost track of time. He knew people were moving around the room, and then he fell into a memory. There was the first trip he'd ever been on with his parents, a winter trip to Italy, the year before he started tutoring. He revelled in the colours, the gold and the green and the whitewashed plaster. This time, he had more smells, the crispness of cypress, the meals they'd had. And he remembered their trip to a painter's studio and the oils and turpentine, the powders of the stones used to make the paint, of his early lessons in what would become his personal Book.

He wanted to linger there forever, back in a time when life was simple. When his parents were there, and they loved him, they explained things to him, they made things work out.

Carillon was interrupted, though, someone coming and sitting down. He blinked, turning his head sideways, trying to make his eyes focus.

Lizzie's voice seemed to come out of nowhere, a slow drawl that didn't sound like her. "Right here, darling." And so she was, and he let himself slide to rest against her shoulder. He tried to explain to her, he opened his mouth, but she murmured, "Right here, don't fuss." There was a different colour there now, a purple, hadn't her dress been blue?

He let his eyes close, leaning against her, his mind flying off on other trips, both the real and the imagined. Watching a glorious sunset from the bow of a boat in the middle of the ocean. Being somewhere in the mountains, maybe that was the Tirol again. Walking through a spice market, now, with all the colours and sounds and smells. All the bliss.

He took a long time to realise that in these blissful moments, he was in beautiful, interesting, fascinating places, but he was not alone in any of them. He could never quite see who he was with, a voice just out of reach. He could feel whoever it was, beside him, no matter what the angles of the sun or the depths of the shadow. It was that he kept wanting, kept walking toward, the thing the drink brought him.

As the hours passed, he lost track of what was going on, letting himself slip down. It was only much later, by the ache in his back, several hours, that he came back to himself. His head was cradled in Lizzie's lap, her hand brushing his hair. She had pulled one knee up, leaning against the arm of the couch. From what he could see she was feigning a stupor, her face half buried in the crook of her arm.

When he moved, though, her arm immediately paused, her head shifted, and she murmured, "May we retreat?"

He did his best to nod, and that disarrayed his sense of balance entirely. More cautiously, he got an elbow under him, then pushed himself upright. At least half the party were slumped in positions that seemed more like the most dissolute illustrations of an opium den than anything else, arms and legs all askew. Some had already gone to other places, he thought, trying to get his eyes to focus.

"Let me help." She was quiet but insistent, and together, they managed to get his arm around her, and himself on his feet. As soon as they were out of the drawing room, Mally was there to offer her arm. He could stagger up the stairs, ridiculous and slow, until they got him to fall into bed.

Someone - he thought Mally, but he honestly couldn't tell - got the jacket and shirt off him. Someone else was holding a glass to his lips and saying, "Drink water, you'll feel better tomorrow."

He sat upright just that long and no more, before he slumped onto the bed again, and remembered nothing else.

# THIRTY-FOUR

## A COUNTRY HOUSE, WALES

**M**onday was a confusing day. Lizzie had lain awake for much of the night, listening to make sure that Carillon kept breathing. He'd been so still when they were downstairs, and again when they got him into bed. She hadn't been sure if it was all right to touch him, given how fragile things were between them.

Everyone was slow to rise except Lizzie. In the late morning, Mally brought a tray, and Carillon managed to stagger into the bathing room. Lizzie was starving and stiff and increasingly anxious about the rest of the day. She changed into a day dress, and by the time Carillon came out, mostly had her things ready. Mally had packed up her case, and most of his.

"Pardon, sir, but they can go down to the portal promptly. Is your man meeting them?"

Carillon nodded. "Any time..." He reached for his pocket watch, did a double take at it. "Is it really half eleven? He will have been there an hour already."

Mally bobbed. "Everyone sleeps in, after." And then a "Miss?"

Lizzie shook her head then said, to cover. "My case is all ready."

Mally finished up the last couple of things and then said, "The gentlemen will meet, sir, downstairs, to be talking. Miss, I can show you somewhere you can sit. If you have a book, miss, I suspect the other ladies may be otherwise engaged."

Lizzie moved to extract a book from her case, and then said, "I'll be quite entertained, darling, however long your meeting is."

Carillon made the most miserable face at her, and they went off in their separate directions.

Lizzie didn't see him until nearly three when he came to the rather neglected library they had stuck her in and knocked on the door frame. "The carriage is ready, do you need anything before we go?"

He looked almost translucent, and she shook her head. "I'm all set, thank you."

It was more her offering her arm to him than the proper way round. She got the sense he needed her to guide him through the halls and that something had deeply unsettled him.

On the way out, Mr Morland came out of one hallway, and said, "Come round the office tomorrow, old man, we can work out the final details." He offered a brief nod to Lizzie. "Regards to your sister, Miss Penhallow."

Lizzie wished that didn't sound so nearly threatening. She wondered, suddenly, if the threat had been for Laura, all along, but if Tibbie Morland wanted to hurt Laura, she was right in his front office, every work day.

Carillon nodded, waved, and said, "I will let you know," before they escaped to the carriage. It was no release, not yet. They had to keep up the act until they were at the

portal, and then Lizzie had to bear up under Benton's disap-
proving glare. She had not returned Carillon in fit condi-
tion, and they all knew it.

Carillon made a gesture toward trying to explain, and
Benton glared again, if much more briefly, until he
subsided.

Once they got back to the townhouse, Lizzie absented
herself for twenty minutes to let Benton fuss. She changed
into a much more relaxed dress and set herself to putting
her hair up more comfortably. Benton came to show her to
the library, and she could explain what the investigation
needed next.

They had set Carillon up on a couch, sipping some
particular concoction of Benton's that was steaming gently
in the cup.

"Did you - "

"Are you - " They both started together, and she had to
stop and say "You first."

He coughed, and said, "Did you manage, last night?"

"I'm fine. I almost got pressed into drinking, but Mally
was a great help. And I have a sample. Well, had. Benton
was going to take care of it when he got a chance."

He lurched upright from where he'd toppled over
leaning against the arm of the sofa. "You what?"

"Benton is taking it to your pocket materia specialist,"
Lizzie said. "I wrapped it up for him. I got a handkerchief
wet with it, the glass I spilt on myself. Pity about the dress,"
she murmured, distracted for a moment.

"And then Mally was able to rescue the dregs of a
couple of glasses, put them in a tiny bottle, bring them up.
Only a few drops each, and a little shimmer of the gold, but
enough, maybe?"

Carillon looked simultaneously like he wanted to leap

up and dance around the room, and like doing so would be a cataclysmic failure. The fact he was visibly torn between the two made her smile.

"I would not have managed without you," he said, finally. "Without you - well, you see me." He gestured. "Entirely useless."

She stood, hesitated a moment, and then came over to the couch, to settle beside him, for all he was trying to sprawl across it. "Stop that," she said, spacing the words out.

He blinked at her, and whatever he'd expected her to say, it was clearly not that.

"You did a very dangerous thing, drinking it. Making yourself vulnerable, like that. I could - I could not have done that." She could feel all the reasons, surging up in her.

He reached to touch her hand, just for a moment, like he was sure she was going to jerk it away. She glanced over, sideways, and then turned her hand to welcome his, palm up.

She was watching him, not his hand, and she could see his eyes soften, something different there, before she felt his palm against hers, his fingers curving. She closed her hand, squeezing his, and then said, "We could go on like this for days. I'd rather not."

This made him laugh, the kind of laugh that was on the border of tears. She held on to his hand, letting him drain out all the things that needed lancing, as best it could. When he came to a gasping halt, she said, more quietly, "What do we do now?"

He rubbed his face with his free hand, and then said, "I'd like you rather closer." It was a cautious offer.

She took a moment to realise how his tone had changed. Warmer. The drawling contraction was back. Not the false image of the confident lordling, but something much more real.

It made her sigh and then try to figure out how they could arrange that. "We have business left. We can't fall into bed. Not and do our duty." She considered, then moved to settle against his shoulder, fitting against him. It would do for the moment.

Carillon nodded, dropping her hand to rub his face, with a murmured, "I wish my mind would come to heel." It sounded decidedly plaintive.

"What happened in your meeting?"

He had to try to rearrange it, in his head. "I'm sure they don't know what it does to the coins. Or at least, I don't think most of them know. I met most of the core group involved, Morland, some others like him, people who made a lot of money on the War, not caring so much how they did. This is a peacetime effort to do the same."

"What was it that bothered you most?"

He looked at her, his gaze sharpening. "How they went about it. That those people were... that it was no problem to get them addicted to something expensive, no thought of how it would destroy families, leave people unable to work. And that's without the coins themselves, and the trouble they could cause, sent back out into the world. They've five deaths that I know of on their hands, now. And we saved Mally from being another."

Even sharper and harder, he added, "I do not care for profiteers, but they are very difficult to avoid entirely."

"Tibbie Morland, among them?"

He nodded. "Tibbie got me alone, at the end, when we were breaking up. His brother was a much better man, and Tibbie's always had a chip on his shoulder, about not being good enough or smart enough or brave enough. And instead of learning how to do things better, he looks for the cheat, the way around. He thought I was like that. That I wanted to be like that."

Lizzie looked up. "You're not like that at all. You might come across as... Well, I agreed with my sister that pavo clearly does nice things for your shoulders and your legs." She blushed. "And you're charming. Everyone agrees you're charming."

That made him laugh for a moment. "I want them to see me as charming, not terribly bright, and cheerfully single-minded about my few public hobbies. No threat to anyone at all."

"That's what Laura told me." She gave enough of a breath for the change back to seriousness before continuing. "So, what did they tell you? About the process?"

"Not much detail. They kept waving it off, saying it was terribly technical, old chap, no need to linger on it. It works, and it's wonderful."

That made her snort. "So they don't understand it either."

Carillon nodded, then sobered. "They asked me what I thought of it, what I experienced, and I did not much want to tell them. It was...." He pauses. "I'd give anything to have more, and yet the experience was not entirely pleasant. Other people told me about things like your sister. About everything being warm and delightful, and dreams of far-away wonderful places. Several people talked about a sense of escape from their troubles."

Lizzie squeezed his hand. "And you?"

"It brought me to places where I'd been with people who cared for me. Last night, it was ... someone I couldn't quite see. Part of me wanted to, to know that was part of what I was dreaming, and part of me couldn't bear to. It was

entirely unsettling, even in what should have been unal-
loyed pleasure."

Lizzie took in a breath, watching his face, then she said,
very softly. "I said, the day I was so hurtful, we didn't have
that kind of relationship. What.... No. Let me try this
sentence again."

She had to stop, rearrange her thoughts. "I have
assumed that you must marry someone of your own class.
That whatever you and I had, it could not be that. It's not
scandal or reputation that makes me unwilling for other
things, but I can't abide cheating or lying about relation-
ships. Not to the people in them. Except for that, I would
gladly be your mistress, or your companion, or whatever
other term you want to choose. If I can keep talking to you,
working on puzzles with you. Exploring your library."

His eyes widened, and she went on. "My sister told me
you'd turned down a lot of women from the proper families.
So now I don't know. I think I'm asking what you want. And
how you see what we've done fitting with that."

He cupped her hand in his, and closed his eyes, clearly
taking time to find the words he wanted. "I could not have
solved this without you. So many times, you had a question
or a thought that changed things. You knew how to speak
with the Belin and you weren't scared to. You thought to
befriend Mally, lead her to trust you, you reassured her.
You've a sharp eye for gossip, and people aren't afraid to talk
around you, even knowing you're associated with me.
Though I do play enough of the fool in public."

He was rambling and clearly realised it, because he
stopped. "I want to find out what we can do together, when
we've time to know each other better. All your skills, and
mine."

This made her blush again, and then murmur, "I like that. I still need a job, mind."

"Oh, I'm quite sure Vivian will keep you on. Even without having come to the final scenes of the plotting, we've brought them a vast treasure trove of information they had no idea about. And if not, well, I'm sure we can come up with something you'd accept."

That got her smiling and saying, "So. We need to talk to Vivian and ap Rhys. And probably lots of other terrifying people. That... that isn't our part, is it? What happens after?"

"Raiding wherever the thing is made, and rounding people up? All the muses, no. We turn that over to the Guard."

She let out a massive sigh at that and let herself relax against him. His arm tightened. "We'll send Benton off when he gets back from taking that sample, and ask Vivian and ap Rhys and whoever else to come visit, then. You rest, domina, right here."

She liked the sound of that. And that he was calling her domina again.

# THIRTY-FIVE

## TRELLECH

B y six that evening, there were rather more people in the library. Lizzie had taken advantage of the pause to change clothing, as had Carillon. Separating had been difficult, but they still could not afford the distraction of doing anything about their desires to be private. Not until everything was well and truly sorted.

Vivian arrived first, arching an eyebrow at them as she settled in a chair, though it was only a minute or two before ap Rhys came bustling in. "Most mysterious note, Verch Hendrek. Are we waiting on anyone?"

Carillon nodded. "Someone from the Guard." There was the sound of hard leather heels on the wood outside, and then a salute from a woman in Guard uniform, all sharp navy jacket and split skirts.

"Captain Lefton, I was hoping you were not called away elsewhere. There's a certain delicacy with some of this."

The woman made a slight bow, and Carillon murmured to Lizzie. "She was in charge of an issue out by Ytene two years ago. Very reliable, particularly with complex situations."

Lizzie nodded, and then he gestured. "This is Elspeth - Lizzie - Penhallow, Lefton. She'll be leading us through what we discovered, I'll chime in. You know Vivian Porter and Iolo ap Rhys."

He took a step back, watching as Lizzie glanced at the notes they had put together, laying things out. "The goldwasser and the loss of magic are related, but two distinct things." She glanced at ap Rhys. "May I speak freely about certain topics?"

Ap Rhys nodded. "You may, in this company. Captain Lefton has proven her discretion repeatedly."

"While at the country house, one of the Belin approached us. The brief conversation it permitted clarified that the goldwasser was a problem, but that the process did something to the coins used to make it, made them die, it said. That otherwise, the coins were renewing, reborn. This process changed that."

Carillon was watching ap Rhys most closely, and his eyebrows went up, though he avoided saying anything too hasty.

"There was more?" That was Vivian, who was leaning forward.

"The Belin mentioned something about dragons, that the metal left was - not healthy for the dragons. Not healthy for anything living, it said, but it especially mentioned dragons."

Carillon coughed, and Lizzie nodded at him. "One of the maids at the house, someone had tipped her a coin that made her feel unwell, and it was someone involved in the making. It's being analysed right now, carefully."

"You clearly have more." That was Lefton, who was tracking this like she might follow a trail in the woods.

He nodded. "They introduced me to many, if not most, of the conspirators. I managed to write down the names they told me, and descriptions, and a few of them I knew enough to identify."

Carillon paced. "They wouldn't tell me where the manufacturing was, but I am certain it can't be far from where we were. On a river, to allow for water power with the bottling, to avoid attracting too much attention, but they were cautious about transporting it by portal. Something about large amounts being potentially explosive."

Benton cleared his throat, and said, "We marked the most likely locations on a map, ma'am, for your consideration."

That got a low chuckle from her, and a purring, almost predatory, "You do make my work easy, your lordship."

Carillon spread his hands, smiling, before he nodded at Lizzie to continue. That led to a commentary on the house they'd been in, an analysis of who was there, the names she'd heard, and Carillon helped fill those in, along with those he was quite sure were pseudonyms.

A few people in, Vivian made notes, and said, as he finished. "I should be able to sort out exactly who was involved with a few hours work, and my notes. Lizzie, those tidbits are a great help, and descriptions of the dresses."

That startled Ap Rhys. "The dresses?"

"Many of the pieces were custom made. Someone with contacts at the dressmakers can often track down the customers rather precisely." Vivian was rather sharp about it. "And of course, I maintain those contacts."

The conversation went on for a bit longer, until ap Rhys said, "So, what happens next?"

Lefton cleared her throat, and he nodded at her. "I will need some time to scout the area and gather the best people for this particular task. Discretion, and ability to evaluate and act without direct instruction, since there are likely a number of innocent parties in the area."

Lizzie was about to say something, but Lefton murmured, "Like the maid, yes."

Carillon nodded. "We could use additional staff at Ytene. I'd be glad to offer her a position, tell her that if it would help."

Lefton nodded. "M'lord." She tapped her fingers on the arm of her chair. "A day, perhaps better two, unless there is some particular urgency."

Carillon considered. "To people given the coins, yes. To others, I'm not so sure."

Ap Rhys and Vivian conferred quietly for a minute or two, and finally Vivian said, "I think better to take the time, even with the risk. Less chance we'll have more problems later. Do you think they suspect you?"

Carillon shook his head. "Not at the moment, no. I made..." He tried again. "I was clearly quite taken with the stuff. By the stuff."

Lizzie murmured. "Sir, ap Rhys, someone will have to go speak to the Belin, I presume I should plan to. They demanded an explanation by the full moon. That seemed far too soon, and I said we should have as much solution as we were going to by the new moon."

Ap Rhys did a little mental calculation and nodded. "That should be no problem. Would you rather Grwn or Halwyn for translation?"

"Grwn, sir, he's got a better sense of the language. And - oh. Warin Burke is... son, I think? Possibly a nephew. To one of the people involved. My sister was likely to have been at a party he was at this weekend, the younger set. I haven't seen her yet."

Ap Rhys considered. "Talk to your sister. Pass on anything else useful she found out. Stay out of the way. I'll set Burke to something where he can't get in the way. Carillon, if you can hole up here, or go to Ytene, that would be best. Verch Hendrek, stay somewhere people can't find you. That home of yours or wherever. We'll manage without you a few days. Badly, but we'll manage."

Lizzie nodded, though she smiled at the implied compliment.

"We'll go confer on the practical issues. We don't need you - or your library - for that. Lefton, arrange a private conference room, and the right staff, for an hour from now."

That got a prompt "Sir." She stood, as if to go, and Carillon murmured, "Do ask Giles when I could come by, would you, when you get a chance? I've something that could use his touch." Within five minutes, all of them were gone, leaving Carillon rather amused.

"They are efficient when they can finally do something. I think it was rather annoying both Vivian and Iolo that they had nothing to get a grip on. And well, Lefton's like an arrow shot true."

Lizzie shook her head, and then said, "Who's Giles? And what do we do now?"

"Where's your sister, do you know? And Giles is Captain Lefton's husband."

That got a cough from the door. "Pardon, sir, the young lady in question sent a note round. It had fallen under some of the other messages. Should I escort her?"

Carillon considered. "Do you want to stay here, Lizzie, or go somewhere else?"

"Let's talk here, that's easier? I'm not sure - " She shook

her head. "I feel all itchy, inside my head. Is that the right word? I don't know where I want to settle."

"Itchy's as good a word for it as any. Here, come have something to drink and settle down with me, we've plenty of books. Did you finish that one you'd started here?"

It was an hour before Benton turned up with Laura, and a carpet bag. "I thought it best the young lady pack a few things."

"You certainly shouldn't go back to work," Lizzie said.

"Couldn't pay me to," Laura agreed, a bit sharply. "Lizzie, did you drink it?"

"No, but - Car - Lord Carillon had to." Lizzie was suddenly cautious. "You?"

Lizzie shook her head. "I left the party early. I was." She stopped, her hand going to the locket at her throat.

Lizzie suddenly leaned forward.

"I wanted to argue with what you'd said. I went to the party because I was sure I knew better. Because the gold-wasser felt so good." Laura gestured at Carillon. "You drank it, you know."

He made a face, wanting to argue and being unable to.

Laura went on, "But Lizzie had asked me not to drink it. And I managed not to, Friday, and everyone else did, and it was horribly boring. Awful. Feeling on the outside again. Saturday, I was going to, only they got to pressuring me. Tourney, especially."

"Tourney Aplin?"

Laura nodded. "He'd been so kind, and so generous. But when I..." She stopped. "He didn't like it when I didn't do what he wanted. He was." She looked at her sister, very earnest now. "It was like Leander. All out for himself. His pleasure. His things."

Lizzie sucked in a breath, and whispered, "I didn't know you'd.... seen."

"Not then. Later." Laura murmured. "And it, it was like they broke a spell. I don't know. Knowing what it had been like for you, enough. What people had wanted me to do when I didn't want to do it." She shook her head. "And people were getting more and more grabby. So I packed up a case with the things I couldn't bear to lose. Put the pendant on. When everyone was dressing for supper, and I walked out."

"Oh, Laura." Lizzie didn't know where to start.

"It was a long walk. Well, I was in bed, more or less, until Benton came."

Carillon offered quietly, "Lizzie's been worried."

Lizzie nodded. "Very. I'm - I'm so very glad you listened."

Carillon nodded, and said, "Can we send for a Healer?"

Laura waved a hand. "Overdid it. Nothing worse. Though I'll see someone if you insist."

Carillon coughed and said "I thought we might consider decamping to Ytene. Private, good protections, excellent cooking, we could get a Healer in." He said it rather cautiously, not quite sure whether it would be welcome.

Lizzie paused, and she was oddly quiet.

Carillon reached for her hand, with a "Lizzie?"

"Trying to figure out how to... solve something."

"Solve?" Carillon was puzzled. They had a place to go.

"I'd..." Lizzie stopped, then said, "Hear me out, please?"

"Of course." Carillon couldn't help but notice, despite his focus on Lizzie, that Laura was leaning forward, looking very interested.

"I'd like to show you my home. Before - before you sweep me away with Ytene, with everything. Talk to you."

And then a wry. "And I suppose I'd better see to the chickens and things and plan to be away another few days."

That drew a laugh out of him. "Is that all? Well, we can manage that. Laura, would you be willing to go to Ytene on your own? My housekeeper and Benton will take good care of you. And I think you might get along well with my head stableman's wife. We'll be along tomorrow."

Laura looked from one of them to the other, and then asked, "I gather you apologised to him, Lizzie?"

Lizzie looked away and said, "In pieces, yes. It was rather a complicated few days."

Carillon shifted his arm around her. "And you want to be somewhere you know."

She looked up at him, her eyes wide, like she hadn't expected he'd remotely understand. Perhaps she thought he'd humour her, but no. He could understand wanting your own place, especially someone who had been so much at sea as she had.

"Cornwall it is."

# THIRTY-SIX

## LANYON, CORNWALL

It was late, nearly full dark, by the time they got to the cottage, and Lizzie looked drawn and tired. Benton had gone off to see to things at Ytene. They had generally agreed that Carillon and Lizzie would appear there at some point the next day.

She was shy, the long walk up the hill. Whether she was asking him for too much, what he'd think of their old worn house.

He let her go first, murmuring, "It's your home." She pressed her hand to the door plate to open the locks and the wards, then inside, to bring up the charm lights. The kitchen was tidy, at least, and homey.

Carillon looked around, nodding. "This is like the kitchen at Ytene. The proper kitchen. Where there's food and people sitting around talking while it's made."

Lizzie was startled. "You do that?"

"Oh, whenever Mrs Mudthon lets me, which is fairly often. I don't steal the biscuits until they're cool." There was a grin, and she saw for a moment the boyish, cheerful man he'd been before the War and everything else.

"Do you need anything? I could make tea..." She wasn't sure what to do now they were here, and turned away, trying to figure out what to offer him. Besides eggs.

"You mentioned chickens?"

"I - yes?"

"Go see to the chickens, whatever they need tonight. Can I make tea? Will you let me make tea? I promise I know how."

The earnestness made her laugh. "All right. Tea there, in the canisters, labelled. Mint for me, please. I'll be five minutes. Maybe ten." She snagged the egg basket from its hook and went out the back door. She went through the evening chores, checking the fencing and warding were still solid, refilling the water dishes and grain, then hunting out as many eggs as she could find.

After several days, there were a baker's dozen from her four hens. She came back with the basket quite heavy and carefully balanced to find a mug waiting for her. Carillon was carefully folded into a chair at the kitchen table, not prying into anything, his own mug in front of him.

She set the eggs where they could wait for tomorrow, and picked up her mug, taking several sips from it, and then letting out a sigh.

"Carillon..." she said, carefully.

"Geoffrey." She blinked.

"Call me Geoffrey," he said, clearly. "Please. Almost no one does."

"It's... presumptuous."

"I want a lot of things with you, Lizzie. I want to see your home, by charm light and candlelight. Tomorrow, in the daylight. I want to see where you read and think and whatever else you do. I want to show you my home, my horses. For you to meet the people there. And I want..."

He had to stop, to catch his breath. "I want to make something with you. I don't know what or how yet. You're right, people will fuss. But I don't - there's no one in my extended family who can do worse than make snide comments. And most of those would rather I marry someone. I want the kind of things that mean you should call me Geoffrey."

She let him run down to a stop, because she wasn't entirely sure what to say. Eventually, she managed a "Ca... Geoffrey." She tried the name out, cautiously. "I - that, yes. All of that. But not right now. Sitting around talking is all well and good, but we've been doing that all afternoon."

That made him laugh and stand. "Have you had enough sustenance, m'lady?" She took another sip of her tea, and one more, then said, "For now, yes." She considered, then led him up through the narrow stair, and along the hallway to her room, under the eaves, looking out to the ocean. "Close your eyes. And, um. Let me guide you, you want to mind your head."

He was obedient in her hands, trusting, and she turned to take him by both hands and draw him into the room. She looked around, checking that the place was not horribly askew, but no, she'd made the bed. It was not broad like his, but wide enough for two if they were fond of each other. The desk in the gable by the window. The chair to curl up and read in. The maps pinned up on the plaster, the places her father had gone, the etchings and drawings of things he'd seen and heard of, from scientific to the fantastical.

"Here." Her voice shook and he immediately caught her hand in his, then drew her close to kiss her. He opened his eyes, before he said anything, letting his hand slide down to her waist to steady her. She leaned against him.

Only when he seemed certain she was reassured did he

look around, taking his time, taking it seriously. He kept his hand cupping her waist, his thumb stroking slowly.

"This is grand. Are the sketches yours?" She nodded. "Some. The ones from places I've been. Some were Papa's and my uncle's."

"That's what I loved about going places. Seeing things, seeing things in a way no one else I knew had looked at them." He inhaled, sharply, and then turned to her, kissing her suddenly much more fiercely, as if seeing her room had unlocked something in him.

"We're a match for each other, Lizzie. Don't you see it? Won't you... "

It took her breath away, but she nodded, then murmured, when he released her from the kiss for long enough, "You. You saw. You understood. This. What..."

He was nodding, fiercely, his hands already working to help undo her clothing, slipping to undo his shirt. Then it was a jumble of hands and snatched kisses, neither of them wanting to stop undressing for long enough to do anything else. Her hair came loose in the middle, and he paused just long enough to run a hand along a curl and murmur, "Glorious."

Then they were both naked, and she could feel the cool air on her skin. He was drawing her down to the bed, getting a sense for how it felt and breathed. "May I, domina, may I delight you?"

She settled on her back, looking up at him, blinking to try to focus on his face. He was so earnest. "May I, the magics I know?"

"Oh, yes, please." She felt like she should take the more active part here, she had apologies yet to make to him, and things to ask him. She could not think further, because he was focusing on something, shifting his hands, and when he touched her again, all she knew was the delight. It was like the first time, only more so, like bottled joy.

"Can you teach me that?" When she could find words, that's the thing she said, needed to say. "So you can feel it?"

The question clearly startled him, before he bent, kissing her fiercely. His hands stroked her, working their way down her body, dipping between her legs. Then he was cupping her breast, arousing her, letting her roll in it like a river surging down to the sea.

"Oh, yes, domina." he murmured, against her ear. "If you wish, I will teach you all I know."

The potential in it, the purr in his voice, it made her buck up against him, urgent now. He steadied her, his hands encouraging her to stretch out. "I want this to last, domina. To revel."

He yielded to her neediness, enough that he spread her legs. His fingers slipped inside to tease and touch and stroke until he pushed her up and over into a glorious climax that left her shaking. That eased her urgency a bit, leaving her wanting more, but with a less demanding need.

"There, domina. Mmm, yes. Spread out like this. I want you like this, in our bed, night after night. Hear your cries, feel you shiver. Do you want that? Will you grant me that?"

Her back arched, she moaned, even before she could think of words, the image of it overwhelming her. What it would be like to be with him, enjoying his sureness, his skill, his patience. And what it would be like to drive him to a point he begged and pleaded.

She reached up, to trace the line of his arm, from the scar on his shoulder, down. "I believe we can come to ... agreements." Teasing, gently. "You don't steal the covers, you know."

That made him laugh, changed the feeling from something full of urgency to something suddenly comfortable and joyful. "Considerate is my middle name. Well, no. But it's a pleasant maxim to aspire to." He was impish, as if something holding him back had loosened, all at once.

She blinked up at him and then snorted. "You are a wit, then?"

"You're more than my match there. And you like the challenge, don't you, domina?"

She laughed. "I do seem to. And you do make things..." She searched for the word. "Adventurous."

Carillon bent to kiss her, and this time, the kiss was slower, tender, as if he was telling her all the things neither of them had words for. Words would come later. All the sorting out what they were precisely, and what they would be to each other, and how they would do it. For now, it was clear he was hers and she was his, and everything else was trifles.

He kissed his way down her neck, to her breast, shifting to suck at her. It had made her shy, with Leander, but with Carillon, it was as if he was worshipping, delighting in her. He paused, shifting his position, so he could cup his hand around his shaft for a moment, closing his eyes and breathing in concentration.

When he looked back at her, it was to smile, and say "I wish... May I, domina? May I give you pleasure?"

Her fingers traced his cheek, and she was quiet for a long pause, searching for words. "Give us pleasure, instead." Emphasis on us.

He threw back his head, laughing, and glowing, so very much the boy who had not been hurt in uncountable ways. "I will."

He did not lie. The instant she felt him press against her, she knew he'd worked some new magic, the way his cock felt like it was pulsing against her. Not just the beat of her heart, or his, the closeness, she could feel that too, and it was different. Something that made him feel like he was swelling and yielding, in a steady, glorious pulse that drove her wild as he pressed into her.

By the time he was fully seated, she wanted to buck her hips, to cry out, to praise him in babble and moans. He would have none of that, guiding her into a steady kiss, a patient exploration of how they were joined, how they were together.

She had no idea someone could draw out the act of love that long. She lost track of the time, it became an endless flow of rocking movements, the pulse of him inside her. He rubbed all the places that felt best, his skin against hers. He built and built, until finally, they sped up, moving to crest like reaching the top of some great wave that would carry them onto entirely new shores.

He thrust three more times, deeper and faster, finally letting his strength and need show. At last, she felt him go over, the explosion of warmth and slickness inside. It drove her over as well, until she felt like she was split apart and immediately gathered up to be made whole.

When they both finally came to rest, he slipped to stretch out beside her, arm loosely over her, a foot across her ankle. She loved how he could curl around her without restricting her own movements.

She closed her eyes, finally secure that whatever this was, it was good, and would be good, and for both of them.

# THIRTY-SEVEN

## SNOWDONIA, WALES

Ten days later, they were busy climbing Snowdon, though the company was improved from the earlier trip. Carillon had sorted out a private rail car to take them and their boxes, then they transferred to a smaller rail line that ran to the top of the mountain. Benton had seen to providing a small host of tents, with all the comforts magic could provide and a few little luxuries besides. That was the reason for the boxes and luggage, more than anything else.

He was amused, mind. Lizzie had looked at ap Rhys, for an explanation, and the giant of a man had shrugged, laughing. "His lordship isn't limited by our budget requirements."

It had earned Carillon a lengthy kiss from Lizzie. Then he had the delight of her slipping a hand into his, as they walked along the ridge. There was a Silence-cloaked area, protected and warded, for the magical folk who came to this mountain. He could feel the magics settle around him, the comfort of not needing to be on his guard against a slip of the tongue.

One tent for Vivian and Captain Lefton and one for ap

Rhys and Grwn. One more for Lizzie and Carillon, and one for Benton and Mally. The housemaid had firmly attached herself to Carillon's household already, much to the protective amusement of both his housekeeper and Benton.

They had, by mutual agreement, put off any significant discussion of their recent activities or future plans while on the train. Even on a private car, there were listening magics and train staff passing through. "Talk after supper," was all Carillon would say, when pressed. "Enjoy the view." Which was splendid, at the moment, the evening light going on and on. It was clear enough to see a vast distance away, down into England.

The six principals in the presentation of information had had little chance to talk without risk of someone overhearing since that meeting in the Trellech townhouse library. Carillon had quietly vetoed a conversation on the train. It was not until the tents were set up, and they ate supper, that they gathered in the little sitting room of his own tent, to discuss.

Grwn looked unsure of what to do.

It was Vivian who broke the silence with, "I hope your sister is doing well, Lizzie?"

Lizzie nodded. "She is, thank you. It's been a bit rough. She - she did the right thing in the moment, and then she went to bits, after. And there's the after effects of the goldwasser, too. Bad dreams." She paused, then shook her head. "Not bad, precisely, but complicated. The kind that make you lonely."

Carillon reached out for her hand. It must be awful, being alone with that. At least two or three times a night, he found himself befogged in a dream. He felt so alone and lost, wanting the glowing warmth the bottle had given him, until he could reach out and run a hand along Lizzie's side or her back, and remember where he was. It was easier to turn away from the goldwasser with that. Doing it in a solitary bed, in an empty house, that must have been far worse.

Grwn coughed and said, "No one's really explained the goldwasser? Pardon, I feel like I'm a dozen steps behind. We're not bringing the usual offerings? And there's more people, and..."

Vivian and ap Rhys started talking and Vivian gestured at Lizzie and Carillon. "I believe this is your explanation, if you wish?"

He gestured at Lizzie. "You were doing most of it, domina, do have at, and I'll fill in around the edges?"

"You are gallant, Geoffrey." The affection in her tone clearly baffled Grwn as much as anything else.

Lizzie settled on the bench they'd set up, as if considering where to start. "Vivian hired me, and set me to work in the office, because she knew ap Rhys was concerned about the Belin. She knew that there were people drinking some new kind of drink - a magical drink - that left many of them with their magic drained."

Vivian coughed and interjected, "It turns out I was wrong, but we'll get to that."

Grwn nodded. "So you were doing other things, besides your job? In our office?" And then, more hesitant, "Do you plan to stay? Please say you will, you're much better than Audrey."

Lizzie glanced at Vivian, who waved her hand. "I'll likely continue consulting, but doing other work for Vivian as needed. A range of things. But no big changes for a couple of months, at least. Plenty of time to find someone to manage the forms."

Grwn nodded and said, "You do them really well." He

was earnest in a way that made Carillon settle a little closer to Lizzie.

She glanced at him, and grinned, before she continued. "My sister Laura, she'd got a job in an office, and she'd been getting invitations to parties. I worried about her - she spent most of her teens and twenties ill, tuberculosis. She's cured now, but that doesn't mean I don't worry." Lizzie said it as if daring anyone to say something about it. No one dared, and Geoffrey squeezed her hand again.

"I went off to - you heard the gossip about the pairs party, maybe? Geoffrey was trying to sneak in, the same way I was, and he fell over me, where I was watching from a bush."

Captain Lefton raised an eyebrow and said easily, "You know I'll tell Giles."

Geoffrey laughed. "Have me to dinner, and I'll tell him myself."

Lizzie paused, puzzled, and Lefton said, clearly, "My husband was blinded in the War, a gas attack. I'm sure he'd give you lessons on keeping your feet under you, your lordship." The gleam in her eyes made it obvious to everyone in the room she was teasing, he was sure.

Geoffrey grinned and said, "Oh, if he's willing." He murmured to Lizzie, "I'll take you to see them play bohort together. They're terrifyingly competent as a team."

Lefton smiled a toothy smile and then waved her hand. "Go on, Lizzie." Geoffrey grinned at her. Watching her unbend that far was a delight.

"It soon became clear that the goldwasser and the thing with the Belin were related, if not the same problem. So Vivian put us both in the same room and suggested we'd collaborate well. It turns out we do." The blush that came up on her cheek was gorgeous, and Carillon leaned to kiss her cheek.

Vivian said, dryly, "I was not actually matchmaking, but that turns out to be a pleasant addition."

"From there, it was going to a series of house parties, and hoping someone would invite us to something suspicious enough we could do something about it. Which they did, remarkably promptly."

"The goldwasser reduces inhibitions in a rather large number of ways." That was Lefton. "Your pet analyst was most thorough, and we've started getting additional reports back now. It made people feel unbeatable. Their little slips wouldn't matter. Everything would work. That kind of thing."

"The dangers of overwhelming well-being." Geoffrey rolled that around in his head for a moment.

Grwn made an inquiring sound, and Lefton explained. "It relies on the distance in the coins to work its magic. Coins that have gone all over the world are more potent, and it would induce dreams of places you remembered fondly, or wanted to go to. Flavoured by where the coin had gone."

"Spice markets featured prominently for many people. Ships." Geoffrey agreed. "At least from the debriefing notes I've seen so far."

Lizzie nodded. "Anyway, in the middle of that, I came up here for the chat with the Belin." Ap Rhys winced at the informality. "Or rather, while you did. And when we were at the last party, one of them turned up."

That sent Grwn into a sudden shiver. "You, without any preparation? You, how?"

Lizzie's voice got gentle. "I'd read the things you lent me. I knew the thing to say to start? And I was very polite." She paused. "I suspected it really wanted to be clear. It was very pleased when I figured out the main points fast enough. That it was the goldwasser and the coins they used for it that were problems."

"But the offerings..." Grwn sounded lost again.

"It said that the truth was the appropriate offering."

Grwn's face went through a series of expressions, ending on a wide-mouthed "Oh." then a "My grandfather, he will be so jealous. I must write it all up. In detail. You'll let me interview you, please, Lizzie? Lord Carillon? For our family records?"

Ap Rhys murmured, "And a copy for our files, please."

"It was very clear we needed a resolution. And when we got home from that party, we went to ap Rhys and Vivian, and then Captain Lefton put a lot of things in motion. So the big thing is telling them at the new moon - tomorrow - like I promised."

Grwn nodded, then said hesitantly, "Um. What are we telling them?"

Lefton took over then. "That the people who were causing the damage have all been arrested and will be tried. That we're learning what they did, so we can reverse it as much as possible. We've been collecting the coins that cause the problem."

"We need to ask what they want us to do with those coins. That's part of why you're here, Grwn. We suspect you can make sense of the answer better. Whatever they say." Lizzie was ever practical.

Geoffrey stretched. "Do we have them all back?"

"We think so." That was Lefton. "There may be one or two out there, somewhere sympathetic magics won't reach. We can put out an official notice, too, if they think it's necessary. And the healers are on alert."

Grwn looked around. "So, tomorrow, we go along the mountain and ... just tell them?"

"Share information, see if there's anything else, and then go do that."

Lizzie glanced at Carillon. "Then we go home."

The musicians had been tuning up and rehearsing on the terrace for twenty minutes or so, but there were no actual guests yet.

"Lizzie, there's someone in the music room. Did you, should I know her?" Laura came through the door into the library, with her sketchbook in her hands. "Oh, you look grand. That blue suits you no end." Her dress was draping, endless folds of a deep blue silk, the colour of twilight.

"No one said the guests were here yet. Mally promised she'd come fetch me." But then Lizzie paused and considered. "Older, hair pinned back, an undefined sort of dress, probably dark blue?"

"Yes?" Laura was clearly puzzled. "Who is she?"

"That's Great-Aunt Matilde."

"I thought your fiance wasn't close to any of his family? I mean, the living ones. This would be a different party if he were?"

"Oh, she's been dead for several centuries. One of the family ghosts."

Laura blinked several times and half-toppled into a side chair.

"Ghost?"

"She's very pleasant. Sometimes she plays the harp."

Laura blinked several times more. "You realise you sound very matter-of-fact."

Carillon opened the door from the other end of the library, entering with a perfectly timed, "Laura, surely you know your sister has an excellent line in matter-of-fact. What about this time?"

"I was explaining your Great-Aunt Mathilde, love."

Laura looked from one to the other, as Carillon came to settle on the couch beside Lizzie. He took a moment to kiss her, the kind of exhibition of affection that could be quite excused at an engagement party. She leaned into it, taking her time.

"See, I was certain you didn't need to fuss about the musicians." Carillon added, for Laura's benefit, "Great-Aunt Mathilde wanders off when she disapproves of the music."

Laura blinked at him a little more, and he said smoothly, "Fifteen minute warning on the portal from Trellech. Are you set to come out and welcome our guests?"

Lizzie stretched. "I believe I can manage that."

Carillon snorted. "Oh, a moment, you are a tad under-dressed."

Lizzie glanced down and said "This dress is lovely. You chose it yourself."

Laura murmured, sotto voce, "He thinks you're gorgeous in everything. And nothing."

That earned a laugh. "I heard that. Decidedly lovely in nothing. But also in that dress. The colour came out even better than I'd hoped from the fabric swatch. It was this I had in mind."

He reached for a drawer in the side table and drew out a long velvet box. She opened it to discover a lovely necklace of amber and sapphire, to pick up the blues of the dress.

"There. Just the thing. And none of the family jewellery, so you have something to start a collection of your own."

Lizzie looked up at him, raising an eyebrow.

"You have been very clear about wanting to be your own person, as much as my inherited commitments permit. And also very clear about not letting me give you things. But even the most restrictive etiquette books say I may give you things once a date for the wedding is set, and we announce that today. So I am starting with this, for your lovely neck."

Lizzie had to laugh, and she said, "I presume you have a list?"

He moved to fasten it around her neck, settling it in place and carefully rearranging the hair draping down her back in loose waves. "A collection. I could not give you things for rather a long time, months and months, and I kept seeing things you would like."

That got Lizzie laughing. "As it turns out, I have rather a collection too." She stood for a moment, walking over to the bookshelf, and pulling a title off a higher shelf, something with a worn leather cover. She opened it gently and offered the interior to him.

"Hiding in plain sight, domina?"

"One of my talents, you've said."

He reached for the volume, opening it carefully, and then blinking. "This is the Duchartre edition I didn't manage to snap up last winter."

"About commedia, yes. The one you quoted the second time we met. That would be because Vivian helped me buy it." She waited a beat.

"How long has it been sitting on my library shelf? In among the... what is that, the farm reports from the 1500s?"

"The afternoon of the auction. I had the cover ready to go in case I found something that needed hiding. Benton was most helpful. And you had just the perfect amount of space."

Carillon grinned and said, "If we had any question we are a match for each other, I believe that is decisively answered. Come along, domina, Vivian will want to see me expounding on the virtues of your gift, I'm quite sure."

IF YOU ENJOYED *Goblin Fruit* and would like to read more of this series, please sign up for my mailing list to get all the latest news and fun extras. As a thank you, you'll get a copy of *Ancient Trust*, a prequel novella about Carillon inheriting his title in 1922.

Your reviews (on whatever review site you use) are much appreciated, too!

Read on for more historical details about this book and an excerpt from *Magician's Hoard*.

## AUTHOR'S NOTES

In the 1920s in Great Britain, the Mysterious Charm series focuses on a magical community living and loving alongside the history we know. This series grows out of my joined love for mystery, parallel world fantasy, and romances. (And a particular fondness for Dorothy L. Sayers and other Golden Age of mystery fiction and for rolling around in real-world history.)

You can read a bit more about Lizzie and Carillon in *On The Bias*, which focuses on Carillon's valet, Benton, and Cassie, the dressmaker you met briefly in this book. *Best Foot Forward* picks up with Carillon in 1935, in the rumblings before the Second World War. (You can find additional books about the Carillon family on my public wiki at bit.ly/celia-lake-wiki under the Series and Arcs section.)

**Lord Geoffrey Carillon** is my homage to Lord Peter Wimsey, the main sleuth of the Sayers novels. (And the ghost in the epilogue is a nod to the ghosts referenced in *Busman's Honeymoon* and some of the short stories).

And if you're wondering about the title, yes, this book is

inspired by the poem **_Goblin Market_ by Christina Rosetti**. We'll be seeing more of Laura in a later book (In The Cards, book 5 of the series.)

**Trellech** is the major magical city in the British Isles of the series, though there are plenty of magical folk who live and work in London and other places. Trellech is a real place, or more accurately was a real place. It's in Monmouth in southern Wales, near the River Severn.

In the 13th century, Trellech was one of the largest towns in Wales, about 20,000 people (at a time when London itself was about 90,000 people). It was a major centre for producing arms and munitions for the De Clare family. After they died and the family lost power, the town became a shadow of its former glory.

Of course, as soon as I discovered it, I realised it fit in beautifully with my timeline for the magical community (which starts to diverge strongly around that point, and splits off into its own community in the 1480s).

**Comedia dell' Arte** is a theatrical style that began in Italy and also flourished in France. Using stock characters, such as Arlechino and Columbina, troupes would create their own stories, often with a highly improvisational approach.

**Pavo** and **bohort** are both real mediaeval activities adapted in the magical community of the series for play. Pavo is played on horseback (a bit like polo, but more complex) and bohort is played on foot. Both are played by small teams who have to solve puzzles or challenges set by the match designers. Think of them like a cross between an escape room and capture the flag, with a dash of cricket scoring.

Laura has spent a number of years being treated for

**tuberculosis,** which killed a tremendous number of people in this time period (before antibiotics were available.) Treatments included long stays in places with cold clear air (often in the mountains), extreme rest or highly regimented activity, and often painful surgeries to collapse or even remove portions of the affected lung. Even if someone survived, the disease lurked for the rest of their lives.

*Spitting Blood: The History of Tuberculosis* by Helen Bynum is a fantastic overview of the disease and treatment if you'd like to learn more.

**The Belin** are my take on a mysterious mention in a bit of Arthurian folklore about someone named Belin (or Beli or Beli Mawr) who is a king of the dwarves, or at least an underground kingdom. There are traditions like this in many places (especially those with a long history of mining), and as Lizzie notes, she's visited some of the German ones in the past.

If you've got questions about these or other things that appear in the books, feel free to reach out and ask. I love talking about the bits of history I've found inspirational.

The best way to find out my latest news is to subscribe to my mailing list.

*Ancient Trust,* my thank you to my newsletter folks, is a prequel novella for the series focusing on Geoffrey Carillon inheriting his title that overlaps with *Outcrossing*. It also introduces various other people (before Lizzie) who are important in Carillon's life. And again, *Best Foot Forward* picks up with Carillon and his life in 1935.

The next book in the series is *Magician's Hoard*, when a research project takes on some unexpected complications.